I FALL TO Pieces

SHIRL RICKMAN

I FALL TO
Pieces

Trish, thank you for always being my sounding board and believing in me.

And all my love for Ryan, who reminds me daily how wonderful life is because I'm married to my best friend.

Prologue

JASPER

Mrs. Connolly enters the room where Cora's dad and I are waiting with an excited grin. We both stand at the sight of her. "It's a beautiful, healthy girl!" she says.

"A girl," Mr. Connolly says reverently as he walks to his wife and embraces her.

Happiness fills me. I have difficulty believing this moment has come; it almost feels surreal. Every second I've spent helping and supporting Cora prepare herself to become a mother feels justified by this moment—a baby girl.

"Congratulations, Grandma and Grandpa," I tell Cora's parents.

They both turn to me, their smiles reflecting their gratitude. "Thank you, Jasper, for everything. Cora specifically asked me to let you know she's eager to see you once the nurse settles her and the baby girl. Your support has meant the world to us."

"Well, you all mean the world to me. Cora is …" God, Cora is everything to me. She's had my full attention since we were nine, and they moved in across the street. But I can't say that to her parents when I've never even told her. So instead, I say the expected. "Cora is my best friend. I'll always support her."

The Connollys have been our neighbors since Cora and I were nine. During this time, Mr. and Mrs. Connolly became my second parents, and Cora became my best friend. Mr. Connolly has often picked me up when I fell off my bicycle and encouraged me to get back up again. Mrs. Connolly has comforted me when I needed it, and my mom wasn't there. They were family, and that makes Cora more than my friend. I'd do anything to support her.

They both walk to me and pull me into a group hug. "And you mean the world to all of us," Mr. Connolly says.

• • •

About thirty minutes later, a nurse comes into the waiting room. "Is there a Jasper here?" she asks.

I stand quickly. "Uh, that's me," I say, pointing to myself. Mr. and Mrs. Connolly have gone to the cafeteria for some coffee. I stayed in case the nurse came to get me so I could see Cora.

Her lips tip up at the corners. "Well, that was easy. Cora Connolly is asking for you, so please follow me." I give her a nod before she turns on her heels and leads the way to Cora's room.

As we turn a corner down the long corridor of the maternity ward, the nurse points to a door just across from the nurses' station. "She is right through there," the nurse says, then takes a seat behind the desk at the station. "Thanks," I tell her.

My knuckles wrap against the door lightly before I turn the knob to enter the room. "Come in," I hear Cora say quietly as I push the door open.

Closing the door behind me, I walk further into the room. As soon as our eyes meet, a smile widens across her face, and I can't help the one I give her in response. "Jasper," she practically whispers. When I'm at her side, I take her hand. "Cora."

"I'm so glad you're here," she tells me as she squeezes my hand lightly.

"There isn't anywhere else I would rather be."

"Wanna meet Avery?" Her smile widens.

Avery, I think, returning Cora's expression. She has gone back and forth about what she wanted to name her baby girl. Even last night, she hadn't made a decision yet. Cora finally shrugged and told me she would know as soon as she saw her, but she couldn't decide before then.

Releasing my hand, Cora throws the blanket off her and slowly swings her legs over the side of the bed.

"Can you walk?" I ask.

Looking over her shoulder, her warm brown eyes connect with mine. "I gave birth naturally, Jas. I can't run a marathon, but walking five feet to pick up my baby is a reasonable expectation of my body." A hint of humor hugging her words.

I grin, shrugging my shoulders, "What do I know about having babies?"

I watch Cora as she walks gingerly over to a small cart on wheels. *Cart? What is that called?* Either way, I didn't even notice it when I came in. I only saw Cora and how exhausted she looked, but still so beautiful. Something in her eyes shone slightly differently, yet she looked the same as she always had. I'm unsure why I feel nervous now that the baby is here; I know things will be different. Cora will be different. Although I can see that nothing about her has changed, the feeling still lingers in the corners of my mind.

Cora reaches down and cradles her baby in her arms. Her gaze never leaves the little bundle she's holding. "Hi, sweet girl…I want you to meet someone special to me," she says, her voice a softer tone than I've ever heard her use. As she steps toward me, Cora looks up at me, her face full of happiness. "Jas, I'd like you to meet Avery." I take a step closer and move my eyes down to look more closely at Avery, nestled into her mother's arms.

Her sweet face is peaceful, her little eyes framed by the longest lashes I've ever seen, blinking slowly and staring. She is such a beautiful little thing, just like her mom. My chest tightens with a mixture of emotions. This little girl isn't mine, but right here, right now, I know I will spend forever doing what she and Cora need me to do to ensure their happiness and safety.

My words choked by emotion, I say, "Cora…she is perfect."

"I know."

I glance up to find Cora's attention is still on her baby's face. I want to tell her she is perfect, too. But I don't. As I have for our entire friendship, I keep my true feelings for her as hidden as possible. Instead, I inch myself closer, wrap an arm around Cora's shoulder, and stare back down at the little girl who lies soundlessly in her arms.

"She's more than perfect, and I promise I will always be here for her like I've vowed to always be here for you."

Cora's head falls to my shoulder, and she releases a soft sigh. Avery's eyes flutter closed, and we remain quiet, watching her. I'm not immune to how natural it feels to be together, the three of us in this moment.

One

JASPER

1 Year Later

Cake in one hand and balloons in another, I kick the door of my Jeep closed with my foot.

I told Cora I would pick up the cake and balloons she ordered on my way to her house for Avery's first birthday party. Spending as much time as possible with her and Avery over this past year has been one of the best parts of my life, especially since I can visit my parents while I'm there. Cora lives with her parents, who still live across the street from my parents.

I promised to be here to help her as much as possible. I mean, what are best friends for, right?

Our thirteen-year friendship has been significant but also ever-changing. How could it not be when you met your best friend at nine years old? We rode our bikes up and down the street well after sundown, and the streetlights came on. Cora and I walked to and from school every day. Our Summers were spent going to the beach and biking downtown to enjoy ice cream. She was my best friend, and we were inseparable. There was rarely a day we weren't at my house or hers. Then, one day, something changed; when we were twelve years old, I walked across the street, knocked on her door, and took one look at her long brown hair in curls and that pink dress she wore with her Converse, and my heart started beating a little harder. Our friendship was still first, but there was something more to it. Over the years, that feeling of love blossomed into something so honest and true. But just for me. Or so I think, because I've never actually told Cora she means more to me than just a friend. I've never wanted to risk telling her how I feel because I didn't want to lose her. So, I watched her date other guys and get her heart broken every time. I was always the one there to help her pick up the pieces.

And when she told me at Rosie and Drew's wedding that she was pregnant from a drunken one-night stand with that asshole, Tommy Warner, I told her once again I would be there for her through it all.

I've been everywhere she's needed me since that day. I've been with her every moment, supporting and helping her in any way she'd let me. My friendship and devotion haven't changed since Avery was born a year ago, and they won't for as long as Cora allows them to.

But this relationship isn't without its critics. My siblings and parents worry about me. They fear I'm in over my head and I'll get hurt. They love Cora, but they are worried that my heart is too involved, especially since Cora and I have never established ourselves as more than friends. I tell them it's not the time, though. Cora is focused on Avery, and I'm focused on both of them.

We're comfortable.

Walking through the front door, I hear music playing in the background and someone banging around in the kitchen. "Cake and balloons are here!" I shout over the noise.

The banging stops, and Cora appears in the doorway to the living room with a bright smile. My God, she takes my breath away. "Awe! You're a lifesaver!" She takes the cake box from my hand as she gives me a hug. "You can take the balloons on the patio to my mom," she says as she disappears back into the kitchen.

As I make my way toward the back door, I stop and peek into the kitchen, finding the countertops covered in platters and bowls filled with snacks. "Good Lord, Cora... this is a one-year-old birthday party. You have enough food for fifty adults."

"Oh, hush, I couldn't decide on one thing to make."

Laughing, I shake my head and put my hands up, "Cool, just making an observation, but glad I brought my appetite." She smacks me on the shoulder and laughs. "Where is my favorite girl anyway?"

"Right here...oh, yeah. I lost that title a year ago." She gives me a wink and looks so cute doing it. "Avery is walking around the backyard with my dad."

"I still can't believe she is walking already. Time has

just flown by." I take one step out of the back door and stop, turning my head to her. "Oh, and Cora, you'll always be my favorite girl over the age that Avery is each year." I grin and wink at her, just like she did to me a few seconds ago, then walk out onto the patio. Her laughter follows me out the back door.

"Balloon delivery," I say to Mrs. Connolly. She places a tablecloth over a table and turns to look at me.

"Jasper, it's so nice of you to pick those up for Cora." She walks over and takes them from me. "You're too good to her."

"It was on my way, and I don't mind."

She gives me the same look my mom does when we discuss Cora's and my relationship. I see it in Cora's parents' eyes every time I'm around them now, too care, concern. Just like with my family, I appreciate everyone's concern, but I'm not as fragile as they all seem to think I am. I wish they would all stop pitying me. Pushing those feelings of frustration aside, I ask, "Do you need some help with the decorations?"

Mrs. Connolly looks around as she ties a balloon to one of the deck's posts. "I think we have everything handled. I'm just going to tie the rest of these balloons to random spots. I think there may be a certain little birthday girl roaming around the yard with her granddad, who might be a little excited to see you."

A bubbly squeal rings through the air right on cue, pulling my attention to the right. Beneath the trees, Avery is toddling around as her grandfather lifts her into the air. She has soft ringlets and the same chocolate brown eyes as her mother. To add to her sweet face, a small dimple sits on her cheek. Avery is the sweetest little girl, so happy and full of love. She makes my heart ache with love for her.

Walking over to where the birthday girl and her grandfather play beneath the trees, I make my presence known. "Hey there, my Avery girl!"

Her shining eyes move in my direction, and a wide grin spreads across her face. Her tiny arms reach out to me as she babbles, "Ja... Ja." My heart fills with a kind of warmth I've never known until I met Avery.

Mr. Connolly releases his hold as I place my hands under her outstretched arms. "Jasper, it's good to see you. It looks like our sweet girl is happy you're here, too."

Pulling Avery to me, I kiss her cheek as her arms wrap around my neck. She squeezes me as tightly as she can and giggles. The sound, music to my ears, and the feeling of her hugging me confirm once again that she has me wrapped around her little finger.

CORA

I watch my dad hand Avery over to Jasper; her little squeal of delight is loud enough to reach my ears inside the house. His smile matches the one spread across her face. My heart aches at the sight. She loves him, and it's obvious he loves her. Jasper is the one constant in my life. The most reliable and safest person I know. I can't take my gaze off them, even when I feel my mom's presence at my side. The sensation that seems to burn from the center of my belly to the center of my heart is there again, just as it has been most of my life regarding Jasper. A desire for something I'm not sure we can have together.

I can still sense my mom standing behind me, yet she remains silent, focusing on the same two people I am.

After a long minute passes, my name crosses her lips. "Cora." Her hand touches my arm.

"Don't, Mom, not today."

"But honey, you can't keep…"

I interrupt her. "Not today. I know what you and Dad think, but not today. I understand I need to tell him, but like I said, not today."

"Fine, Cora. But you need to talk to him soon, before this situation changes your friendship and relationship. Jasper deserves honesty." She takes the bowl of chips from the counter and leaves me alone, still watching the two most important people in my life through the window.

It seems life is constantly testing me. Every choice I've made in the last couple of years has led to change: both good and bad decisions and the consequences of those choices. Avery is a consequence I didn't think I would be able to handle. Yet, I did, but not alone. Thanks to my parents and, most importantly, to the support Jasper has given me every step of the way.

As my parents have recently pointed out, I can't count on Jasper to constantly drop his life to be by my side. It was my choice to take this new job in Arizona last week, which requires me to be there in three weeks. I made the decision to leave everyone I knew for a new place and a new start. I need a fresh perspective to become a responsible single mother.

Except I didn't think about Jasper and how he would feel. I didn't even think about how it would make Avery or me feel not to have him around when we need him. How do I give up my confidant? My safety net. My best friend. How do I give up having Jasper around nearly every day? The one person who has been by my side unconditionally for the last thirteen years.

I didn't even try to put Jasper and his future first. I let him promise to always be here when I needed him. And I needed him because the day-to-day is so much better with him. Selfishly, I allowed him to give us all his attention, but what did he get out of this promise? He spends every free moment coming to my parents' house to be with Avery and me. To spend time doing the day-to-day things a parent does, but he isn't the parent. We aren't his obligation, and I've allowed him to feel like we are.

But, why? That's the question my mom and dad asked me when I told them I applied for a position in Arizona two months ago. It was after Jasper had once again spent the weekend with us, helping me assemble a new big girl bed for Avery. They wanted to know what was happening between me and Jasper. Dad asked me what Jasper was to me. Did I love him? My response was easy: of course, I love him. At first, I didn't understand what they meant, but then Mom said, no, we know you love Jasper, but are you in love with him? Then, I got it. Yet, I got frustrated and resisted the truth behind their implications. Was I in love with Jasper, or was I putting him in a role that wasn't meant for him? My one night with some asshole resulted in this beautiful little girl, yet it was one night that was my mistake and changed my life forever. But it wasn't Jasper's, and he deserves more than just playing the role of parent with a child who isn't his. Because he is a friend I love, but was I in love with him?

I've been trying to determine the answer to that question since that night. I don't have the liberty to consider how I feel because my priority has to be Avery. I can't take a chance on something Jasper may or may not feel. On top of that, what if it didn't work out? Then, not only would I hurt myself, but I'd hurt Avery. And Jasper. I could never hurt either one of them. If we had tried something deeper, I would never have taken this dream position in Arizona. I would never ask him to leave his home, job, and family.

The call came last week with an offer I couldn't pass up. And I accepted without even giving it a second thought. Now, Avery and I are moving in three weeks, and Jasper has no idea. But he deserves an explanation. He deserves better than me. Better than a girl who only thinks of herself and was blind to the fact that he was giving up his life for them. Yet, I find I can't be honest with him.

Mom is right; I have to talk to him soon.

JASPER

The party was everything a one-year-old's first birthday should be. Avery played so hard that she was out like a light after she took a bath, and Cora put her to bed. While they did their nightly routine, I helped clean up all the decorations.

When everything was mostly cleaned up, I promised Mr. & Mrs. Connolly I would take care of the rest. I knew they were exhausted and wanted to relax. They said their goodbyes to me and sought out Cora before heading upstairs.

Cora's first role as birthday party host was perfect. She seemed excited about the party for Avery and a few kids from her Mother's Day out program, but something was off with her today. If I'm honest, she has seemed a little off the last few times we've talked on the phone over the past week—maybe even longer. I just can't put my finger on it. It's like one second, we're just like we've always been with each other. Then suddenly, it's like she's distancing herself from me.

I place the last dish in the dishwasher and start it as I hear footsteps walk into the room behind me. When I turn around, Cora is standing there, watching me quietly. She looks contemplative and worried, like she can't figure out the answer to an important question.

"Everything is all cleaned up," I tell her. "I think Avery loved her party. She may not fully understand it was her birthday party since she is only one, but she was happy and laughing all day, so that is something to feel good about, right?"

"I think you're right. Have I thanked you for all you've done for me?"

"Cora, you don't need me to thank me. I only picked up the cake and balloons. You did all the hard stuff."

"No, Jasper. I don't mean just today. I mean, for our friendship over the years. For being there for me when I found out I was pregnant and not judging me for one second. To make sure all my pregnancy cravings were satisfied." She runs a hand through her hair and lets out a soft sigh. "God, Jas, you rushed to the hospital when I went into labor and stayed there all night until Avery was born. You've been there for me at every good and bad point in my life, and you never questioned my decisions. You spend every free weekend coming over here to help with anything I need, and you even help take care of Avery when you're here. All for nothing."

I stare at her, unsure of where this is coming from. She's thanked me before, I'm sure of it. But even if she hasn't, I don't need her to. "Cora, where is this coming from? Yeah, I did all those things and would do them again. I'm sure you've thanked me in the past, but you don't need to because you're my best friend. And I love…Avery." I look away momentarily because I almost said more than I should. Shaking my head, I look back at Cora. "I don't need a thank you, Cora."

"You do."

"Fine, if it makes you feel better and gets that worried look off your face, then I will accept your thanks, and you're welcome."

Cora walks closer to me until she stands inches from me. She's tall, but I'm at least four inches taller than her, so I'm forced to look down at her. Suddenly, she wraps her arms around me. A knot grows in my chest, feeling a lot like fear. I'm not sure what's happening, but I return Cora's hug and hold a little tighter than I intend.

"Cora?" I whisper. Her name comes out like a question. "Is everything okay? You're worrying me."

She takes a minute to respond before finally saying, "No, but let's not talk about it now. Soon. Tomorrow. But not tonight. Tonight, let's do what we always do when I put Avery down when you're here. Let's make popcorn, curl up on the couch, and watch a movie."

I want to tell her no and make her tell me what is making her act so strange, but instead, I agree. "Okay, if that is what you want."

"It's what I want and need tonight. Let's be Cora and Jasper tonight...the neighborhood best friends who are inseparable and never let the other get hurt."

I pull back from our embrace and put a smile on my face, hoping to lighten the mood. "Well, that will be easy. Isn't that exactly who we are?" However, now I'm even more confused by this conversation.

Cora half-smiles, "Yeah, that's who we are. You're too good a friend to me."

"Well, not that good. I'm not letting you pick the movie this time."

This makes her laugh, and if I didn't know better, I might think everything is just as it always is and the last few minutes mean nothing.

But the knot that formed in my stomach a few minutes ago feels even tighter.

Two

JASPER

I strap Avery into her car seat while Cora puts our beach bags in my Jeep. When I make faces to distract her, she lets out a loud giggle. She is the cutest and sweetest kid. There are so many things about her that remind me of her mom.

I was so worried for Cora when she first told me she was pregnant. I couldn't help wondering how it would change her life. I wasn't wrong; having a baby completely set Cora in a whole new direction. Avery changed everything; I just never expected how much she would change me, too.

Watching her grow and develop into her own little person is incredible. I never imagined I would love a little girl as much as I love Avery. It's partly because of Cora, but at the same time, it has nothing to do with her. Avery has become an essential part of my life, and I can't imagine it without her now.

I lean in, kissing her little forehead, and start to close the door when I look up and catch Cora watching us from the other side of the car. She looks so sad. "Cora?" Her name comes out like a question.

It seems to bring her out of her thoughts. She has that same look in her eyes that she had last night. When she realizes she's staring, she gives me what is obviously a forced smile. "Let's get to it and have our fun beach day!" She smiles widely. Avery squeals with excitement in response to Cora's sudden enthusiasm.

Cora's invitation for a beach day with Avery was an easy yes; I'd jump at any chance to be with them. But our conversation from earlier is on my mind, mainly because I can tell she is still pointedly ignoring it. I could feel her holding back, so I chose not to push it, giving her this day to avoid it, giving her a little peace. However, that single look on her face just now conveyed the opposite of peace. Her distress is obvious, and my willingness to wait is fading. If she doesn't share what's bothering her soon, I won't be able to stand by and ignore this uneasy feeling that something is up. I push my thoughts aside.

"Avery and I are ready, Mama." I tickle Avery in her seat, and she goes into a fit of giggles. "The question is, are you ready?

"I am!" She says, closing the door and hopping in the front seat.

If she is going to pretend that she's fine, then I guess I have no choice but to do the same. I recheck Avery's seat to ensure it is adequately fastened and climb into my seat, starting the Jeep.

As we approach the beach, everyone's quiet for a few minutes. Avery is looking out the window, content to watch the world go by. I glance over at Cora; she is doing the same out the passenger-side window.

I can't resist trying to see if she'll open up to me. "Are we still being Cora and Jasper, neighborhood best friends for today?"

Her head swivels in my direction momentarily, that worried look back in her eyes, before she returns her gaze to outside the car.

"Just for a few more hours," she finally says.

Releasing a sigh, I turn my attention back to the street in front of us. I can't help asking, "And then what?"

"Then we talk. It just isn't the time. Please, let's enjoy this day together," she pleads.

With everything I have in me, I accept that simple request and do my best to make the most out of the day with Cora and Avery.

"Anything for you."

CORA

This day was everything I hoped it would be. Jasper, Avery, and I played in the sand. Ate our picnic lunch. At one point, Jasper carried Avery out into the water while I stayed on shore and snapped photos. I took so many photos of the two of them. And of all three of us. I'm trying to capture memories because who knows when we will be able to have another day like this once Avery and I move.

I spent the day working so hard to savor every moment I could before I broke all of our hearts.

We decided to head home in the late afternoon, and Avery was knocked out before we even drove ten feet. Jasper and I rode home in silence. I could feel his worry and the questions, although he hadn't brought up the conversation again since this morning. I know he is confused as to why I've been so vague. I just needed more time, and in typical Jasper fashion, he has allowed me the time I told him I needed.

"I'll get her inside while you unpack our stuff," he tells me as we pull into the driveway.

"Are you sure?"

"Cora, I'm much better at picking her up without waking her than you are." He laughs. "And sweet girl needs the rest after all that fun and sun."

"Whatever! You're stronger than I am, and she is getting heavier by the day!" I say, rolling my eyes at his teasing.

Jasper carries Avery into the house and puts her down to continue her nap. Before he arrives to pick us up this morning, I ask Mom and Dad if they could stay with Avery while I speak to Jasper when we get back. Neither of them hesitates because they feel like this is a conversation, I needed to have weeks ago, if not before.

I sit on the porch, waiting for Jasper to come back out, trying to work on my courage. I've been thinking about this conversation for so long, and I'm still unsure of what I will say to him. I mean, where do I start?

Do I begin with the job opportunity? My feelings? His promise and my selfishness? There are so many things I need to say, and we need to lay them out on the table, metaphorically, between us.

I'm startled when the front door swings open, and Jasper walks out. "Oh, God! You just scared me."

He comes and stands before me, not even responding. Jasper takes me in, and his scrutiny overwhelms me, so I shift nervously in my seat.

Suddenly, he asks, "Are you ready to tell me what has been bothering you lately?"

"No, I'm not sure I will ever be ready, but I can't keep avoiding it either," I tell him. "We're running out of time."

Jasper drops to his knees in front of me and takes my hands in his. "Cora, what the hell do you mean we're running out of time?" His gaze locks with mine, and I see fear in it.

His voice quivers as he continues, "Are you sick?"

"What? Oh, God, no, Jas. I'm fine." As if my guilt couldn't consume me anymore, I feel like I'm drowning in it.

He runs a hand through his hair. "Then, what?"

"Jasper, I accepted a new job. Avery and I are moving."

"Cora! That's fantastic! You had me worried it was something serious. Do you need me to borrow Drew's truck to help you move?"

His excitement for me is so typical Jasper, but I obviously wasn't clear enough.

Pulling my hands from his, I stand up, step around him, and lean against the front porch banister. "I don't think you understand, Jas. The job isn't here in Santa Cruz."

I can feel him standing behind me now.

"What…uh, well, where is the job?"

"The job is in Arizona, and we leave in three weeks."

"Arizona! Three weeks! What the hell, Cora? How long have you known? I didn't even know you applied for a job out of state."

The hurt I can feel behind each of those words is exactly why I feared having this conversation.

"I know. I'm sorry," I tell him. I'm afraid to face him because of what I will see in his piercing green eyes, but I turn around anyway. When our eyes meet, I can't even describe what I see. Pain. Sadness. Emotions I'm not used to seeing reflected in Jasper's eyes. How do I explain this away? "Jas, I didn't even think I would be offered the job. I just kind of did it on a whim."

"But you wanted the job, Cora, or you wouldn't have applied." His gaze drops to our feet, and his hands rest on his hips.

"You're hurt. I'm…" I begin, but Jasper cuts me off.

His head snaps back up, and his gaze bores into mine. "Yeah, I'm hurt that you didn't tell me. Even if you didn't think you'd get the job. But you did get it. So, the thing that hurts the most is that you obviously waited to tell me. You couldn't have just found out. You've known for weeks, right?"

What can I really say, so I just nod my response.

"God, Cora. I'm with you and Avery nearly every day. So, why? Why didn't you tell me? Why did you accept this job?"

Now, he sounds a little angry, which makes me feel defensive. "Because I needed to do this for me. For Avery. I need a fresh start where I stand on my own two feet," I shout at him. Jasper and I have never spoken like this to one another.

He sits in the chair I was sitting in and rests his elbows with his head hanging down. Jasper looks so defeated. I can't see his face anymore, but I still feel his hurt and disappointment.

"I didn't do this to hurt you. I don't want to leave my parents, my hometown, where everything is familiar, and I definitely don't want to leave you. But, Jasper, I have to do this, not only for myself but for Avery, too. I can't pass up this opportunity."

Without looking up at me, he asks, "What about the last year? Things haven't been so bad. There is a routine. Aren't you happy?"

This time, I'm the one who drops to my knees, taking his face between my hands and forcing him to look at me. "Of course, I'm happy. Avery has been the best thing to ever happen to me, and having my best friend by my side every step of the way made it all easier...better."

His hands wrap around mine, and he moves them gently from his face. "I would do it again without hesitation." His eyes glisten with unshed tears, and I feel my heart crack slightly. "I'm just supposed to say goodbye to you, to Avery? As if the two of you aren't the most important part of my life?"

Jasper's words spread a warmth through my body. It's how he's always made me feel — like I'm the center of the world. Safe and protected. I think of my parents' question. *Do you love him?* And that is the thing; I don't know how to answer that because what if I said yes…and it destroyed us? Because I do love him. I've always loved him. But what if he doesn't feel the same? Too many what-ifs, and I have Avery to think about. She is my priority, and while Jasper is amazing with her, we depend too much on him. My parents were right when they said I needed to recognize that Jasper had given up too much and I was offering him nothing in return. Dad told me once, many years ago, that things could get messy if friends fell in love and it didn't work. Avery upped the stakes.

"We aren't saying goodbye forever. We just won't see one another every day. We'll still have phone calls and…"

"I could come with you. Find a job," Jasper suddenly blurts out. "I can still help you take care of Avery."

My heart skips a beat for a split second, and I want to say yes, but then, it falls back into its natural rhythm, bringing rational thinking back with it. "I can't ask you to do that, Jasper."

"You didn't ask me! I offered."

"You can't leave your life here. Your job. And there is no way you can leave your family."

"But you and Avery are my family."

"But we're not." When I say it, I don't mean it as harshly as it comes out. He pulls back as if I'd hit him. "I don't mean it like that. I mean, we aren't your responsibility. It's not fair to you, Jasper. You deserve a life. One you choose…where you find a girl. Fall in love. And have your own children. We've already kept you away from finding your own life for a year. I've been selfish." Saying these words and imagining Jasper in love with a family of his own makes me feel slightly unbalanced. Nauseous even.

"This is crap, Cora, and you know it. I'm a big boy, and I wanted to be here. I love Avery. I love being with the two of you. It's my choice. You didn't make me do anything."

"It's also my choice, and I choose Avery. I choose to protect her by making her my one and only priority. I choose to give her the best life I can. God, Jasper. I know you love her, but it's inevitable. You are incredible, and everything that is amazing, and one day, someone will come along who falls in love with you and can give you everything you deserve. And sure, you will always love us, but we won't be able to be your priority anymore. It's unfair if I allow us all to be hurt like that, even if it is completely unintentional."

"Let me get this right. You applied for and took a job without telling me because you are trying to do what's best for me while also doing what is best for you and Avery?"

I stand up sharply, back straight and shoulders back. "Yes! I'm trying to do what is best for all of us."

"If you said you wanted to focus on Avery, I would do my best to accept this all. But using my future well-being as a crutch is bullshit. Just like you control your life and choose your future. I choose mine. I've been choosing mine for the last year, and I had hoped you would see it. I guess I've been stupid."

"I'm sorry, what?"

We stand face to face for a long minute. "When do you leave?"

I'm a little taken aback by the sudden shift in the conversation. I'm not even sure what he was saying.

"Cora, when do you leave?"

Snapping out of my confused shock, I whisper, "We leave in two weeks."

"Two weeks? I thought you said three."

"I have to start my job in three weeks."

"Two...three, what does it matter, I guess? I have to go to dinner with my family. Mom wanted you and Avery to come over tonight, but we should plan it for next week. I need a minute." He moves past me and steps off the porch. It feels like that bond between us is being stretched beyond the point it has ever had to endure.

I turn and run a few steps behind him. "Jasper, wait...," I say with a little desperation.

Jasper stops just before stepping onto the street without turning around. He doesn't say anything, but he doesn't move further from me.

"I didn't mean to hurt you. I would never intentionally hurt you."

There is only silence, and I'm not sure he will acknowledge me, but I wait.

Still facing away from me, he says, "Deep down, somewhere, I know that, Cora. You say nothing will change because we will always be best friends, but I already feel the change. And, damn, if I'm not standing here trying to figure out how I'm going to put my heart back together when you and Avery leave."

A tiny sob escapes, and I cover my mouth, trying my best to hold it in as I watch Jasper disappear into the house across the street like I've done what seems like a million times for more than a decade. As soon as he's gone from sight, I quickly rush into the house and shut the door behind me. I slide to the floor, release the emotions I've felt since I took that job, and realize I've just made a choice that will change more than just my life. I changed our whole world.

Three

JASPER

Walking away from Cora and into my parents' house took every ounce of willpower I could muster. For one, I want to beg her not to leave. I want to tell her I'm proud of her for all she has done over the last year. For taking this single mom thing and giving it her all. For being the kind of mother, she is to Avery, for holding down a job and still being everything her kid needs. I even want to tell her how proud I am that she went after the job of her dreams and got it. But that last one means she must leave, which isn't okay.

I'm so hurt she kept this from me. And I'm hurt she didn't even consider how her and Avery's leaving will impact my life, too. I'm not even sure what hurts more. I feel so numb that I can't even think clearly.

Even though I didn't turn back and look at her, I heard

her pain when she sobbed. It took everything in me not to turn back and pull her into my arms. Tell her it's okay. But if I did that, I would be lying because I'm not alright. I can see she's hurting, but I don't know what to do or say at this point because this was her choice. I'm sure she needs me to be supportive. I just need time to process exactly how I'm going to do that. I need time to think before we both end up saying something we'll regret. Nothing good comes out of charged emotions. I was blindsided and thought that space was what we needed.

When I reach the door of my parents' house, I pause a minute, taking a deep breath because I know Mom and Dad will wonder where Cora and Avery are. They don't join us every Sunday for family dinner, but they do join us at least two to three times a month. Tonight was supposed to be one of those nights.

I'm not up for being around anyone, but this is not something I can easily get out of. My family is a whole other ball game when it comes to having any privacy or even private thoughts. Plus, I'm the baby, so they all feel the need to take charge of my life when anything big happens. And this feels big. So, I take one final breath and put on what I hope is the best game face I've ever attempted before walking inside.

As I close the front door behind me, I hear my parents chatting from the kitchen, the sound of pots clanking. I already know my mom's hovering over the stove while my dad's washing dishes. It's their usual routine. She cooks, and he washes everything, so there is less to do after dinner. My siblings and I switch off each week for after-dinner clean-up duty. My turn comes around less often now that my new sister-in-law, Rosie, and my brother Parker's girlfriend, Abbey, have joined the family.

So, to avoid startling my parents, I call out, "Mom! Dad! Happy Sunday!" Nothing about this Sunday feels happy, but I have to act like I would at any other dinner.

Mom peeks around the corner of the kitchen doorway into the entry hallway. "Oh, Jasper. You're a little earlier than I expected."

"Yeah, is that okay?"

"Don't be silly; of course, it is," she says as she meets me halfway down the entry hall. As soon as she reaches me, she pulls me into a hug. Her hugs always feel like they could heal you, and I could use some of that right now. I pull her tight and hope she doesn't question why I hesitate to let her go. But she seems fine to let our hug linger a little.

I finally start to pull back before I give her a reason to question me. When her bright green eyes meet my identical gaze, she has a gentle smile on her face. "Well, that was a nice hug. Haven't had one of those from you in a while."

"Yeah, well, it felt like the right time."

Her smile widens. "I'm glad, and I'm happy to accept one anytime. Now, where are my favorite little one-year-old and her mother? I thought they were coming tonight."

My stomach sinks, and part of me wants to tell her everything. I know she is going to be upset, too. But it's not the time because my brothers and sister will be here any minute. "We had a long, eventful day at the beach, and Avery was so exhausted she fell right to sleep. Cora thought it might be a good idea to skip tonight," I say, avoiding eye contact so she doesn't see I'm holding something back.

Except my mom is perceptive. I can feel her watching me, but I know she won't pry. She will wait until she is sure I will open up to her. Gwen Nallen has the patience of a saint, which I guess you need when you're the mother of four sons and a daughter. She has no problem waiting any of her children out.

"Huh, well, that's too bad. Come in here so I can make sure your dad isn't adding any extra seasonings to my sauce. You know he tends to overdo it when he thinks I'm not looking," she says as we head into the kitchen.

"I heard that," my dad shouts from down the hall.

"I swear, if I'm standing next to him, he can't hear a thing, but I'm in a different room whispering, and he can quote me verbatim." She rolls her eyes before shouting back, "You know it's true, Richard!"

I laugh as I walk through the doorway into the kitchen behind my mom. My dad has a wide grin across his face and winks at my mom. "Hey there, Jasper. Where are the girls?"

Before I could answer, my mom placed a hand on my dad's shoulder and answered him first: "They had a big day at the beach, and sweet Avery was exhausted. Cora thought it best that they stay home tonight." My mom's eyes were on me the whole time. She definitely knows something is up. Tyler may be right; she just might very well be a witch. Psychic, at the very least.

"Well, that's too bad, but I'm glad you all had a good day."

"Yeah, the beach was perfect. What can I help with?" I

want to move away from the topic of Cora, Avery, and our day together.

"How about you start setting the table?" Dad says. "I'm sure your brothers and sister will start trickling in sooner rather than later."

"You got it," I say as I reach into the cabinets and start pulling plates out for the entire family. "Are we sitting inside or outside tonight?"

"You choose," Mom says.

"Outside. The temperature is perfect tonight, and no fog for once."

I carry the plates onto the deck, and as I set them out, I can't keep my mind from drifting to thoughts of Cora and Avery. The worry of what will happen to all of us slips in. It feels like it's eating me from the inside out.

"Hey there, little brother. What's with the sour look on your face?" Drew interrupts my thoughts. I glance up and find Drew and Rosie looking at me as they carry out the glasses and utensils, and I place the last plate on the table.

"Oh, hey, guys," I say, trying to sound nonchalant.

"You good?" Rosie asks quietly as she comes close to me, placing a glass next to the plate I just placed on the table.

Looking in her direction, the concern is apparent on her face as her forehead crinkles between her eyes, and I shake my head. "Yeah…yeah…, I'm good. Just a long day in the sun."

My sister-in-law, Rosie, stares at me for a beat longer. It's weird that my brother, Drew, married a girl as similar and perceptive as our mother. She gives me a simple nod and starts setting up the utensils in her hand. Drew, on the other hand, is completely oblivious, which is much more in line with my intentions of not discussing how I'm feeling right now. "So, little brother, where are our favorite neighbors? Mom and Dad said they were joining us tonight," Drew asks.

Never mind. He may be oblivious, but it would be nice if he also avoided the topic of contention altogether. Except, why would he when he has no idea? If everyone keeps bringing Cora and Avery up as soon as they see me, I'm going to have a hard time keeping this game face on. And that will only open the door for them to start pressing me for information.

Mom walks out just about that time, Parker and Abbey on her heels. "Avery was still asleep after their long day, so Cora decided they should stay home for the night. Isn't that right, Jasper?" I don't know if I should thank her since this is the second time she has come to my aid in answering that question or be upset that she seems to be fishing to see if I give anything more away.

"Yep." I keep my response short and notice the looks exchanged between everyone. "Hey, Parks. Abbey." I greet them to change the subject.

"Hey," Park and Abbey say in unison. Rosie puts the last fork down and embraces Abbey, and they exchange greetings.

Rosie and Abbey are best friends, and they both fell in love with my two older brothers. Although they're different in many ways, Abbey is just as sweet as Rosie. My brothers got lucky because, from my perspective, they can be idiots. Or maybe that is just a little brother's point of view.

"Let the party begin!" A shout comes from inside the house.

"Sounds like Ty is here," Parker says.

We all roll our eyes as our brother Tyler steps out on the deck, hands in the air. He is the loudest and most melodramatic of all of us. But he is also the most loyal and protective, too, so we overlook what we affectionately call his annoying traits.

Suddenly, Kelsea appears behind Tyler and slaps him on the back of the head as she steps around him. He reaches up to hold his head with a shocked look. And just like that, she knocks him down a peg in typical Kelsea fashion. As the only girl, she had to be smart and tough to keep up with us. The thing is, she turned out to be smarter and tougher than any of us. She doesn't take crap from anyone, and while we always aim to protect her around others, she can stand on her own with no problem. We make it a point to treat her like one of the brothers, or she will make sure we pay for being "misogynistic a-holes," as she puts it.

"Damn it, Kelsea!"

"Tyler, your mouth, please," Mom scolds as she walks back into the house. We all laugh, and Tyler flips us all the bird as soon as Mom is out of sight.

Seconds later, Dad comes out, carrying some platters of food, and Mom follows with more. "Tyler, make yourself useful and grab the pitcher of tea, please," Dad says, then continues, "Parker, you grab the salad bowl, and then we will be all ready to eat."

Tyler and Parker disappear into the house without a word while the rest of us take our normal seats around the outdoor dining table. The temperature outside is perfect for eating on the patio tonight.

Our usual family banter starts as soon as Parker and Tyler take their seats. Drew and Parker tell my dad about a project they started working on together. The girls all start talking about a new boutique that opened downtown. Tyler adds to everyone's conversation. I take them all in and how the conversations float effortlessly between us. Tonight, I'm content just listening. Maybe the less I speak, the less likely they will start prying into my life.

This Sunday dinner seems to be like every other week. There's laughter, arguing, and more laughter. It's my favorite day of the week because nothing feels better than being with my parents and my siblings…except being with Cora, and now Avery. God, what am I going to do? Is this really happening? I feel the knot forming in my stomach again. That same gut-wrenching feeling I had an hour ago when Cora first told me they were moving. It felt like I was losing my life then, and I still do now.

"Hey, little brother, speaking of, why aren't Cora and Avery here? Did you finally wear out your welcome?" Tyler asks when Kelsea mentions a new shade of lipstick Cora recommended to her.

I don't know if it's the thoughts I was just having or that everyone in my family insists on bringing them up, but Cora's name sets me on edge, and I snap. "Screw you, Tyler. Contrary to belief, I don't always know why Cora does the things she does. And who knows, maybe they do need a break from me. We were together all day. I don't make Cora's life decisions. I don't even get a say in them!" I'm practically out of breath, standing up abruptly, and begin to leave the table.

I only get five feet before I hear my dad's booming voice: "Jasper Nallen, I'm not sure where that little outburst came from, but you will not act like that at the family dinner table, and you have not been excused. I don't care how old you are."

I take three deep breaths and turn around to take my seat again. Everyone is staring at me in shocked disbelief. My mom and Rosie have a sympathetic frown that confirms my suspicions that they both caught on to my sour mood and preoccupied thoughts earlier. "My apologies, everyone."

If there is one thing I'm certain of, its that I've never raised my voice like this to anyone in my family. It's just not like me. Tonight, I'm not really feeling myself.

"Uh…sorry, Bro," Tyler says, a sincere apology in his tone and maybe some confusion.

"Jasper, do you need to talk about something?" Mom asks.

Keeping my gaze on my dinner plate in front of me, I feel all their stares on me. What do I say? That the girl I've been in love with most of my life is taking her daughter, whom I love like my own, and moving to another state. Although we spend practically every free moment we have together, not to mention we are each other's best and most trusted friends, Cora didn't even consider me in her decision? That she didn't even tell me for weeks, and then we both said some regrettable thing, and I acted like a little bit of an ass because I was hurt? Is this really the conversation I want to have at the family dinner table?

They've all teased me for years about being in love with Cora. They know how I feel for her and even showed some concern when Cora first became pregnant because I practically never left her side. But they all love Cora, too, and so they moved past their concern for me and gave her the support they would give anyone else in our own family.

"Jas?" Dad says, concern filling the air because I haven't answered my mom.

Finding my voice because I have no choice, I start, "I…" I haven't said this out loud yet, and I know as soon as I do, it won't be just a conversation I had with Cora. It's going to be even more of a reality. I look up, and they are all still patiently watching me. "Cora and Avery are moving to Arizona. She received her dream job offer, and they leave in two weeks. She just told me tonight before I came over."

Mom lets out a soft gasp. Rosie's hand covers her mouth. My dad and siblings' eyes fill with sympathy, along with Abbey's, who reaches over and puts her hand on top of Parker's.

"If it is alright with all of you, I'd appreciate it if you would all stop looking at me like I'm about to shatter, whether it's true or not. And I would like you all to finish family dinner and excuse me tonight because I think I'd like to go home and be alone for a bit."

"But Jasper…" Mom starts until my dad places his hand on her shoulder.

"Whatever you feel you need, but don't hide from us for too long," Dad says.

"Thanks, I appreciate it." I push my seat out and stand to leave. "Goodnight, I'll see you all next Sunday. Have a good week." I turn and head to leave.

Just before I step through the door, Drew says loud enough for me to hear him, "It's cute he thinks we're going to let him avoid us and this conversation for a week."

I actually want to laugh, but only a little. Instead, I keep walking and leave my family to finish family dinner, one member short for the first time in…well, ever.

Four

CORA

It's been twenty-four hours since I told Jasper I was moving to Arizona with Avery, and he stormed off. And I still haven't heard a word from him.

I put my notice in at work today, and it wasn't easy. He was the first person I wanted to talk to about it, and for the first time since I've known him, I didn't feel like I could call him. Instead, I called my mom. She has been struggling with her own sadness over us moving, but her perspective is that of a mother. The tug of war, wanting to keep us with her and my dad, and her desire for me to find my own way. I'm not sure I truly understood that feeling until I had my own child.

As I walk out of my office building and into the cool afternoon air, I wonder how I will fix this with Jasper. I know he is going to miss us, but I can't fully understand his reaction. I made it through a whole day without talking to him, but it was miserable.

Walking up to my car, I look up and find the person I've been missing leaning against it, waiting for me. "Hey," I say, unable to think of anything else to say.

Pushing off the car, Jasper puts his hands in his jean pockets. "Hey," he says, looking down at his feet and then back up to me. "Do you think we can go somewhere and talk?"

A loose strand of hair whips across my face, and I push it out of the way, as I watch him for a moment, trying to read his face for what he is feeling. We've always known each other so well, but this one conversation made me feel like we were a million miles apart. He waits patiently; his gaze locked on my face.

Of course, I'm going to agree. There is so much I need to understand, not to mention many things I need to explain. "Sure, I just need to call my parents and ask them if they can give Avery her bath tonight."

"Yes, okay…umm, should we go to the cove?"

"That's fine; I will drive my own car and call them on the way. See you in a few minutes."

"Yep, sounds like a plan. See you there," he says. Jasper turns away from me, and I watch him until he's in his car before I get into mine.

He pulls out first, and I follow behind him. Once we turn out onto the street, I press the talk button on my steering wheel and tell Siri to dial home. My dad picks up almost immediately. "Hey, Dad."

"Hey, sweetie. Did you just get off?"

"Yeah, and if you don't mind, I'm going to be a little late. Can you and Mom give Avery her bath? I should be home in time to put her to bed."

"No problem. Are you okay? We didn't see you last night after you gave Avery her bath. You seemed upset when you came inside after Jasper left, and we know you told him about moving."

After Jasper left, and I broke down just inside the doorway, I did my best to keep my emotions as quiet as possible before I picked myself up and coaxed Avery awake for a little dinner and her bath. My parents didn't ask me any questions while we ate, and I purposely didn't go back downstairs after Avery's bath. Instead, I tossed and turned until I finally fell asleep.

"Actually, I'm going to be late because I'll be with Jasper. We have some things to work through together." Surely, he and I can work through whatever we need so things can be as they've always been with us.

"Cora, yes, take your time, and please work out whatever you need with Jasper. I know you will, and I'm certain he'll be the supportive and kind friend he has always been. All will be right," my dad always says before we say our goodbyes.

As we hang up, Jasper and I pull to a stop, parking next to each other near the cove. One of our favorite hangouts growing up. The perfect little beach hideaway. I grab my sweater from my passenger seat because I know it will be chilly as the sun goes down and get out of the car. Jasper is already waiting for me.

We silently walk together down the path until we are on

the beach. There is a large piece of driftwood where both of us take a seat. Neither of us talks for several minutes, our attention looking out at the waves crashing against the shoreline. I'll miss the sound and feel of the sea air—not nearly as much as I will miss the man next to me.

"Cora, first, I want to apologize for not congratulating you and being more supportive," his voice filled with sincerity.

"Ja…" I begin, but he stops me.

"Please let me say some things first, then we can discuss things." He looks over at me, waiting for me to agree. I give him a silent nod, and then he continues, "I'm so proud and happy for you. You obviously want this new life, and as your best friend, I want you to have whatever makes you happy. I do want you to be happy, Cora, and I know it didn't come across that way last night. I'm sorry for that."

I watch him for a moment, and this is my Jasper. The Jaspe, who has always lifted me up and cheered me on until I believed in myself. Yet, I can see he isn't finished.

"But I don't want you to leave. Just like you said, I don't have a part in your decision; you don't get to decide what is good for me. You and Avery are good for me. How am I supposed to let you both leave without saying how I feel? Things changed the day she came into this world."

"Jas, I didn't intend to hurt you the way I have. I would never do anything to intentionally cause you pain. But I don't know what you want from me. You're my best friend, but this is my future…Avery's future."

"I get that, but it's my future, too."

"Don't you see, I know that! I told you last night I can't keep holding you back from the future you deserve."

"Who made you the authority on what I deserve?"

We start arguing back and forth, as we did last night. This is not how I was hoping this conversation would go.

"God!" I yell and push myself up off the log. "Why can't you see I'm trying to do what is best for all of us? Why can't you see that this changes nothing about us but our day-to-day? You are, and will forever be, my very best friend."

"And I want to know why you can't see this," he motions between us, "is so much more!" He shouts, rising and comes to stand in front of me.

"What?" I ask.

Jasper stands before me, staring at me, his gaze boring into me with such intensity that I feel like I could catch fire. "If you can't see what I mean, then maybe it's all in my head, and there really isn't more to discuss except how we spend these remaining couple of weeks with the least amount of impact on Avery."

I want to ask him what he means again. Instead, I remain silent, worried about the answer to that question and even more scared that I'm not prepared for it. Finally, I find my voice again. "I think we should gradually reduce the amount of time we spend together so Avery feels less impacted by your absence." It sounds harsh and cold, even to my ears. Why does this keep happening?

"Okay, whatever you want. She is your daughter. I'm just…well, I'm whatever I am."

Without thinking, I reach my hand up and cup his cheek

gently. "Jas, you know I … you're my best friend, right?"

He hesitates a moment, "Yeah, sure I do. Like I said, I just want for you and Avery to be happy. That is all I've ever wanted for you, Cora." He pulls me into one of his strong and comforting hugs. We stand in this embrace for a long time, wind whipping around us.

When he pulls back, he gives me a sad smile. "Goodnight, Cora. See you tomorrow night for our usual dinner, right?'

"Yeah, we will see you."

"Good."

Jasper steps away. "I'll walk you to your car." I nod, and we walk back to where we parked our cars.

"Goodnight, Cora."

"Goodnight, Jas."

This conversation ended differently than last night, and it felt like more of a shift in our relationship—like a breakup—and worse than any I've ever experienced.

JASPER

Last night, Cora, Avery, and I met at our favorite burger joint for their Tuesday night special. Cora and I have been doing this since we were teenagers, and over the last year, it has become even more of a ritual.

The night went as well as it could, given the tension between me and Cora. I gave Avery all my attention, and she was as happy as she always was, so I would say the night was a success. Typically, I'd see them on Thursday, too. In fact, the only nights we don't usually spend together are Monday and Wednesday. But not this week; this week begins our new arrangement. A change for all of us, and one I'm already dreading. But we agreed that this will make it easier for all of us when the move actually happens.

A loud banging on my front door pulls my attention away from my thoughts and the baseball game I'm watching on the television.

I let out a groan because I know who it is. It's one of three people, or all three of them at once. I contemplate not even answering the door, but I'm pretty sure they know where the key is hidden. I guess they deserve a reward for making it to Wednesday, three whole days before they butt into my business.

"Jas! We know you're home, so get off your ass and answer the door."

It was either Parker or Drew; they often sound similar. The fact that he said "we" means it's most likely all of them. Great.

"Why can't you leave me alone?" I ask as I open the door.

"Because Mom, Drew's wife, and my girlfriend will never stop nagging us to check on you," Parker says. He and Drew are each leaning against the wall on either side of the doorway. Tyler is standing directly in front of the entrance as if they are expecting me to make a run for it, and they're blocking me in.

"I was just hoping for a guy's night," Tyler adds, a crooked smile on his face.

I stare at all three of them for a few seconds and turn, heading back to the couch, my beer, and the baseball game. I hear the door close behind me. I throw myself down onto the couch and glance over at my brothers. Tyler opens the fridge and pulls out a beer.

"Help yourself," I say, sarcasm hanging on my words.

"I am, thanks. These two prefer that pale ale crap, and I know you have a stout," Ty responds.

Drew and Parker place a pizza on the counter, start dishing out slices of pizza on four plates, and ignore Tyler's remark. They each fall into either a chair or onto the couch around me.

"I'm not hungry," I tell Drew as he hands me a plate, but I take it anyway. He doesn't acknowledge that I said anything. I take a bite of the pepperoni pizza.

"Who's winning?" Parker asks.

"Oakland, surprisingly," I tell him, then take another bite. Maybe I was hungry after all.

"Nice," Tyler says, kicking his feet up onto my coffee table.

I finish my slice and put the plate on the side table next to me. I pick up my beer and take a long guzzle before setting it back down. "Let's get this over with, say what you need to say," I tell them.

Drew and Parker look at one another, but Tyler, of course, is the one who speaks first. "So, Cora and Avery are moving away. Did you finally tell her how you feel, or are you just going to let her walk away?"

"Well, right to the point is one way to do this," Parker says.

"They're leaving, and I tried, but Cora doesn't want to hear it."

Drew leans forward, his elbows resting on his knees, "For the past year, from our perspective, you two have been in a relationship. Were we wrong? What is the deal?"

I shrug.

"Dude, you mean you still haven't defined your relationship?" Tyler chimes in before I can answer Drew.

"Tyler, shut the hell up. Let Jas explain," Parker says.

"Look, he's right. I should have told Cora. But I've loved her since we were kids. It never seemed necessary to say it. I was content just building this life with her, and the path we seemed to be on. Avery just made that path a hundred times clearer for me. It's just shit luck that Cora and I weren't on the same page."

"Okay, and now what?" Parker asks.

"Now, they leave. Cora reaches for her dream of working for a successful national marketing firm. She takes Avery, and they find their place in the world. I stay here and be her childhood best friend. She calls on occasion and sees me when she comes to town for visits."

My brothers all stare at me. I can practically see the words hanging on their tongues written across their faces.

Tyler shakes his head. "Jasper, you…we all know you and Cora are more than that; letting her walk away will be a mistake. You deserve to have the life you want with her." Parker, Drew, and I stare at Tyler. I think we're all a little shocked because it's rare for Tyler to open up his sensitive side. We know it's there, but he doesn't often let anyone in. He continues when he sees our faces. "Oh, come on, you guys know I'm right."

"This won't happen often, so don't let it go to your head." Drew looks directly at Tyler when he says this and then turns to me. "But Tyler is right."

I stand up and walk to the fridge for another beer. "I hear you, but I'm obviously not a part of the dream Cora has envisioned for herself. She keeps mentioning that I will fall in love with someone one day and start a life…a family with that person. She says it's unfair of her to depend on me so much and not allow me to find that person."

"And did you tell her she's the one you want?" Parker questions.

"Yes, in a way. Hell, I told her I would go with them," I tell them.

"You, what?" Drew demands.

"I told Cora I would go with them. Because I would."

Tyler laughs, "Mom would freak."

"Maybe, but it doesn't matter anyway because Cora said no."

"It sounds like you've already given up," Drew says.

"I wouldn't say I've given up. I've just accepted what she says she wants. I've always loved Cora, and I've always respected her. I won't stop now, no matter how bad it hurts me."

"Sounds like your mind is made up. Just know we'll be here," Drew says.

I downed the rest of my beer. I know my family means well, but I don't know how to tell them what they want to hear. This is something I can't even answer for myself. I don't know how I will move forward when my whole world feels like it's ending. The only thing I can do is give them a Jasper-type answer to keep them from worrying.

"Support Cora. Support Avery. I will be fine and find my way."

They all look at me skeptically and then raise their beers in the air before downing them.

Five

CORA

This week's Tuesday night dinner with Jasper went well...at least for Avery. She adores him, and I worry about what his absence will be like for her. He doted on her as usual, and they were like they always are, connected and happy. I can see how much he loves her, and it's breaking my heart. He was cordial with me, and I could tell he was doing his best to make everything feel normal, but that wall between us just seemed to get higher.

As we wrapped up for the evening, we agreed to spend Saturday together and have one last Tuesday night meal together before Avery and I leave. We are usually together almost every night, but we must get used to life without one another. So far, it's been really hard this week because we haven't seen Jasper since Tuesday.

Sometimes, I worry that I'm crazy—for pushing him

away, leaving here, and going out into the unknown with my baby. Then I remember why I'm doing this and shove everything else out of my mind. Jasper and I have been friends too long not to get through this.

Avery and I will make the most of these precious last days with Jasper while we can. Today, we're driving to the aquarium in Monterey for the day, and then we'll have lunch. It's something we've wanted to do with Avery for a while, and we finally decided to take her after her birthday.

"So, Jasper is going with you?" My mom asks as she walks into the kitchen. She stands next to me as I pack some snacks for the road.

"He is." I continue to pour Goldfish into a small Ziplock bag.

"Good, we haven't seen him much in the last week."

"Mom. We talked about this already. Jasper and I decided it's best for all of us, especially Avery, to limit the time we spend together over the next couple of weeks."

"Cora, I just want you to be certain of your choices. I'm worried about you."

"I know you and Dad just want to protect me and Avery. I know Jasper wants to protect me and Avery. But I need to protect us. It feels like this is my opportunity to do that."

"Cora, I'm not trying to say you shouldn't take this job. I'm just saying not to alienate the person you trust and who has stood by you for more years than you can remember."

I lean against the kitchen island and let out a long, drawn-out sigh.

"I'm not trying to alienate anyone, especially Jasper.

God, Mom. It's breaking my heart to think about leaving him and separating him and Avery. But this is my dream job and an opportunity I need to take for myself and my baby girl. I have to prove to myself and everyone that I can stand alone."

"You have nothing to prove to your father and me. Or Jasper."

"Fine, I do to myself then." I turn to face her. "Mom, I feel like I've made one wrong choice after another. Starting with getting pregnant by Tommy. A person I never loved, and someone who could so easily sign away his rights to any relationship with his daughter. It seems that with every turn, I couldn't get it right and made a string of mistakes. Of course, I would never change having Avery. She is the best part of me. And I need this. I need this chance to prove to myself that I can do all of this without you and Dad. And without Jasper."

Just saying that breaks my heart. She's right, I can't remember a time I've done anything without Jasper standing right by my side. Supporting and cheering me on, no matter what I got myself into.

Mom reaches a hand up, gently running it over my cheek. "I love you, my girl. I wish you wouldn't judge yourself so harshly. Childhood and youth are the time for mistakes. Growing up is learning from them. I'm so proud of who you've become, and I only want you to be happy. Your father feels the same."

I pull her into a hug and allow myself to soak up all her motherly love. "I love you so much, Mom."

"I love you too, baby girl."

SHIRL RICKMAN

We pull back and hold hands.

"I'm hurting Jasper, and I don't know if he can forgive me."

"Cora, we both know Jasper will forgive you for living your life the way you need. He may be hurting because you two created something special and safe. Jasper…well, I won't speak for him, but you both need to clear the air between you before you leave. That's all I'm going to say about that."

"Do you think I'm making another mistake? Leaving? Leaving Jasper?"

"Cora, honey. Only you can answer that for yourself. Just know that sometimes you only realize the right choice after making the wrong one."

My mom and her wisdom. My entire life, she has always forced me to find my own way, and that may be why I feel the need to make this life change.

Before we can say more, Avery comes toddling around the corner, my dad hot on her trail. Seeing her reaffirms that some poor choices allow you to receive the greatest gifts.

JASPER

"Mom. Dad. Anyone around?" My voice echoes through the house as I walk through the door. "Hello?"

Closing the door, I make my way to the back of the house. Maybe they're outside in the backyard. It is Saturday, and as early as it is, it's already sunny and warm. Usually, at this time of the year, we are used to early morning fog and cool temps.

When I reach the back door, I notice it's open and hear my mom's voice from the outside. She's talking to my dad, and when I hear my name, I stop and listen.

"I'm just worried about him, Richard. Jasper is so good and always puts others first. He never asks for anything, especially for himself."

"You're right, but this is Jasper's life. He must handle it for himself. I don't want to see him hurt as much as you, but we can't involve ourselves too much. It helps that I'm certain Cora cares for him, too. She would never intentionally hurt him; that's all we can ask for."

I hate my parents worrying about me, and their words, even if they weren't meant for me, comfort me. I feel bad enough as it is, listening in on their conversation, so I call out to them again to give them a warning. "Mom...Dad!"

I wait momentarily, and my dad answers, "Out here!"

I push the door open and walk out onto the deck. They're sitting at the table, both holding coffee mugs. "Morning," I say.

"Morning, Jasper, we weren't expecting you," Mom says, trying her best to act as if they weren't just discussing me. It makes me want to smile. I walk behind her and lean down, kissing her cheek.

"What brings you by so early?" Dad asks as I walk around the table and take a seat across from Mom.

"I'm picking Cora and Avery up; we're going to the aquarium in Monterey today."

Mom's eyes widen in surprise. "Oh."

"That sounds fun," Dad says, sipping his coffee. "Remind us of when they leave again."

My chest instantly knots. I wonder when I might finally get used to the inevitable and not feel sick when someone mentions them leaving. "Uh, in just over a week, so the Monday after next. Cora wants a week to get things in order once they get there. Mr. and Mrs. Connolly will be going with them."

Dad nods, "Makes sense. We sure are going to miss them. You should have them join us for Sunday dinner tomorrow or next." He says it so matter-of-factly. My parents are trying their best not to ask all the questions I know are on their minds—the same ones they were obviously just discussing. I love them both so much for respecting me. I know my mom, though. She is going to need a little more, and she will find a way.

"I'll ask Cora today and let you know."

"Your brothers mentioned they went by your house on Wednesday night," Mom broaches, trying to sound blasé.

"They did." I raise an eyebrow at her teasingly. She raises hers right back in challenge, which is one of my favorite things about her. "It was more like barging in, taking over my living room, and drinking all my beer."

Both of my parents smile and just look at me. Ugh. This is how they do it. I see it, and I still can't avoid it. They are letting me talk, and the more I talk, the more I will open myself up. The thing is, I knew this would happen, and it's the real reason I came here.

"You know how they are. They wanted to make sure I was okay, and I am."

"Are you?" She questions.

Shrugging, I glance between my parents. "What choice do I have?"

My dad, who never really says too much, and when he does, it's with intention, leans toward me and looks directly into my eyes. "You always have a choice, Jasper."

"Well, I have to be okay, Dad. I'm choosing to support Cora, even if it is tearing me apart." I put my head in my hands and grunt in frustration.

"Oh, Jasper, you love her," Mom whispers softly as if she is physically feeling my pain.

"Son, that's one of your best qualities, but you should be honest with Cora, too. You should tell her how you really feel, whether it changes anything or not," he says.

I look at both of them, knowing they're right. I just don't see why I would do that to Cora or me if it won't change anything. I don't want to put any pressure on her and guilt her in any way.

"She should know you love her. What she does with that information is her choice, of course, but regardless, be honest," Mom adds.

"I'll think about it," I tell them. And I will because, in the end, Cora…Avery and their feelings are what matter most. For me, my feelings aren't the priority.

"We love you, Jasper," Dad tells me, placing his hand over mine. "We will be here to support you no matter what happens."

"I know, Dad, and I'm thankful for that. I will figure out what is best, and I promise I'll do it soon."

I spend the next half hour with my parents before I'm supposed to pick up Cora and Avery. They don't mention Cora, her leaving, or my choices again. In true Richard and Gwen Nallen form, they leave me to make my own decision.

Six

CORA

I look around the dinner table at all the familiar faces who make up most of my core childhood memories. Jasper isn't the only Nallen who means something to me. All those years of our friendship growing up, I was always treated like I was a part of the Nallen family. From the moment I brought Avery home, they all embraced her as one of their own. Tonight is no different, and it weighs heavily on me. A sadness I knew was hanging around inside me, but it only became real when I saw the everyday love we'd miss by not having our loved ones in our day-to-day lives.

Over the last two weeks, I've made it a point to visit Mr. and Mrs. Nallen with Avery. More than once, one of Jasper's other siblings was here, so we got to spend time with them, too. When Jasper told me that his parents wanted us to come to Sunday dinner before we left, I didn't hesitate. I knew I not only owed it to them, but I owed it to myself and my daughter.

I'll miss these warm, casual family dinners with this amazing group of people. Rosie bounces Avery on her knee while Kelsea and Abbey make faces at her to get her to laugh. Drew is relaxing with his arm slung over Rosie's chair, an admiring grin on his face. Tyler and Parker are having a heated discussion about baseball and some sort of stats while Mr. Nallen referees the two. Mrs. Nallen went inside a moment ago to get dessert.

When I glance Jasper's way, he's looking at me. His features are hard to read, but his eyes have a melancholy look to them. Our gaze holds one another, and I can't help the shiver that comes over my skin. He abruptly stands up and moves in my direction. When he is standing in front of me, Jasper leans in a bit and whispers, "I'll walk you and Avery home tonight; there are some things I need to say to you."

"Oh…okay," was the only response I managed to get out before he turned and disappeared into the house. When I look back up, Kelsea's attention is focused on me now instead of Avery. She slowly stands up and walks over to me.

"Hey," she says.

"Hey," I reply, refocusing my attention on Avery's smiling face.

Other than Jasper, Kelsea and I have been the closest over the years. For one, she is only a little over a year older than Jasper and me. Also, I was a female buffer for her since she is in a house full of brothers. She has always been a trusted friend, and I looked up to her my whole childhood. Kelsea is probably the strongest and smartest person I know.

"How are you doing?" Kelsea asks. I glance over, and her gaze meets mine. I see friendly concern and understanding.

"I'm good. How about you?"

"Honestly, Cora. How are you?"

I don't look her way. I think about that question and the real answer, not the automatic one. She says she wants the honest answer, but I'm not even sure I've allowed myself to think out what that is, even though my parents have been pushing me toward it.

"I guess I'm unsure how to explain how I am."

"Just a little unsolicited advice—you should figure that out before you leave tomorrow."

"That seems to be a popular opinion," I retort without animosity.

"I love you, Cora. But I don't want to see Jasper hurt."

"Neither do I," I tell her. "Jasper is…but I need to make the responsible choice for Avery and myself."

"I can respect that," Kelsea says. "I should probably say, I don't want to see you hurt either. I hope you and Jasper can be honest about how you feel."

My gaze darts to her. "I'm sorry?"

"You heard me," she says. "If you aren't, I fear you will lose one another. Now, I'm going back to steal my favorite little girl from Rosie and get as much loving as possible while I can."

Kelsea leaves me standing alone, feeling as confused

as ever. I feel as if Jasper and I have been nothing but honest with each other. He doesn't want to lose Avery or our friendship. I don't…well, I don't want to lose our friendship either. We've never known life without each other, and understandably, it will be hard for us to get used to it.

"Dessert is served," Mrs. Nallen says, walking out with a bundt cake. Jasper follows behind her, ice cream in hand.

Mr. Nallen begins cutting the cake while Mrs. Nallen serves it. Jasper walks around, scooping out the ice cream. I take Avery from Kelsea and put her in her seat, sitting next to her. Jasper hands me a scoop with a spoon, then sits on Avery's other side. Before I have a chance to give Avery some, he is sharing his cake and ice cream with her. This isn't an unusual occurrence. Jasper has played this role since Avery came home from the hospital.

And I'm suddenly struck with knowing that this is exactly why everyone is worried about me leaving and how it will impact Jasper. But it's going to impact me, too. This is why I said those things to Jasper when I told him I was leaving. He has always felt a sense of responsibility for me, but he deserves more than just feeling responsible for someone else's kid. He deserves a chance at finding his own love. And as his best friend, as someone who loves him so deeply, I need to stop taking advantage of him and his reliability. I need to release him. I need to stand on my own two feet, so he no longer feels obligated. Jasper has always saved me from myself, and I can't let him do that anymore. It's time to save myself.

Avery giggles and reaches her tiny hand out until she touches Jasper's face. She pats him softly on the cheek, and his face lights up. Every second we're with him makes all of this so much harder.

Mr. Nallen stands up, stealing my attention from Avery and Jasper. "I'd like to say something on behalf of everyone sitting here." Every person sitting around the table stops talking. "Cora, you have practically been part of our family since you and your parents moved in across the street. You captured all of our hearts from the start. Gwen and I have watched you grow into a beautiful, smart young woman. Then you brought Avery into our lives, and we can't imagine life without either of you. The only reason we are able to let you go is because we know this new adventure is a chance of a lifetime. But please don't be a stranger. Don't be shy if you ever find yourself in need and never forget where you came from. Cheers to you."

I don't even realize tears have escaped down my cheeks until Jasper hands me a napkin. "For the tears," he says.

I look over at him, in stunned silence, and accept it. Then, I slowly stand and make my way around the table to Mr. and Mrs. Nallen, embracing them both. "Thank you so much." I turn to the rest of the group. "You can't know what you all mean to me. I will miss you all, and I know Avery will, too." My teary gaze locks with Jasper's, and I feel my heart crack slightly from the painful reality that this will be our last night together for who knows how long.

JASPER

I'm surprisingly calm sitting on the Connolly's' front porch, rocking in the chair, waiting for Cora to put Avery down. The night is cool, and quiet surrounds me. The only lights are coming from the other homes along our street. A street that Cora and I rode our bikes down daily to school, where we drove our first cars, and played hide and seek as children. So many memories. So much time.

The last year has changed our relationship in many ways. We just never talked about it. We just let it happen, and now I'm not sure that was the best idea. I can't change it now, though. All I can do is be the Jasper I've always been and support her. The sound of the front door opening and closing brings me back from my thoughts. I don't look over at Cora, though, mostly because I don't even know where to begin. She takes a seat in the rocker next to me, and we fall into a rhythm. Until recently, we've always been in sync.

Cora remains silent, knowing it's what I need right now, and I'm sure it's what she needs, too. We both have things to say, and, unsurprisingly, we both need a minute.

"Cora," I say, breaking the silence between us.

"Yeah, Jasper."

I reach over and take her hand in mine. She accepts the gesture willingly.

"I'm going to miss you," I tell her.

"I'm going to miss you, too. So much, it hurts."

My chest begins to fill with overwhelming emotions.

I'm nervous and scared. Normally, I'm not afraid of anything, but I now realize that isn't true. I'm afraid of telling Cora how I feel, being rejected, and then losing her. I'm afraid it will change everything. Except everything is changing anyway.

Releasing my hold on her hand, I stand up and walk out into the yard, a sudden need for space and air. I can feel Cora's stare on my back when I come to a stop. I keep my back to her, considering how I'm going to move forward and what is best for all of us. Suddenly, she's behind me, "Jasper." Her tone sounds desperate and full of worry.

"Cora, I don't want you to leave."

"Why?"

"You know why," I insist. I can't bring myself to say more.

"I don't think I do. It's like you've been talking in circles for weeks around what you really want to say. I do know this: you have been the one constant in my life, Jasper. You've always been honest and forthright with me. What is different now? Tell me."

As I turn toward her, we're inches from one another. I search her eyes for a sign that if I take this chance, it will change things, and she won't leave here... leave me. But I see something in her eyes; I see fear. She says she wants honesty, but I don't think she's ready for it. This revelation breaks my heart.

I reach my hand up, gently cupping her cheek. Her eyes widen but remain locked with mine. Then she closes her eyes and leans into the palm of my hand, like she is savoring the touch. I'm going to tell her, but not with words, because I knew the moment I turned and looked into her eyes, she was going to leave regardless. There is nothing to lose, so I lean forward and slowly and gently place my lips against hers. Cora's eyes flash open, but I don't move. I just linger there, looking right back at her. After a moment, I allow myself to move my mouth over hers, and she moves with me...one...two...three caresses, then I pull back. Cora looks stunned and flush and perfect. It feels almost impossible to walk away, but that's what I need to do.

"That is what I needed to tell you. Goodbye, Cora," I whisper and turn away, walking toward my Jeep.

After a few steps, Cora calls out, "Jasper!"

I turn around but keep moving backward toward my truck, a small, sad smile on my lips.

"I...it's not goodbye, it's I'll see you later...you..." she stutters through her words. "Nothing is changing. I'm just moving. We will talk and... right?"

I still don't say anything. I just keep smiling because I know deep in my heart tomorrow, when she drives away, things will never be the same.

I turn just before I reach my Jeep, open the door, and step inside. Instead of getting in, I raise myself up into the Jeep, still leaning out until I can see Cora again standing there. "Be happy, Cora." And with that, I get in and close the door. As I drive away, I feel the final brick in the wall I've been building the last couple of weeks go into place.

CORA

I stay where Jasper left me standing long after his taillights fade into the distance. As soon as he walked away, I felt the loss of his soft lips against mine. Jasper kissed me. It was sweet, gentle, and completely unexpected. We've never…best friends don't kiss like that because even though it wasn't filled with uncontrolled passion, it was intimate.

And then he just walked away, and it felt so final. I shake that thought away, walk back to the front porch, and sit in the chair he was sitting in. A tear forms and escapes down my cheek. Reaching up, I wipe it away.

Be happy, Cora. That was the last thing he said to me. I'm wondering if I can truly be happy without Jasper. And what does it mean if I feel that way? I love him. I know I love him. But I'm not what he needs, and I know it. That is what this ache deep inside me means.

Seven

JASPER

Four Years Later...

"Have you gone to see Jim today?" my mom asks, pouring me a cup of coffee.

"Not yet; Mrs. Connolly says he usually sleeps at this time. I don't want to bother him when he should be resting."

Mom takes a sip of her coffee and reaches for one of the scones she put out on the plate in front of us. She places one on the napkin in front of me before taking one for herself. "Have you spoken to Cora?" And just like that, she cuts to the chase.

"Mom, you know I haven't. Cora and I haven't spoken in I don't know how long, and our last text was six weeks ago when we learned that Mr. Connolly was ill."

"All this time, and I still don't understand that. Maybe it's not for me to understand. She's coming home, you know," she says, taking another sip of her coffee and then continuing. "Julia said that Cora insisted she and Avery come back and live with her now that they've put Jim on hospice care."

I didn't know, and that knowledge is like a punch in the gut. After all these years, she still holds some power over me. Of course, she's coming home. Her dad is sick. It was sudden and quick, like cancer is sometimes. Strikes out of nowhere and leaves a person reeling. The day they told me; I felt devastation like I've never known. Mr. Connolly has always been like another dad to me. I immediately called Cora, and when she didn't answer, I texted her. It took her half a day to reply. I know what this prognosis did to her. Her dad was her hero and her world. I still wanted to save her from the pain, but it didn't matter; that had never been enough to keep her close before.

"No, Mrs. Connolly didn't mention it, but I'm not surprised that she'd come home at least to see him. He can't travel to her like they've been doing for the past four years. It's good she will be with her mom during this time."

"Jasper, she isn't just visiting for a little while. She's moving back home, for good. I just didn't want you to be blindsided when she stayed. You know I worry…"

I cut her off before she could finish that statement: "Mom, today is no different than every other day that you've worried about me when it comes to Cora, so stop. I'm fine. It will be fine."

I hope my words are more convincing than what I'm

feeling right now. I don't really believe that having Cora and Avery back will have no impact on me.

"Oh, sweetie, I'm not trying to be a bother about this, so let's change the subject. You know yourself better than any of us," she pauses. "Rosie and Drew sent me a text this morning with a new ultrasound. I can't believe she is already twenty-six weeks along!"

I want to laugh at my mom's attempt to shift the topic. She certainly picked a happier one—a new life. A topic that my whole family is excited about.

"Yeah, Rosie sent it to me, too. I just happened to text her about the Connolly's meal train she and Abbey started."

"Those two are just too sweet for doing that for Julia."

She's right, my sisters-in-law couldn't be more compassionate or thoughtful. Abbey always gives the credit to Rosie, but we all have her number. She's just as kind. The Connollys mean something to all of us, and this has been hard for the entire family to accept.

"They are. Drew and Parker got pretty lucky because we both know they are much nicer now that they are married to those two," I say with a laugh.

Mom playfully swats my hand and laughs, too.

"Well, Mom. Thanks for the coffee, scones, and chat. I think I'm going to head over and see Mr. Connolly before I meet up with Tyler for a little surfing."

We both stand, and I take our mugs to the sink, rinsing them out first, then placing them in the dishwasher. Mom comes to my side, "Tell that brother of yours he better not be late this Sunday for dinner again."

I laugh, "I'll do my best."

She wraps me in a hug. "I love you, Jasper."

I pull back and look down at her. That worry is still lingering in her eyes. "I love you, too, Mom." I decide not to bring it up because I know it will only start the same conversation we've had countless times...my happiness, a girlfriend, my future.

What I haven't been able to tell anyone for four years is that I gave up on the possibility of any of those things for myself the day Cora drove away.

CORA

"Mom, yes. I'm sure we don't need you to come out here and help us move," I explain over the phone to her for the tenth time today. "I have some friends who have volunteered to help me get everything I'm bringing into a small moving trailer, and everything else I've sold, or I am selling."

It only took me a few weeks to make the decision to move home and be with my parents once I heard the news about my dad. They gave up everything to help me and Avery from the time she was born, and even when I took this job four years ago, and I owe them. Not to mention that I can't live with myself for being so far away and missing all the time I have left with my dad. It makes me sick just thinking about him not being here on earth with us anymore. I force the thought from my mind.

"Well, I guess that works out better anyway. I probably shouldn't leave your dad," she says through the phone.

"No, you shouldn't."

"When is your last day of work?" she asks.

"Tomorrow, and then I will spend the next couple of days packing. I plan on loading myself and Avery in the car bright and early on Friday."

"Cora, I want you to be safe and take your time."

"Mom, I will, but I want to be there on Monday, when the new hospice nurse starts, which is why we're leaving on Friday."

"I hate that you're having to uproot this life you've created for yourself."

"No, Mom. Don't do that. I won't regret for one minute leaving this job or Arizona if it means I get to be with those I love most. I miss home anyway."

I walk into the living room with a basket of clothes to fold and set it on the couch. Avery is lying on the floor in front of the television, drawing and occasionally glancing up at the cartoon that's on.

"Speaking of, have you let Jasper know you're coming home yet?"

Somehow, our conversations always end up on Jasper one way or another. They have ever since the day we drove away in the moving truck. Both of my parents can't let go of the fact that Jasper and I just kind of drifted apart. Not on purpose and not for lack of trying on my part. However, he may see it differently.

"No, and I don't plan on it. I don't even think he would care anyway."

"Cora Anne Connolly, you know that is not true. He would certainly care, and we both know he would be over the moon to be with Avery again."

"Mom..." I start, but she interrupts.

"Don't you, Mom me. Jasper has sent Avery gifts periodically and always for the holidays, including her birthdays. And I know you send him pictures of her, too."

"You're right, but I'm still not telling him. He may care that Avery is coming home, but I think I may be a different story."

"I think you're wrong," she insists. "Oh, the doorbell just rang. Must be a sign, because I'm certain it's Jasper. He always comes to see Dad at this time each week."

"He does? I ..." She interrupts me again.

"I'd better get going, honey. I love you. Have a good last day, kiss my girl for me, and we will talk tomorrow."

As we hang up, I can hear someone talking through the phone.

Hi, Jasper.

Hi, Mrs. Connolly, I hope I gave Mr. Connolly enough time to rest.

And then the phone call ends. Silence. I hold the phone up like it's going to keep me a part of their conversation. I haven't heard Jasper's voice in over six months, except in voicemail messages. I can never bring myself to answer the phone when he called, and it takes me some time to find the right responses to his texts. The weird thing is that I'm not sure how it got this way between us.

At first, we talked almost daily, then it became weekly, and finally, it just got harder to connect. We played phone tag, and then he stopped answering my calls for days. I tried to get him to talk to me, but the distance only grew between us. So much so that after thirteen inseparable years and one year apart, we were no longer Jasper and Cora.

No matter how much I wanted things to be the same, they weren't. I stayed connected with Santa Cruz and my past through my parents and Jasper's parents. The Nallens never pry about my life or give me the details about Jasper's life. They really try to stay out of it. On the other hand, my parents have always tried to find a reason to keep us connected.

So instead of mourning the loss of my relationship with Jasper, I threw myself into work and being a mother. That's the reason I moved her anyway, so I focused on that. I made friends in our apartment complex and at work, but no one like Jasper. As for dating, I haven't. Avery has been my life and my happiness. Financially, things have been good, but not good enough for me to afford daycare, expenses, and visits home. So, I chose the two we needed to survive here, and my parents made it easier on me by coming to visit us, sometimes for months at a time. I haven't been home in four years.

I look over at Avery; her artwork and the television still enthrall her. Her laugh is like music to my ears, and I can't imagine my life without that sweet sound. Sinking down on the floor next to her, I pull her into my arms and squeeze her tightly. This only sends her into a fit of giggles. She throws her arms around my neck. "Oh, Mommy!"

"Oh, Avery! I love you so much, you know?"

She sighs, "Of course, silly! I love you, too, but can you let me go so I can finish watching *Bluey*?"

"Oh, well, excuse me," I say, laughing and releasing her. She scurries off my lap and back to her position on the floor in front of the television.

I pull the basket of clothes down to the floor next to me and fold it while I watch *Bluey*. There isn't a moment I regret choosing to make this life for the two of us. But I regret breaking my promise to Jasper...that things wouldn't change between us.

My nerves feel like they are standing on end, but I'm a big girl, and my daddy needs me. So, if that means facing my past, then that's just what I will have to do.

Eight

JASPER

My brothers and I have been put to work before we're allowed inside for dinner. We should've known something was up when my mom asked us to come an hour earlier than usual.

"Why did Dad think buying new outdoor furniture was a good idea?" Tyler asks as we each lift a chair out of the back of our dad's truck. "Did they really need this? I mean, I love the old chairs."

"Ty, those things are you eating one helping too many at Sunday dinner from breaking," Drew tells him. Parker laughs so hard that he has to put down the chair he's carrying.

I shake my head at them and laugh to myself. Just before I reach the front porch, Jake, Drew, and Rosie's three-year-old darts out of the house. "Jakey, where do you think you're going?" He giggles as he runs by.

"Jacob Nallen, you better stay in the yard and out of the street, or your mom is going to throw a fit," Drew tells him as he walks by, chair in hand. "You got him?" he asks me as he passes me into the house. I give him a nod.

Parker and Ty follow him inside with their chairs, and I start toward my favorite little guy.

I run over to him and scoop him up. His laugh gets louder, and I whip him around onto my back. His favorite is when we play Cowboys. "Get'em up," he says, a grin on his face. What he means is giddy-up. We just haven't quite mastered that phrase yet.

I gallop around the front yard as he pretends to shoot the bad guys. I even give a neigh here and there. It doesn't even cross my mind that the neighbors or someone driving by may see me. My mom says it's cute, and of course, Tyler tells me he is taking my man card.

Jake and I are so involved in our Cowboys and Robbers game that I don't notice the car pull in across the street. Or the little girl who stands watching us at the edge of the yard with a huge grin on her face. Until I hear a familiar voice shout, "Avery, don't go in the street, I'm going to put this inside really quick!" I nearly trip over my own feet when it hits me; I know why that voice and that little, brightly smiling face are so familiar. Cora and Avery. I see the back of Cora's head disappear into the house. I don't think she even saw me.

"Okay, Mom," the little girl says.

I can't stop myself; I want a closer look at her. So, I walk across the street, with Jake still on my back, and stand a few feet from her.

"Hi, can I play?" she asks, like we're not strangers.

"I... " I begin as Jake starts shooting again.

Avery laughs and looks up at me expectantly. I laugh, too. "I'm Avery. Your Jasper. I've seen your picture. You send me presents. I like presents. Is he your little boy?"

She spits out her questions rapidly, reminding me of the first time I met Cora.

"Hi, Avery. You're correct, I am Jasper. This little guy is Jake. He's my nephew."

"Since you're not a stranger, can I play with you and Jake? What is a nephew anyway?"

I can't help the grin that forms on my face. She is exactly like her mom, and it warms something inside me that's felt cold for a long time. "If your mom is okay with it, then I think Jake here won't mind. And a nephew means I'm his uncle and his dad is my brother."

"Oh, I don't have an uncle, so I guess I'm not a nephew. Let me go ask my mom if I can play." Avery turns to leave, but Cora appears at the edge of the porch before she makes it a few steps. She has a shocked, nervous look on her face as she stares at me. I can't help but stare back. She's as beautiful as the night I left her standing in this very yard. "Mom! Can I play with Jasper and Jake?" Avery's questions break the lock time just had on us.

"Jasper and Jake," Cora repeats our names.

"Yes, Mom. They're playing cowboys and robbers. Jake is the cowboy, and Jasper is the horse. I want to be a robber!"

"Oh, well then, how can I say no to that? You need to

say hello to Granddad and Grand first."

Avery turns back to me and throws her fist into the air. "She said, yes!"

"I heard. I guess you'd better hurry and say hello to your grandparents so we can gallop back into the Wild West."

Avery laughs and looks up at Cora as she walks by, "He's funny, Mom."

Cora's attention never leaves Avery. "Yeah, I know. He always has been." Avery is inside before Cora even finishes responding.

Turning back toward me, her eyes lock with mine again. "Hi, Jasper. It's been a while," she says after a minute.

"Yeah, four years is a long time. Oh, wait, you did text me back a couple of times in the last six months."

She flinches, and I don't allow my face to show a single emotion. I don't know why I'm being cruel. This is Cora, and she is hurting right now.

"I'm sorry; I didn't mean to be so rude."

"You did, and maybe I deserved it in some way. Jasper, do you..." Avery comes running out of the front door, guns blazing, interrupting whatever Cora was about to say.

I shrug my shoulders and jump into action because as soon as Avery began shooting, the cowboy on my back joined in the gunfight and began kicking my sides.

We wind around the Connollys' yard, and eventually, I signal to Avery it's safe to cross back into my parents' yard. From the corner of my eye, I can see that Cora is watching us, smiling, but she looks a little sad.

Finally, she calls out, "Avery, don't leave Jasper's sight."

Avery answers by waving as she ducks behind a tree to hide from me and Jake. Cora makes one final eye contact with me and then disappears into her parents' house again.

CORA

The instant I saw Jasper, I was struck by how much I've missed him. The comfort of just being near him. He looks the same yet completely different. Still as handsome as I remember, but his features seem more manly instead of boy-like. The years have only complemented him. I have the urge to check myself in the mirror.

Then there is the easy way that he and Avery just kind of fell back into a natural state of being together. Watching Avery with him makes me question ever separating them. They always had a special connection between them, and it's even more apparent after just a few minutes back together. She acts as if they haven't been separated for the last four years.

The guilt sets in. I shake the thoughts away, like I have a million times since the night Jasper left me standing stunned in the front yard.

"What are you looking at out there? And where is Avery?" Mom asks, peeking over my shoulder out the window. "Oh, I see things have fallen right back in step like no one missed a beat."

I shrug and mutter under my breath, "Looks like it… at least for some of us."

Mom looks over at me, "Oh, Cora. You had to know that life went on without you around here, and you're the one who pushed Jasper away."

My head whips around at her in shock. "I did not!"

"You did, and we both know it. It started as soon as you told him you were leaving when you set the new 'we can only hang out so much before I leave' rules, and then it continued once you settled into your new life there. You missed him, but you pushed him away instead of telling him how you really felt and pulling him closer."

"Mom, you know I had to make that move, and if I continued to lean on Jasper the way I've done our whole lives, he wouldn't have had the opportunity to find his own life and be happy."

"Keep telling yourself that, Cora. Did you ever think that maybe you were the life he wanted…you and Avery?"

I look back out the window as my sweet five-year-old daughter falls to the ground pretending to have been shot while the little cowboy on Jasper's back throws up his fist in victory. Jasper prances around Avery, smiling. I think about that brief, gentle touch of his lips to mine, like I've dreamt about for the last four years. Like always, I push away any feelings that lead me down the path of possible heartache.

"No, I wasn't what he needed. He deserved better."

Mom's arm wraps around my shoulder, and she pulls

me closer to her. "Cora, I wish you could see yourself clearly instead of focusing on your missteps in life. Everyone else in your life sees you for what and who you really are and always have. Then you became one of the best mothers I've ever known; Avery is proof of that." She kisses my temple before continuing, "Maybe coming home will help you finally realize that you deserve happiness and help you figure out what you want from life, too. And you don't have to give that up because you had a baby out of wedlock. I love you, my girl, and I'm so grateful to you that you came home. I needed you."

I turn and throw my arms around her neck. I'm unable to speak as tears fall down my cheeks. For the words she just said and for the sadness that I feel realizing it will soon just be me, my mom, and Avery. Dad will be gone, and I don't know how we will make it. I know I need to be strong for Mom and Avery, who seems like she gets it, but how can she when she is only five?

"Mom, all of this is just so hard."

"I know, but I'm strong, and in turn, you're strong. As it goes, Avery is strong. We will be okay because we have one another and friends like the Nallen family. Remember that Dad would want us to live our lives as happily as possible until the end because that is how he has lived."

"I love you," I tell her.

"I love you, too. I'm going to go check on your dad. We'll start unpacking your things tomorrow."

"Sounds good. I will come in to see Dad soon. I'm going to go check on Avery and try to pry her away from Jasper, so she doesn't wear him out on our first day back."

I turn back and see Jasper, Avery, and little Cowboy heading into his parents' house.

"Hey, Mom, who is the little boy, anyway?"

"That's Jake, Drew and Rosie's boy. I thought I sent you pictures before."

"Oh, you did, but he was much smaller." Mom starts down the hall, and I walk outside. The air is much different from that in Arizona. I almost forgot how good the humid sea air feels on my skin.

I take a deep breath, realizing I'm about to be forced to face the Nallen music, and I've barely been home an hour.

Nine

CORA

I amble up the walkway to the Nallens' front door. A path I've traveled more times than I can count since we moved in across the street. But this time, it feels different. Nerves sizzle through my body. While I've stayed in touch with Mr. and Mrs. Nallen and, occasionally, Kelsea, I've left everyone else hanging, including Jasper.

When I step up onto the porch, the door is ajar. I can hear conversations bouncing off every wall; I guess some things don't change. It's oddly comforting.

"And Mom and I drove for two days. We drove by Disney, but Mom said we couldn't stop."

"Well, that's no fun." I hear Mrs. Nallen's familiar voice say.

"Yeah, but she said we can maybe go next summer."

"That's something to look forward to then. Jasper,

don't you think you should walk Avery back across the street? You can invite Cora to come back to dinner if you like."

"Sure, I can walk her back, but I'm sure Cora has some unpacking to do."

Ooof. That hurt.

"Wow, little brother, your subtlety could use some work."

I'm pretty sure that was Drew.

"What? I'm just thinking that it must have been a long trip and…"

I can't bear to hear his next excuse for not wanting me to join them for family dinner, so I knock and step through the doorway, interrupting him.

"Hey," I say with a little too much enthusiasm.

"Mom!" Avery runs to me, hugging my legs like she hasn't seen me for days.

"Hi, baby. Did you have fun playing Cowboys and Robbers with Jake and Jasper?"

She's looking up at me with a wide, toothy grin. "Yep, and then we came inside for something to drink. They have juice. Then Jasper's mom showed me a picture of me when I was a baby. Jasper was holding me, and you were there, too. You looked so pretty, Mommy."

"Thank you, and that is so cool. I'm sure they have a lot of pictures we can look at from when you were little."

"Oh, they do. Jasper's dad told me he has a bunch of you, too, from when you were little."

I finally look up to find the entire Nallen clan watching me patiently while Avery talks away.

"Hello everyone, it's good to be home. I've missed you."

Everyone smiles and rushes toward me, giving me hugs and warm hellos. Everyone, that is, except Jasper, who stands off to the side with an unreadable look on his face.

"Cora, you've been missed, but I think we can forgive you for being such a stranger. We are so glad to have you both back; we just wish the circumstances were different," Mrs. Nallen says.

"I'm sorry about that, and I hope I can make it up to you…to all of you." I allow my gaze to drift back to Jasper.

"Do you and Avery want to stay for dinner?" Mr. Nallen asks.

I don't take my eyes off Jasper, and he turns away from my stare at his dad's words.

"That is so kind of you to invite me, but I want to see Dad before he goes to sleep. Not to mention, I have some unpacking to do."

"Fine, but soon you'll join us."

"Yes, I promise," I say, then look back down at Avery. "Let's go, sweet girl."

We head for the door as everyone says goodbye. Suddenly, Avery turns around and darts across the room, hugging Jasper's legs like she did to me earlier.

"Thanks for letting me play with you and Jakey. It was fun. I hope we can play together again soon," she tells him, then darts back past me and out the door. Jasper smiles at her until she disappears.

I watch him in surprise. First, I'm constantly amazed

at Avery and the way she communicates at just five years old, and second, I can't believe the trust she's already given him. When Jasper realizes I'm staring at him, he gazes back with that same look he's had since I saw him again for the first time earlier today—a weird indifference I'm not used to from him.

Someone in the room clears their throat, bringing me out of my staring contest with Jasper. "Well, this is awkward," Tyler says under his breath, then releases a grunt when Kelsea jabs him in the stomach with her elbow.

I glance around the room, and everyone looks between me and Jasper.

"Uh, well, I'd better catch up with Avery," I say as I back out of the house.

"It's nice to have you back, Cora," Rosie says. I give what I hope is a warm smile. It really does mean so much.

"Yes," everyone agrees. Jasper remains silent.

"It's nice to be back. See you soon," I say, closing the door behind me.

Avery is waiting for me at the edge of the yard. She knows my rules, and she is a stickler for them. I hope she always stays that way.

"Mom, it took you forever to say goodbye," She yells, with mild annoyance in her voice.

I want to laugh because she's already acting like a teenager.

When I reach her, I take her hand. "Sorry, baby girl. Jasper and his family are like our second family."

"They're our family?" she questions, looking up at me with a smile, but not sure she understands my meaning.

"They are our chosen family. Jasper and I were best friends practically our entire lives. You may not remember, but he took care of you when you were a baby."

"He's nice," she says, then stops mid-stride. Looking up at me again, she asks, "Is he still your best friend, Mom?"

Straight and to the point. "I sure hope so, sweet girl."

"I hope so, too. He seems like he would be a good best friend."

"He is the best best friend."

JASPER

As soon as Cora left, I needed a little space, so I snuck out of the room while everyone else chatted about how sweet Avery was and how happy they were to have Cora back.

I thought seeing her and having her home would be no big deal. I believed I could remain unaffected by her return, but the thing is, it's easier to pretend not to give a damn when she's thousands of miles away. It's much harder when she's right across the street.

Sitting on the bottom step of my parents' back deck, I stare out over the yard. Every part of this house holds a memory of her; it's taken me nearly all four years she's been gone not to see her in everything.

I don't even hear Kelsea come out until she sits beside

me. I glance in her direction briefly and find her looking out at nothing like I was a moment ago.

She's a lot like our mom when it comes to things like this; they worry, but instead of barraging you with questions, they patiently wait for us to settle into the idea that they're about to pry. It's kind of annoying how good they are at waiting it out.

"I think we've sat in silence long enough, so tell me what's going through that brain of yours, little brother."

"Nothing special."

"Don't treat me like I'm an idiot, Jas. You see, I think you're pissed that Cora Connolly still holds every bit of your attention. No matter how hard you've tried to change that in the years since she left, you never stopped loving her. That wall you thought you carefully constructed wasn't quite as sturdy as you presumed, and all it took was for her to pull up in that driveway across the street and to knock it down completely."

"Kelsea." My voice feels tight with annoyance.

"Jasper," she retorts.

"How'd you get the job of coming out here and analyzing me?"

"I volunteered."

"Well, you shouldn't have. Because I know what I do and don't feel about Cora. I don't need your help putting it into perspective."

"Oh, really? So that little display of indifference and, quite frankly, rudeness to the girl who was your best friend for most of your life was a clear-minded perspective?"

"I wasn't rude."

"Jasper, you practically shoved her out the door. I think if it weren't for Avery, you would've. Not to mention the way you watched her. The look on your face was icy. That's not you. You've never been that person, and there is no way in hell you're starting now. I'm telling you, you need to be honest with yourself, and then you need to apologize to her. Regardless of how much she hurt you, I don't believe it was intentional, and it doesn't make it okay for you to lose your manners and treat her like this. Leaving hurt her too, whether you see it or not."

"Quit mothering me."

"Fine, do you want Mom or Dad to come out here and tell you the same thing? They were on their way out here when I intercepted them and said I would talk to you."

I blow out a long breath and turn my gaze to the sky. Kelsea does the same. The silence between us stretches out. I know she's right, and I hate it. I hate that every word she said is true. It's even worse because I know she's trying to wait me out again. Playing me like a fiddle.

"Part of me wants to hate her," I admit.

"Yeah, but you don't. You don't because she doesn't deserve it, and you aren't meant to hate her. In fact, you feel the complete opposite of hate."

"I hate that you're right, calling me out on my attitude. I'll figure it out, and then I'll apologize to her and to Mom and Dad. But Kels, I don't know if I can go back to who I was before she left. I'm different, and I don't know if I want to go back to that Jasper."

"You've grown up, which is expected, but who you are on the inside hasn't really changed."

"We'll see," I tell her.

"Wanna make a bet with me?"

"Not really," I laugh.

"Chicken!" She stands up and reaches her hand out to me to help me up. "Come on, let's go inside and get something to eat. Hopefully, Tyler hasn't eaten all the food."

Taking her hand, I pull myself up. "Thanks, Kels."

"Don't thank me; just get yourself together and be the Jasper we know and love."

She kisses my cheek, and as she walks inside ahead of me, she announces, "Hey, guys and gals, Jasper said he's doing kitchen duty solo because he was such a shithead."

My family cheers, and I shake my head. I guess I deserve that.

I have to figure out how Cora and I can move past this hurt and repair our relationship. In the last few years, she's been gone. And I had to deal with my feelings of hurt and loss for the last four years. I felt like I was left behind. And I didn't think it was still that big of a deal. I thought I'd dealt with all of my feelings… that is, until I saw her again today after all these years. I didn't take it well, having her back today. I was a jerk, and I'm sorry for my bad behavior, and I have to apologize to her. Since I still need to work through my feelings, I'm going to focus on Avery and what an incredible little girl she is. I've always known she was special, but I also know how she's turned out has to do with Cora and what kind of mother she's been to Avery. Kelsea is right; I need some time to gain perspective, and then maybe my friend and I can find our way back to one another.

Kelsea and I sit at the table, and everyone continues eating as if today has been like any other day.

"Avery has grown into quite the little lady," my dad says.

"Isn't she darling?" Mom says.

"She's definitely still drawn to Jasper. It's like they've never been apart," Parker states.

It did feel good to be with Avery again. And I'd be lying if I didn't feel some extra resentment toward Cora for keeping us apart for all these years. I feel like I missed out on so much.

"It was so cute the way she just glowed any time she looked at him," Rosie adds, rubbing her belly affectionately.

"Cora's done a great job raising her," Abbey states as she spoons a bite of mashed potatoes into her daughter Livie's mouth.

"Jakey seemed to have fun today, too. Right, Jakey boy?" Drew says, tickling his side. Jake laughs and puts his hands out to defend himself from the tickles.

"Can we talk about how good Cora looked?" Tyler chimes in, and everyone's head swings in his direction.

"Seriously, dude," Kelsea scolds. "You're so dumb sometimes."

"What? Jasper doesn't care anymore, right, bro?"

Tyler is just trying to get a rise out of me, as usual, but I'm not going to give in to his antics.

"Tyler, stop talking now," Dad states sternly.

My mom and dad are the only ones who can get him to stop his sarcastic comments and his need to stir the pot, so to speak. When my parents aren't looking, I flip Tyler the bird.

"I just want to say one thing," I tell them, then wait until they all look in my direction. "I may be on clean-up duty tonight, but that means Tyler is in charge of dessert next Sunday."

"I like that idea," Mom says.

My siblings, aside from Tyler and my dad, all concur. Tyler just stares at me, and as soon as he sees that Mom and Dad are distracted, he returns my hand gesture from moments ago. I actually laugh out loud, and everyone stops talking and looks at me.

"Uh, sorry."

They all give me a look but then go back to talking. Like every Sunday, I'm struck by my family's love, kindness, and connection. Maybe I need to think about the roots of our family dynamic and how it all works. Then, I might be able to figure out my feelings for Cora, and maybe even gain that perspective that Kelsea just lectured me about. Having Cora back is just a little bump to overcome.

Only time will tell me how well I can adjust to having her and Avery back.

Ten

CORA

I can't believe it's taken me two days to get by The Roasting Company, the best coffee shop in town. And they have perfected my favorite drink. I've never been able to find any place that can make it just so perfectly. Four years without tasting that delicious creaminess is too long.

"Hi, Andrew," I say as I walk up to order.

The long-time barista looks up from the register. It takes him only a split second to recognize me. "Cora, darling," he says in his beautiful British accent. "When did you return?"

Smiling, I tuck a loose strand of wild, curly hair behind my ear. "Just a couple of days ago." He moves around the counter and pulls me into a hug.

"It's so lovely to see you. It's been too long." He pulls

out of our tight embrace. "Let me see if I can recall your favorite drink," he pauses, tapping his chin like he's thinking. "A hazelnut matcha breve latte."

"Your memory is astounding!"

He jokingly pats himself on the back as he walks back around to ring me up.

"Will you be having a croissant or treat?"

"No, thank you...actually, yes. I will bring one home. Can I get a blueberry muffin?"

The bell above the door rings, signaling that a new customer has walked into the shop behind me.

"Anything for you, sweetie." Andrew glances behind me and smiles. "Well, I guess I should've assumed that when one comes in, the other follows. Good morning, Jasper. Beth."

Jasper. Beth? I freeze, my thoughts racing, and then slowly turn around. I practically come face to face with Jasper and a petite blonde, who I'm assuming is Beth. Her hand rests lightly on his arm. She's smiling. She's pretty. Jasper's eyes are staring directly into mine. His face looks just like it did Sunday, void of real emotion. Unreadable.

I instantly regret leaving my hair down today because the curls are wild and chaotic. I nervously shift my stance and tuck that same damn errant lock of hair behind my ear again.

Jasper is the first to speak. "Good morning, Cora."

"Morning."

"Is Avery with you?" He glances around me.

"Oh, no. She stayed with Mom. They were actually going to go over to your parents' house to have lunch with your mom. I'm just running some errands to grab a few things we need."

"I see. I'm sure my mom is over the moon about lunch. You'd better watch out or Avery will end up spoiled with treats like my nephew and niece," he smiles.

"I'll be sure to watch for that, but I'm sure it will be a losing battle, knowing both your mom and Avery."

He laughs. A deep throaty laugh. One that is so familiar, but only as a distant memory. Something warm fills my chest. I haven't seen a single bit of the old Jasper until now, and it feels good to be the reason he showed up.

Suddenly, a hand hangs out before me. "Hi, I'm Beth."

Startled, I take it and look at the blonde standing next to Jasper, whom I had completely forgotten about. "Oh, I'm sorry. I'm Cora."

Her handshake is firm, her eyes wide, and she has a wide smile plastered on her face. "How do you know Jasper?"

Jasper stiffens, and the grin that had appeared quickly disappears. "Cora grew up across the street from my family."

"Yeah, we're best friends...I mean, we were best friends...I hope we're still friends; I've been gone for a while."

My eyes dart back to Jasper; his features have reset to someone I don't recognize. One of the other baristas behind me calls out my order.

"Well, okay, then. That's me." I turn my attention back to Beth, whose hand is gripping Jasper's elbow a little tighter now. "It was so nice to meet you, Beth." My eyes drift briefly back to Jasper. "Jasper, see you around."

"Yeah, I usually visit your dad on Wednesdays, so maybe I will see you then."

"Oh...sure, okay. Bye."

Turning, I pick my drink and muffin up off the counter, then look behind the counter at Andrew, who is bouncing his eyes from me to Jasper. "Andrew, it's good to see you again. I look forward to seeing you regularly now that I'm back."

"Absolutely, darling. You've always been one of my favorites. I've missed you. Glad to have you back. Enjoy your day."

"You're too sweet. See you soon."

I awkwardly step past Jasper and Beth. "Bye, see you."

I walk out the door, then glance back. Just before the door closes, I catch a glimpse of Jasper. He's turned toward the door, and our gazes meet for a split second before the door shuts.

Now that I'm outside, I can breathe again. It felt like I was holding my breath that entire time. And how is Beth? Is she his girlfriend? Mom never said Jasper was seeing anyone. By the way she was protectively holding his arm, they are an item. Why wouldn't he be seeing someone? Except in all the years of our friendship, I've never known Jasper to have a girlfriend. He barely dated.

My mind feels so full. I'm not sure what is happening, but I suddenly don't feel like myself. Things have been quite a whirlwind in the last week, with all the travel and everything going on with my dad. And speaking of Dad, I'd better get home before the nurse's shift changes. I have some things I need to go over with her. I push thoughts of Jasper out of my head and try to focus on why I'm back in the first place. Unfortunately, not thinking about Jasper feels impossible.

JASPER

"How'd your lunch date go with that girl...Beth, right?" Parker asks as he grabs a beer from the fridge.

"Yeah, wasn't it like your fifth or sixth date with her?" Tyler chimes in. He's already kicked back on the couch with his feet on the coffee table.

"Rosie said that Abbey said that she's sweet," Drew says.

"Dude, if that's the case, then I'd say something is wrong with her. Do we trust Abbey's sweet meter?" Tyler chimes in and laughs.

Abbey originally set up the blind date with Beth. She's a new co-worker of hers and Rosie. She's sweet and pretty. I've enjoyed spending time with her. It doesn't take any effort to be with her, and as usual, there is nothing at risk. I like her enough. But there's no chance I will fall in love with her.

"She's nice, and we have a good time," I say, hesitant to mention that we ran into Cora. But since I'm a masochist, I do anyway. "We ran into Cora." Since I say it with little enthusiasm, I'm hoping they won't make it a thing. I spoke too soon. Tyler howls in laughter, and Parker's eyebrows shoot up as he sits down across from me.

Drew tries sounding nonchalant, but I can see every question like rapid fire in his facial expression. "Hmm, interesting."

I try to steer the conversation back to my dating Beth and away from running into Cora.

"Not really," I say, trying to play dumb. "Beth is great. I've tried telling you that I'm not interested in anything serious or long-term, so I'm not sure why it's interesting."

Tyler's laugh gets louder and more obnoxious.

"What the hell, dude?" I ask.

"We heard what you said about dating, but we also didn't miss that you said you ran into Cora."

"Yeah, so."

"Don't play stupid, Jas," Drew says.

Tyler finally stops laughing and takes a long swig of his beer. Shaking his head, he says, "Look, bro, we all know that Cora coming home has shaken you. It was super obvious after you acted like such an asshole on Sunday. Just admit it."

It's my turn to take a long pull of my beer and focus on the game on the television because this is definitely not a topic I'm into discussing further. I also know my brothers, and there is no way they will let this go. I can feel all their eyes on me, so I heave a heavy sigh.

"Freaking fine, since I know you losers aren't going to let this go until I start spilling my guts, and we can all analyze this like a bunch of girls."

"Nah, we just want you to admit you're still in love with Cora, then we won't need to talk anymore, and we can focus our attention on the game," Parker says. The three of them laugh.

"I'm not in love with Cora."

"Sure, and she's not in love with you," Drew says.

My head snaps in his direction. Why would he say that? She's never given me a reason to believe she had any interest in me beyond friendship.

"That's not true. About six months after she left, I think she made it pretty clear that she wasn't even that interested in being my best friend anymore."

"Bullshit," Tyler says loudly, then continues, "I call bullshit." He seems pissed.

My eyes widen as I look over at him. Tyler rarely gets passionate about anything. When he keeps his gaze locked on mine, I feel uneasy under his scrutiny and look at Drew and Parker, but they have the same looks on their faces.

"Tell us how it went when you ran into Cora while you were on your date," Parker says.

My gaze shuffles between the three of them, hoping they give this up and stop the inquisition, but I finally realize they won't, and I give up.

"Fine, it was awkward. Not just to me, but I could see Cora was uncomfortable, too. I've been walking that thin line between love and hate for her since the moment I saw her standing in her parents' yard on Sunday. And every time I see her, it's just hard to know where I stand and how I feel."

"So, what are you going to do about that?" Tyler asks.

This time, he sounds less agitated and more concerned.

I set my empty beer bottle on the side table and shove my hands into my hair.

"I don't know because I don't feel like I can trust her, and I don't want to go backward. Maybe I do love her, but I learned a long time ago that I can't make her love me. And I don't want to allow myself to fall right into the same pattern with Cora again. It is the one thing I'm certain of."

"You're right, you can't, but you can get to know her again, focus on your friendship again, and then see what comes next. I've never seen anyone with a bond quite like you and Cora have. Then add Avery to the mix, and the three of you are an incredible kind of complete unit. Whether that's as friends or more, that's yet to be seen," Drew says.

"Drew's right; it's worth being the Jasper we love and seeing what the future holds. That guy, he is compassionate and loyal. But you'll have to start by forgiving her and letting her off the hook for leaving. Take it slow and feel it out. You will know. The greatest triumphs and rewards are always about patience and timing. I think maybe right now it's about you stepping up and being the friend, she most definitely needs to help her find her way through this tragedy she has been thrown into with her dad."

I hadn't even thought about how bad she must be hurting right now with her dad's illness. Between Kelsea calling me out on my crap the other night and now my brothers, I can see I've been too hard on Cora. I've pretty much been a complete jerk. She needs me, and if I'm honest, that still matters to me. Despite the years and distance, her happiness and safety have never stopped being something that matters to me. Even if I didn't always show it.

"You three really should consider starting a relationship advice podcast," I joke.

They all laugh, and I join in, too.

"Does that mean we were right? You're still in love with our favorite little neighbor?" Tyler asks.

"It means I'm going to get my head out of my ass and get back to being me. Supporting Cora is just a piece of that. Whether I love her or not is irrelevant right now."

Parker reaches over and raises his hand for a high five, which I reciprocate. "Hell, yeah!"

"Now that that's settled, who's ordering the pizza? I'm starving, and Rosie is having dinner with Mom and Dad tonight. Apparently, Jakey and Avery had a playdate today," Drew says.

"It's Parks' turn," Tyler says, standing, walking to the fridge, and grabbing each of us another beer.

"Already done. Food delivery from an app is a beautiful thing," Parker says.

My brothers are pretty incredible to have on my side, despite each of them being a pain in the ass in their own way. These Tuesday night bro nights were the best thing to come out of my family's meddling need to make sure I wasn't lonely after Cora and Avery moved. As much as they annoyed the shit out of me that first year, it is really great to have a family that cares so much for each other.

I kick my feet up next to Tyler, and the subject quickly changes. My mind occasionally drifts back to Cora and Avery. I guess I'll have to bite the bullet tomorrow and apologize to Cora when I'm visiting Mr. Connolly.

The doorbell rings, and we all celebrate the arrival of our food and the home run our team just hit.

Chapter 11

JASPER

As a financial project manager, the days are usually long, but I decided to leave work early today and drive to my weekly visit with Mr. Connolly; part of me hopes Cora isn't home. But I see her car parked right behind her mother's, so that wish has been squashed. It sounds cowardly, but I've gone over every scenario since that conversation with my brothers, and I'm unsure what to say to her. What can I say to make things normal between us again? She and Avery are here, and while things may never return to what they once were between us, she needs support. Her dad's prognosis can't be easy on her, and I need to get over whatever happened between us. If she needs my friendship, then I need to be here for her like I would've been in the past, before all the changes happened.

Walking up to the door, I raise my hand to knock just as the door swings open, startling me. "Whoa!" I jump back a little. Then I see one of my favorite little humans standing there.

"Hey, Jasper." Avery stands in the doorway, beaming at me. "What are you doing?"

I return her smile. "Hi, Avery. I'm here to visit your granddad, like I do every Wednesday."

"Alright. You can come in, but only because I know you. I'm not supposed to let strangers in the house."

"Thank you, and no, that wouldn't be a good idea. It's probably best not to answer the door at all if you don't know the person knocking."

"Yeah, that's what Mom says, too, but I was watching you get out of your car from the window. When you knocked, I already knew I knew you."

I laugh. Could she be any more precocious? "Well, then, I guess we have nothing to worry about."

"Nope," she says, turning away from me and leaving the door ajar for me to follow her in.

Walking into the house, I hear nothing but silence. Avery skips down the hall and stops in front of the room where Mr. Connolly is staying. It was once his office, but since he couldn't get up and down the stairs anymore, they cleared it out and made it their bedroom. When I reach the door, Avery walks in first, and that's when I hear the quiet, one-sided conversation going on.

"I got Avery registered for kindergarten. Can you believe it?"

Silence.

111

Mom said Mr. Connolly is asleep most of the time and hasn't spoken much since the last time I visited last week.

"Yeah, I know. You told me it would fly by, and I should savor the moments, and you were right. I've tried my best, and I think she's ready. You'd be so proud of her." Cora pauses, and I can see her head swivel toward Avery when she walks up beside her. "Hey, baby girl. Can you say hello to your granddad?"

Avery nods and walks closer to her grandfather, "Hi Granddad. Jasper is here to see you. I really like him."

Cora's head whips around at Avery's words. When our eyes meet, I smile and raise my hand in greeting. She stares for a moment, a look on her face I can't quite read, and then a slow smile creeps onto her face. She nods at me, and I nod back, and then we both turn our attention to Avery.

Avery continues chatting, "Mama and Jasper used to be best friends, or maybe they still are. Mama says she doesn't know, but we hope they still are."

As if she opened a door for me to walk through, I decided not to hesitate and take this as an opportunity to extend an olive branch. "Cora and I will always be best friends," I say, stepping forward and squatting beside Avery at Mr. Connolly's side.

Avery beams at me. "See, Mom, sometimes hoping does work."

I hear a sniffle and then, "Yeah, I guess it does." I keep myself from looking at her, but I can feel her gaze resting on me. "Well, Avery, let's go make some lunch and let Jasper visit with Granddad."

"Can Jasper have lunch with us?"

"Oh, uh…sure, if he has time and doesn't have somewhere he needs to be."

"Jasper, will you have lunch with us? I bet we're having PBJ, and it's strawberry jam! Strawberry jam is the best, don't you think?"

Cora is smiling at Avery and shaking her head slowly. I can't help smiling at her, too, and there is no way I can turn her down.

"Heck, yeah! I wouldn't miss out on peanut butter and strawberry jam. It's my favorite."

"Wow, it's my favorite, too. Mom, peanut butter and strawberry jam are his favorites, too."

"I know, it has been since we were kids. Come on, we'd better go get those sandwiches made so we can eat after Jasper sits with Granddad for a bit."

"Okay!" Avery shouts and then starts to take off. Then suddenly, she stops and turns around, running back to Mr. Connolly's side. "Bye, Granddad. I'll come tell you a story later." She places a soft kiss on the top of his hand, resting on top of the blanket, and runs out the door.

When I look over at Cora, a lone tear falls down her cheek. She wipes it away quickly. "Have a nice visit with Jasper, Dad." We make eye contact one last time, and then she disappears from the room, leaving me with her dad.

Turning back to him, I sit next to his bed just as I've done every visit.

"Well, you must be happy to have those two back here," I say. There's no response, but I keep talking anyway. "I know you've told me to be patient with her, but

I think I failed at that. When Cora left, I was so hurt; the more time passed, the more hurt I grew. And then the next thing you know, they're back here, and I've just been so mad at Cora for all these years. And I've been a jerk and took it out on her. I'm sorry about that. You know I would never intentionally hurt her, but maybe I did. You should know I'm letting it all go. I'm forgiving her for leaving and for not choosing me."

"About ti…time, "a raspy, stutter responds.

My eyes widen in surprise, and I reach for his hand. "Hey…do you want me to get anyone?"

"Heck no, those women have been chatting my head off all morning. I can talk to them later." His voice is low and weak, but he manages to get out the words.

"Do you need anything? Water, maybe?"

"A drink of water would be nice. Do you mind?"

"Not at all." I grab the cup of water from his bedside table and gently rest it against his lips while helping him lift his head slightly. He takes small sips at a time, and I give him all the time he needs. After a few sips, Mr. Connolly pulls back and gives me a slight nod of his head. Pulling the cup back from his lips, I gently help him rest his head back against his pillow and place his water back on the side table. We sit in silence, and I hold his hand, just as I've done for the last few months that he's been sick.

"I want you to know that you're our family, son." He says it so clearly and out of nowhere. The words hit me right in the heart, and now it almost feels like I can't breathe. I begin to respond, unsure of what to say, but before I can find the words, he continues, "Thank you for being the friend Cora has always needed and deserved. Thank you for loving her."

My head snaps up, tears in my eyes. "I don…"

"There's no need to say anything, especially to deny what I've always known—probably even before you." He coughs, I reach for his water, and his words hang in the air. He waves me away when I try to give him more water. "Find a way to tell her."

"I don't know if that is something she wants to hear," I tell him honestly.

He squeezes my hand weakly and says, "You'll know when she's ready. You haven't given up on her after all this time. Don't give up on her now."

I start to say something when Avery comes running into the room. "Granddad, you're awake!"

"I am, sweet girl," he says as she takes his hand.

"Your hands are so soft and wrinkly," she tells him. "I love the way they feel."

Mr. Connolly and I laugh, which causes him to start coughing again. This time, he has a hard time stopping, so I pick up his water, and he accepts it.

"Avery, my girl, is lunch ready?" I ask, trying to distract her. I can tell his cough has scared her; she's widened her eyes, and fear is creeping into their depths.

This gets her attention, and she looks up at me, nodding her head but still looking concerned.

"Okay, that's good. Your granddad and I were chatting a little too much, probably making his throat dry. We should let him get some more rest."

Avery looks at her granddad and then back at me. Reluctantly, she nods her head and then turns to him and says, "Okay, I love you." He kisses his hand.

Standing up, I lean forward and whisper, "I won't give up. Thank you."

Mr. Connolly gives me a closed-lip smile and reaches for my hand, squeezing it lightly before letting go.

"Let's go eat some lunch," I tell Avery, and she nods. Together, we walk out, leaving Cora's dad to rest peacefully.

CORA

I place each sandwich on a plate along with a small bunch of grapes and set them on the table. In some ways, this is reminiscent of when Avery was still a baby, and Jasper would spend his free time with us.

"I hear lunch is ready," Jasper's voice sounds through the kitchen as he and Avery walk in, hand in hand.

Smiling, I point toward the table. "That's right. Lunch is served."

"Oh, grapes, too! I love grapes! Do you love grapes, Jasper?"

He and Avery take a seat at the table, and I sit, too.

"I love grapes. This looks delicious, Cora. Thank you."

My eyes land on his, and the sincerity I see there makes my heart skip a little beat. I'm not sure what has changed since I saw him a few days ago, but I can see more of the old Jasper.

"Yeah, thank you, Mommy." Avery beams at me and gives a side-eyed glance in Jasper's direction to make sure he's looking at her, too. And he is. It's one of Jasper's best traits—he's always present with the people he's surrounded by. I'm not sure if this is a younger child thing or if it's just who he is. I imagine it's a little of both.

"How was your visit with Dad?"

"Mommy, Granddad was awake. He and Jasper were talking. I talked to him, too."

My head whips towards Jasper for confirmation. He's watching my face intently and gives me a nod. Dad hasn't been awake for over twenty-four hours. The hospice nurse said this would start happening more and more. But that still doesn't make it easier.

Looking back at Avery, I smile. "That's fantastic news, baby girl. Was he happy to see you?"

As she takes a bite, she nods and says with a full mouth, "Oh, yes. He seemed happy to see Jasper, too."

"Yeah, well, he's always loved Jasper."

"I've always loved him, too," Jasper adds to the conversation. "He was actually carrying the conversation. It was nice because it's been a while since he's been able to talk much during my visits."

I give him a tight-lipped smile, hoping to keep my tears and worry at bay for Avery's sake. We quietly finish our lunch. Avery hums while Jasper and I remain silent. It's comfortable and the most at peace I've felt for some time.

"Mommy, I'm done. Can I go over to Mrs. Nallen's

house?"

"Baby, we don't know if she's home."

"She is. I saw her earlier in the yard. I stood in our yard and yelled to her." I quirk my eyebrow up at her in question. "I didn't go in the street like you and Grandma said. Mrs. Nallen said I could come for cookies after lunch if you said it was okay."

I look over at Jasper. He just grins at me.

"Sound familiar?" Jasper laughs.

"Just a bit, and now I know what my mom felt like when I always wanted to be at your house. Your mom's cookies are hard to resist."

"Huh, and here I thought it was always me that kept you at my house," he laughs.

"You were, but the cookies were just a perk," I grin and give him a wink.

"I just want to go for the cookies," Avery says matter-of-factly.

Jasper and I look at her and can't hold back our laughter. Her blunt honesty is one of my favorite things about her.

"How about we all go together after we clean up from lunch? I always go visit my mom and dad after I come here for my weekly visit anyway," Jasper says.

Again, I watch him, trying to figure out what has changed in the last few days. I wonder if I should bring up this change to him or let it go and let him lead.

"Sure, but if there is only one cookie, I call dibs," Avery tells him.

He laughs. "Avery, there is never just one cookie left

at my parents. Everyone in my family makes sure of that."

"I still call dibs just in case only one is left this time."

"It's yours," he smiles.

Shaking my head, I stand and pick up everyone's plates.

"Thank you again for lunch," Jasper says, standing. "Why don't you let me help you clean up?"

"Don't worry about it. This won't take long, and we can walk together."

He nods.

"Sweet girl, go get your shoes on, and make sure to wash your hands and face."

"Okay, Mom," Avery says and runs off. "Don't leave without me," she calls out over her shoulder.

"She is something else," Jasper says, smiling in the direction she just disappeared.

"That she is."

I begin rinsing the dishes and placing them in the dishwasher. I can feel Jasper's presence close behind me.

"Cora, do you think we can find some time to talk soon?"

Placing the last dish on the rack, I press start and shut the door. With my back still to him, I release a small sigh. A talk can be either good or bad. Our more recent track record of talking hasn't been all that positive.

"Cora?" he says my name like a question.

Turning, I push a loose strand of hair behind my ear. "Yeah, sorry. Of course we can, Jas."

"Good," he says.

Before I can say anything more, Avery comes running back into the kitchen, shoes on and smiling. "I'm ready!"

"Then let's go," Jasper says.

Avery looks at me. "Yeah, let's go," I say. "I just need to let the nurse know we're leaving. Why don't you two go ahead, and I'll be right there."

"Sounds good. What do you say, Avery, wanna go eat all my mom's cookies?"

"You bet I do, man!"

We all laugh, and I follow the two of them to the door. Watching from the doorway for a moment, I think about the turn today took and the talk to come. If I let it, my imagination could run wild on me. Too many years have passed for me to be certain what Jasper thinks or what he might want to talk about. I guess I will just have to wait and see.

Twelve

JASPER

As promised, Avery and I ate all of Mom's cookies, which made Mom just as happy as it made Avery. Cora was quiet most of the day, and off and on, I caught her watching me. Sometimes, she'd watch me when I was playing with Avery, and other times, when I was just a bystander, she'd watch my parents interact with Avery. It wasn't a sad kind of quiet, though—more content and contemplative.

The three of us stayed for dinner since Mrs. Conolly told Cora she wouldn't be eating dinner that evening. Mom instantly took the opportunity to have us stay longer, and we accepted. Spending time together felt natural, and it made it easy for me to pretend that nothing had changed. Except it has, which is precisely why I must apologize for how I acted and fix this crack in our friendship that has been broken for too long.

When I asked Cora to talk at lunch today, I still wasn't sure what to say or how to express my feelings. I know I need to apologize for how I've acted since she's been home, but that's the easy part. The hard part is telling her how I feel about her, mainly because I'm not even sure. My mind drifts to my conversation with Mr. Connolly earlier. I made promises to him, but those promises aren't for today. They're for the future. Today is for our friendship and the past.

As we walk back across the street at the end of the evening to Cora's house, she and Avery are hand in hand just ahead of me. "Mommy, today was a fun day."

"I agree, baby. It was one of the best in a long time."

"I think we should have more days like today."

I listen to their conversation without interrupting. I like the way they talk to each other. It's pretty impressive, especially since Avery is only five, and it's a clear sign of their bond between the two of them. Cora glances down at Avery as they step into their front yard.

"You mean more days with what seemed like endless cookies?" I notice Cora's mouth tilting up at the corner at her own sarcasm.

"Yeah, but also more days with Jasper." Avery drops her mom's hand and turns in my direction. "Don'tcha think, Jasper? Wasn't today the best?"

My heart squeezes at the way her little heart-shaped face shines up at me. "It was, and having days like this more often sounds like a great idea," I tell her with a wide smile. "Especially the part with the endless cookies," I add with a smile.

"Oh, yeah," she exclaims, rubbing her tiny hand in circles over her belly, then she turns back, taking Cora's hand once more.

Cora glances in my direction and smiles. Man, I missed seeing that beautiful, shining look on her face.

When we reach the front door of the Connollys' home, Cora turns to me. She slightly stutters when she asks, "Di...did you still want to talk?"

"I do, if that's okay with you. Maybe I can hang around until you get Avery settled for bed?"

"Yeah... of course."

"Cool."

Avery opens the door, and the three of us walk in together. She runs toward the clanking sounds coming from the kitchen. Cora and I follow. When we walk into the kitchen, Mrs. Connolly is making a cup of tea, and Avery starts to regale her with our day.

As soon as Avery stops talking, Mrs. Connolly looks up at me and Cora. "Hey, you two. Jasper, it's nice to see you."

"Nice to see you. I missed you earlier today when I was visiting with Mr. Connolly."

"I was out running errands. It's much easier now that Cora is here," she says with a half-smile. It's a little sad, and I know it has to be so hard on her, watching the person she loves disappear.

"It is nice to have Cora and Avery back where they belong."

I can feel Cora's eyes on me. Mrs. Connolly nods in

agreement, and her grin spreads a little wider on her face.

"Okay, kiddo. It's time we get you ready for bed," Cora says.

Waving her hand in Cora's direction, Mrs. Connolly says, "I've got my sweet girl; you visit with Jasper some more. Plus, I promised I would read some Shel Silverstein with her. Right, baby girl?"

"Yes!" Avery hops off the stool she had climbed on and takes her grandmother by the hand, who is already pulling her from the room. "Night, Mommy. Night, Jasper. I love you."

The easy way those three words came out of Avery's mouth stunned both me and Cora for a split second. Realizing we didn't respond, we both say, "Good night."

Silence hangs between us while we fidget and stare down at our feet. Finally, Cora clears her throat to bring my eyes up to meet hers. She looks nervous, "Well, okay. It looks like I'm relieved of bedtime duties."

I try to ease her worries by starting the conversation. "Should we go out and sit on the back patio?"

It takes a few seconds for her to respond, "Yeah … yeah, that's a good idea. Are you thirsty?"

"Maybe some water," I tell her.

Cora walks to the cabinet, pulls out two glasses, and then fills them with some water from the filtered water pitcher. Watching her, everything I want to say swirls through my mind, as if I'm trying to decide exactly how I should begin my apology. How should I tell her she's still important to me? I can't decide where to start. Cora hands me a glass and gives me a half smile before turning for the back door. I follow her.

Taking a seat, I sit opposite Cora, our knees brushing under the table. We both take a sip of our water, her gaze locked on mine. One more beat of silence, then she says, "When did things become so awkward between us?"

"When you decided to leave without warning," I snap, immediately regretting it when a look crosses her face as if I'd slapped her. I don't know why I said that. I'm ready to put those feelings behind me, even if the sting of the situation still lingers a little.

"Jas, you know…"

"No, stop. I'm sorry; please let me start over and say what I really want to say," I interrupt.

"Okay, but maybe that is what you really want to say. Maybe it's what you need to say."

Shaking my head slightly, I say, "No…maybe…" She remains silent as I trail off. I can see it's hard for her to stay quiet and not say what she is thinking, but I can see she also wants me to go first. I start over, "No," I begin with more confidence in my feelings. "What I want to tell you first is how sorry I am for how I've acted since you've been home. You need friendship, love, and support. I should've been all those things to you, and I haven't been. That changes now." I take a deep breath because what I need to say next feels harder. It's jumping into the past and acknowledging things that, in all honesty, we've never dealt with. Her eyes widen, and I see some relief mixed with a little pain there. She seems to want to say something, but again she remains silent. "But I do want to clear the air about things we've left unfinished."

"I agree," Cora says, quickly.

"You hurt me," I tell her. My voice is getting a little clogged with the sudden emotions I've kept pushed down for so long.

Cora reaches across the table. "Oh, Jasper, I ..."

"You hurt me, Cora. It felt like I lost everything when you and Avery left."

"I really did think it was best."

Best? That statement stokes the flames of the past hurt and anger I'm trying so hard to tamp out. "Oh, come on, Cora. It was best for you, but it definitely wasn't best for me." I take a deep breath before continuing because I truly don't want to be resentful toward her any longer. "Honestly, I think what hurt the most is that you didn't even talk to me about it. And even if I really had no right to an opinion, I deserved to be considered when we had created... well, when our whole lives before and after Avery were so intertwined." Instantly, some of the weight I had carried from all these emotions lessened. I realize I should have said these things to her a long time ago. "I think if we had just talked it over together before you took the job, then we could've figured out a way to keep our friendship alive even with the distance. That's why it hurt so bad when you just told me you were leaving. I felt like I wasn't even important to you anymore."

"God, Jas. I never even ...I'm sorry," she says with a look of deep sadness on her face. "I messed up so bad. I completely disrespected our entire friendship and everything we've been to each other for all these years. I didn't even think of it from your perspective. And now that I know how you feel, I regret the way I handled it. You'll never know how sorry I was--- am."

This time, I'm the one reaching across the table for her hand.

"The fact we didn't stay connected isn't something you can solely take the blame for; I could've tried harder, too. I could've done better. I guess I just assumed you didn't want me a part of this new life you'd created because you didn't make it seem like it when you left him without any discussion. So, I played it safe and stuck to sending Avery gifts and let you take control of what our relationship would be at that point. It was immature and cowardly, but I was worried that you'd reject me. I was afraid, and I guess the more time that passed, the harder it was to put my hurt feelings aside and risk being vulnerable."

"Yeah, maybe so, but I didn't try either."

"Why?"

She looks startled by my directness.

"I think I was afraid, too."

"You were? Of me?" I ask, confused. I know what scared me, but I can't see what would've frightened Cora. "Afraid of what?"

Standing up, she walks to the edge of the patio, looking away from me and up at the sky. I can tell she is trying to find the words, so I stay silent because I want, no, I need, to hear what she has to say. I need to understand. Slowly, she turns back to me and locks her gaze with mine.

"Jas, that last night before I left when we were fighting and standing out front," she starts, then sighs, "When your lips touched mine, I felt something I'd been fighting for a long time—this thing between us that came on so naturally but so unexpectedly. And I was terrified. Fearful of what it was going to do to us...to you. What if I screwed it up? What if you were meant for a different life ...your own life."

I get up and walk toward her, stopping a few feet away. "Cora..."

"Please let me finish," she interrupts, so I stop talking and let her finish. "I didn't think it was fair to you to have an instant family that wasn't your own, so I ignored everything that I was feeling and minimized what you meant to me and Avery. Yes, you've always been my best friend, but I denied to myself that you were anything more than that. I will regret hurting you like that forever...and hurting myself and even Avery. She missed you for so long after we left, and based on how quickly she's reconnected with you since we've returned, you never left her heart. Thank you for staying connected with her as best as you could. I guess we could also say the only way I let you stay connected. But I also know that as much as I regret how I handled things with you, I can't regret the life we built in Arizona. I became the person I needed to be as a mother. And I grew up emotionally, so I can be everything I need for my life now; I'm just sad it was at the expense of us."

Tears slip down her cheeks, and she wipes them away. I'm overwhelmed by my need to comfort her, so I walk to her and pull her into an embrace. She comes willingly and wraps her arms around my waist, laying her head against my chest. We stand together in silence for a while. I savor the feel of her body against mine, a feeling that is so familiar, yet it seems like I've never held her this way before.

"Cora, I wish we had said all these things four years ago. But we can wish we'd done things differently, but we didn't. And we can't go back and change it now. What's important to me now is that I stop being angry with you because that feels wrong. Having you back makes me feel like I can breathe again, and I didn't even realize I had been gasping for air ever since you left. All that matters right now is our friendship. You're my best friend, Cora. And you need me right now, so please know that I'm here for you in any way that you need me."

She pulls me closer. "I've missed you so much. I don't know how I've gotten through the last four years without you."

"Well, I think you had the best remedy for losing your best friend. Someone to focus on and spend time with. Avery is so amazing, Cora. You've done an incredible job."

"She is pretty terrific." Cora releases me and glances up, a grin spreading across her face. "Thank you, Jasper, for pushing us to clear the air. Your friendship is everything, and you're right; I need my friend now more than ever."

"You've got me. You, Avery, and your mom. Whatever you need."

She wraps her arms back around my waist. This time, I'm the one who pulls her into a tight embrace. I haven't felt this whole in years. It feels like finally coming home.

When we step out of our embrace, I stick my hand out. "Friends forever," I say with a grin. Cora looks down at my outstretched hand; a tiny frown moves across her face so quickly, I could've missed it, and then she replaces it with a smile. She takes my hand. "Friends forever," she says back.

I leave that night feeling better than I have in years. Having Cora in my life again makes sense. It's the way it's supposed to be, and I'm grateful for this second chance.

Thirteen

CORA

Sitting with my legs curled beneath me and a hot cup of coffee in my hand, I think back to last night. I haven't been able to think of much else; even my sleep was filled with thoughts of Jasper, my dreams jumping between him still being angry with me and then telling me he loves me and everything in between. What in the hell is wrong with me? If I'm honest, I'm not sure which of those scenarios bothers me most.

"What's on your mind, baby girl?" The weak whisper of my daddy's voice breaks through my thoughts.

Immediately, I put my mug on the table next to me and lean forward toward him, taking him by the hand. "Daddy?"

He tries to speak again, but his dry lips stick together, not allowing him to open his mouth to form the words.

"It's okay; don't try to talk. How about some water first?"

His frail hand lightly squeezes mine in response.

Standing, I pour more water into the cup sitting at his bedside. Bringing the straw to his lips, I gently lift his head to help him. He takes small sips, and I wait for him to signal that he's had enough. It kills me to see him so delicate. My dad has always been so strong and capable. And now, everything feels so upside down. He shakily touches my hand again to let me know he is done.

"Better?"

He gives me a slight nod. "What's bothering you?" Dad asks, this time clear enough for me to make out the words.

Shrugging, I sit back down. My eyes focus on my hands; I anxiously pick at the skin around my nails. I'm uncertain if Dad is waiting for me to answer or if he is too exhausted to ask the question again. He's always been so patient with me when it came to making decisions. When he knows I'm struggling to come to terms with something, he waits quietly beside me, letting me know he's there to support me in whatever way I need, whenever I know what I need.

Finally, looking up, I find him watching me, a softness in his eyes that I will miss. No one has ever looked at me with that kind of love. "Daddy, I'm so confused about my life and what I'm doing. I'm not sure I've made the right choices, and I don't know if I can do what I need to do for Mom, Avery, and me without you here to guide me."

"Sweetie, what about your life is confusing? You're an

incredible mother. You're successful and have made a life for the two of you. Your mother and I are so proud." He takes a deep breath when he finishes. He signals for more water, so I help him once again.

"Thank you, Daddy. But things are changing, and now that I'm back, I'm unsure of where I fit. And I don't know how I will be able to go on without you."

"Cora, I will always be with you, even when I'm not here anymore. And you have your mother and Avery. You have Jasper."

"That's just it. I know we will all have one another. Yes, Jasper and I talked…we've made up."

"About time," Dad interrupts with a laugh that leads to a cough.

I give him more water.

"I agree, but that's also what I'm confused about. I feel like there might still be a wall between us."

"Until you both admit how you feel for one another, there always will be, Cora."

"Dad…" I begin to argue, but the words leave me. I don't really have anything to say to that. He remains silent, watching me.

"Be happy, Cora. Please stop fearing what might be and embrace what could be."

How does he do that? How does he seem so sure about something I can't seem to accept? Just when I'm about to say more, Avery comes running into the room.

"Good morning, Mommy and Granddad! Gran and I made breakfast!" Avery immediately goes to Dad's side and places a kiss on his cheek. She crawls into bed next to him, wraps her little arms over him, and gently squeezes. "I'm so glad you're awake so I can hug you."

A small smile shows on my dad's lips. "I'm glad I'm awake so you can hug me, too. I love your hugs."

"Mommy, Granddad loves my hugs."

"I heard, baby. It's because you give the best hugs."

"I like giving hugs," Avery beams and looks back to my dad. "Oh, Mommy, Granddad is asleep again."

Looking over at my dad, his eyes are closed, and his breathing has slowed once more. I'm grateful for the short spurts of energy he gets so he can be awake, even if it is just for a few minutes. I'm even more thankful for when I'm here to witness those times.

"Yes, he is, baby. He's tired and needs his rest. Let's go have breakfast with Grand."

Avery slowly and quietly slides off the bed while I lean forward and place a soft kiss on Dad's forehead. "Love you, Daddy," I whisper.

As Avery and I silently leave the room, I wonder what my dad meant when he told me to embrace what could be instead of fearing what might be. He seemed to have more to say, and I know I have more to ask him. I feel just as confused as I did this morning.

When we enter the kitchen, Avery immediately runs to her spot at the table.

"Morning, sweetie," Mom says to me.

"Morning, I hear you've made breakfast with a little help."

"Yep, Avery and I thought it would be nice to sit and eat together."

"Well, I completely agree," I reply as I take a seat at the table. Mom places the eggs in front of us as she joins us. We all look around at one another. Avery is beaming, her young innocence sheltering her from wallowing in the sadness of our family's current situation. My mom and I, on the other hand, try to display some amount of normalcy in our demeanor, but we can't completely hide the sorrow reflecting in our eyes. It hurts that this isn't a normal breakfast when we're all together. Typically, my dad would make breakfast while we set the table. He would always announce, "I love making breakfast for my girls." I shake away the sadness that thought brings when I hear Avery say, "Mommy, can we see Jasper today?"

I can feel my mom's gaze boring into me as I give my attention to Avery, who has a hopeful look, and I answer, "I'm not sure, sweet girl. It's a workday for Jasper."

"But after work, Mommy. I think he would want to see us after work," she says.

"Oh, you think so?"

She nods her head fervently as she spoons in a mouthful of scrambled eggs that my mom had put on her plate. I dish out my portion and grab a slice of bacon. "I will let you call him later this afternoon when he is off work and see what he is up to. I think the polite thing to do would be to ask him rather than assume, don't you?"

She shrugs her shoulders and sighs, "Ugh, I guess."

I try not to laugh at her exasperation with me because she is so serious. My mom coughs, and I look in her direction. She's covering the smile on her face and trying to hide the giggle that slipped out. Apparently, she is amused by Avery's reaction, too. I have to quickly avert my eyes, so I don't lose my composure.

"When does Jasper get off work? Is he off now?"

Good lord. My child is relentless. Giving her my full attention, I answer, "It's still early. It won't be until later this afternoon. And, Avery, we can't spend every waking moment with Jasper."

"Why not?"

"Well, he has other things he needs to do, and he can't always be with us."

"But I bet he wants to be with us. He even told me that he likes hanging out with us."

"Seems like some things don't change, and the apple doesn't fall far from the tree," my mom chimes in.

I turn my attention back to her. "What do you mean?"

"Do we have apples? I love apples," Avery comments.

"No, sweetie. I'm sorry, we don't have apples. I will buy some when I go to the store," Mom says.

"Mom, don't ignore me. What did you mean?"

"Oh, Cora. Don't get a tone. It was a harmless comment, but frankly, it's the truth," she stands and takes her plate to the sink while I stare at her back. Why am I feeling annoyed suddenly? She turns to me, wiping her hands dry. "Avery has shared a special connection with Jasper since day one and wants to be with him every moment she can. And you, Cora, have been the same since the moment we moved into this house and you made friends with the boy across the street."

I stare at her and know everything she just said is impossible to deny. There is just something about Jasper Nallen. He's like gravity—impossible to resist and the only thing on earth you can count on.

"Mommy, is it afternoon yet?"

I look over at her, and this time I can't help myself. I laugh. And it's a loud, shoulder-shaking, stomach-clinching laugh that I can't contain. Tears streaming down my face, I can see Avery through blurred vision, grinning ear to ear before she joins me in laughter. She has no idea what she's even laughing at, which only makes me laugh harder. This girl of mine is both the hardest and greatest thing in my life.

Still laughing, I feel my mom pat the top of my shoulder as she walks past me, leaving me and Avery in this moment.

• • •

Five hours later, Avery and I are out in the front yard hunting for snails. I hate it and she loves it, but I love her more than I hate it. Not to mention, I'll do anything to occupy her. I'm pretty sure she's asked me one million two hundred and seventy-five thousand times if we can call Jasper yet. It's only been twenty minutes since she last asked, and I'm certain we're due for another request.

Glancing down at my watch, I decide to beat her to it. It's four-thirty, and I'm fairly certain Jasper works until four since he goes in at seven.

"Hey, baby girl. What do you say to us calling Jasper now?"

She lifts her head, grinning, and darts across the yard, forgetting about her snails and the menagerie of yard treasures. "Yeeeeeeeeeeeeessssssssssss," she shouts the entire way until she is standing in front of me.

I pull my phone from my back pocket and dial his number, pressing the speaker phone button so Avery and I can both hear him when he answers. One ring and then straight to voicemail.

"You've reached Jasper. Leave me a message, and I'll call you back," his voice echoes through the speaker.

Avery looks up at me, and I say just before the beep, "He must be busy; we have to leave him a message." She looks a little defeated but nods her head.

After the long beep, she says, "Now, Mommy?"

I nod and give her the brightest smile I can, although I think I'm feeling her same disappointment.

"Hi, Jasper! It's me, Avery and Mommy. We were wondering if you could come over for a play date. I wanted to call this morning, but Mommy wouldn't let me because she said you were at work. Anyway, can you come play?"

"Baby, this is his voicemail, so he can't answer. Hi, Jas...uh...call us back when you can. If you can't, that's okay too. Maybe we..." Time is up on leaving a message before I can finish my sentence.

Avery frowns, "I wanted to talk to Jasper."

"I know, baby. I'm sure he will call back as soon as he can."

"Okay, Mommy."

"How about we go inside, check on Granddad, then help Grand by making dinner?"

"Okay. Can we get ice cream tonight?"

I begin to say no, but she still looks so disappointed that we didn't reach Jasper.

"Absolutely! We'll go right after dinner. Now let's get inside and get cleaned up." I tell her as we make our way to the front door.

"I'm not worried, Mommy. I know Jasper will call us back."

I take her small hand in mine as we walk side by side. "I have no doubt." And I don't, but there is a tiny feeling of insecurity lingering deep inside, unsure if we completely fixed everything we needed to last night.

Fourteen

JASPER

Slinging my gym bag over my shoulder, I make my way out of the building and onto the sidewalk. Instead of going straight home after work, I headed to the gym. I've been a little tense all day; add that to the lack of sleep I got last night, and a workout was just what I needed.

Making my way back to my apartment, I realize I didn't turn my phone back on after I left the gym, so I reach into the side pocket of my bag and pull it out. As soon as I power it up, the screen lights up with several messages. I press the voicemail icon to listen to the one message I have before I read the text.

Avery's sweet, tiny voice sings through the phone—she wants to see me. Just hearing her voice creates a warm feeling in my chest. While she's always had that pull on my heartstrings, today's version of the little girl I've adored since the first time I held her pulls a little tighter at my heart. I laugh out loud when she throws her mom under the bus. Then Cora's voice echoes in my ear, asking me to call them back, but sounding pretty nervous. I hate that our once easygoing relationship is still on unsteady ground.

When I'm done hearing their sweet voices, I check my text messages. One from Mom and Tyler and one from Cora. I go to hers first. Around six, she and Avery were planning to head to Maryanne's for some ice cream, and she's inviting me to join them. I glance at the time on my phone; it's six-fifteen. Most likely, they're still there, and I'm just a three-minute walk from Maryanne's.

Instead of texting Cora back, I decide to just show up and surprise them.

As I walk into Maryanne's Ice Creamery, I'm overwhelmed by the buzzing sounds of conversation. It's a typical summer night in a touristy beach town. Families with children and couples, young and old, are enjoying their ice cream at the small parlor-like tables or trying to choose which flavor to get in their waffle cone. It brings back so many memories of good times over the years.

My eyes search through the faces for Cora until I spot her. She squats eye level with Avery, handing her a tiny taster spoon with a small taste of bright pink ice cream on the end. Cora's wild sable curls are pulled back in a ponytail. I like her hair in any style she wears it, but when it is tied back, away from her face like this, her features are even more striking. Cora's eyes shine just as brightly as her smile. And man, I've missed that smile.

Striding in their direction, I reach them before they notice me. Their gazes instantly shift upwards in my direction as I tower over them.

"Hello, ladies," I manage to get out with a grin before Avery screams my name.

"Jasper!" She throws her little arms around my legs. "You're finally off work!"

"Sure am."

My eyes never leave Cora's face. She is grinning from ear to ear and mouths, "Thank you," at me. Giving her a slight nod, I reach down and pull Avery up into my arms, and she comes willingly, replacing her arms wrapped around my legs with my neck.

Pulling back from our embrace, she places her small hands on either side of my face and turns it gently to focus on her instead of her mom. "Jasper, I'm going to get pink bubblegum. I just tasted it, and it's delicerous. What flavor are you going to have?"

"Delicerous, huh?" I smile.

"Delicious, baby. It's pronounced delicious," Cora corrects her, softly.

"That's what I said, Mommy," Avery retorts.

"Oh, well, my apologies," Cora smiles.

Turning her attention back to me, she asks again, "Do you want pink bubblegum, too?"

"Well, rocky road is my favorite, so I'll probably get that kind, if that's okay?"

"Rocky road! That's Mommy's favorite, too! Right, mommy?" Avery beams between us.

"That's right, baby. Jasper, it looks like you still have

good taste."

I grin, "I'd say I have great taste." Looking at Avery, I waggle my eyebrows. She giggles while Cora rolls her eyes and smirks in my direction.

"What can I get you?" the teenage boy behind the counter asks.

"We'll take two rocky roads in waffle cones and one scoop of pink bubblegum in a sugar cone."

"Sure thing," the kid responds.

"Oh, and can we get a small empty cup?" Cora looks over at me. "Just in case things start getting messy for Ms. Pink Bubblegum."

"That's me. I'm Ms. Pink Bubblegum," Avery announces proudly.

Cora reaches over and tickles Avery's belly, causing her to squirm and laugh.

"That will be twenty-four seventy-six."

Putting Avery on her feet, I pull my wallet out and wave off Cora as she tries to pay. "My treat."

"But…"

"No but. It's my treat."

Cora hands Avery's cone to her as she reminds her, "Both hands, please." Then she turns back, taking our ice creams from the kid while I hand money to the young girl behind the register.

"Mommy, can I start?"

"Wait until we sit down so you don't accidentally drop it, please."

"Okay, but I really want to take a bite."

"Me, too. But I think the wait will only make it taste

much better."

Avery gives her mom a skeptical look; it takes everything I have to keep from laughing.

Once I pay, I take my ice cream from Cora. We make eye contact, and her gaze holds onto mine with a sort of longing and peace in it. It's a look of familiarity that I haven't seen in a long time. It takes me back to a time when I thought our relationship was moving in the direction of something more than friendship. To something even deeper than what we already had.

"Shall we?" I ask, interrupting the course of thoughts running through my mind. Cora gives me a slight nod and quickly turns her attention to Avery.

We weave through the tables until we find an empty one and sit.

Taking Avery's cone, I wait for her to climb into her chair and settle before handing it back to her.

"Now?" Avery questions.

"Yes, now," Cora and I answer in unison.

We all dig in, remaining silent for the first few bites, then I ask, "How's your dad today?"

Shrugging, Cora frowns, "Pretty much the same. However, he was briefly awake this morning."

"I don't know if I've told you how sorry I am that this is all happening."

"You don't need to because I know. I know you and your whole family love him as if he were your family. I'm sorry, too."

"I love Granddad, too," Avery chimes in.

Cora and I look over at her; she is already taking another bite of her ice cream as if we're having an everyday conversation. We probably should've waited to discuss these things when we were alone.

"How was your day?" Cora asks, a smooth change of subject.

"It was pretty good, long, but good. What about you two? What did you do today?"

"We played outside and hunted for insects!" Avery exclaimed, flittering her fingers in the air toward me. Her facial features contort into a silly, wide-eyed grimace.

"Eeeeewww," I respond, leaning away from her in pretend horror.

She giggles and takes another bite of her treat. When I look back at Cora, she is watching me with a look I'm not sure how to decipher.

"What?" I ask.

After a second, she snaps out of it, "Oh, nothing." She shifts her attention back to the rocky road ice cream in front of her.

I watch a few moments as she looks at everything around us but me, then I break the awkward silence, "Mom is wanting you, Avery, and even your mom if she is up for it to come over for family dinner on Sunday."

Her eyes snap in my direction, "That's nice, I can ask Mom to see if she is up for it."

"Yes, please," Avery states, a pink mustache forming over her lip.

Cora and I look over at her and then back to one another, and we can't help the smiles that have formed on our faces. The awkwardness disappears once more, and we all settle into easy banter while we finish our dessert.

• • •

After we finished our ice cream, I walked Avery and Cora to their car. Avery made me promise I would see her the next day. I couldn't do anything other than agree.

Cora tried explaining to Avery that I might have other plans and not to make me promise such a thing. I explained to Cora that I absolutely had nothing better to do, and if I did, I wouldn't have promised her.

She conceded, and I hugged them both goodbye.

Now, as I throw on some shorts and flop back on the couch, I reflect on everything that has happened in the last few days. Cora and I agreed to start over, rebuild our friendship, and find that comfortable rhythm between us again. Just when I thought it might be easier than I expected, I could feel Cora pull back tonight. She seemed to get lost in her thoughts, and it was like she was a million miles away.

Then my phone rings, pulling me from my thoughts.

When I look, it's lit up with Tyler's face. I swipe the screen, "Yo, what up?"

"Yo…yo, Mom said to call you about possibly helping them pick up a new grill. She said it would take both of us."

"Sure, glad to hear Dad finally caved and agreed to get rid of the rust bucket he couldn't seem to part with."

"Right? I think he even got a smoker and grill combo.

It's like he's moving up into the advanced bracket of bar-becuing, haha."

I laugh. We've all been trying to convince him to buy a new grill for years. He always said he didn't need one, even though the bottom of his was nearly burned out and rusted.

"Well, when are we supposed to be doing this pick-up?" I ask Ty.

"Tomorrow, after we get off work, if that's okay with you. I should be out by five," he says.

"That works perfectly. I promised Avery when I walked her and Cora to their car that I would see her tomorrow anyway, so I was going to head over that way."

"Oh, yeah? When you walked her and Cora to their car? You were with her and Cora tonight?"

"God, Ty. Don't make a big deal out of things that aren't a big deal," I tell him, my words showing my irritation.

"Hmmm, well, from what I heard from Parks, you had a nice little chat with Cora. You two both waved your white flags, and not even a day later, you were out with her and Avery. Smooth."

"I'm hanging up now," I say.

"Oh, come on, lil bro! I'm just trying to understand where this is going. I don't think I can deal with you falling back into the ass you've been since she left."

"I wasn't an ass."

"You were."

"Look, Cora and I did talk. We're good. We agreed that we messed up. Both of us. We should've been better at keeping our friendship together; it was worth more than we gave it credit for. We made a mistake, and we're going to do better, for our friendship and for Avery."

"Friendship, huh? That's bullshit. You two need to have another talk."

"What's that supposed to mean?"

"You know what it means; you're not stupid, Jas. And before you can say it, I will just tell you that I'm going to hang up on you now." And then the phone goes silent.

I drop my phone, and my head falls back onto the couch. I wish I were an only child sometimes. Privacy would exist. Yeah, I really would like to know what having a little privacy felt like.

Asshole, I think before clicking the television on and forcing my mind to focus on anything but Tyler's word and Cora.

But it turns out that Cora is harder not to think about than my family's opinions.

Fifteen

CORA

"**A**very, please put on your shoes so we can leave for dinner at the Nallens'," I shout up the stairs as I walk toward the kitchen.

It's Sunday dinner night. I just spent time with my dad, and Mom is making him food. She decided to have dinner with him tonight and promised Mrs. Nallen she would come next week. She feels like she needs to be with him whenever he's awake and feels like eating.

Walking into the kitchen, I go to the fridge and pull out the fruit platter I made to bring with us. "Mom, are you sure you don't want us to stay?"

"Sweetie, yes. I'm positive. I think a little alone time with your dad will be nice." She gives me a sad smile and pats my shoulder as she passes me to the cabinet to pull out a few dishes. "Not to mention, Avery loves spending time with all of the Nallens. She'll even have someone her age to play with. Besides, she needs to get out; she has been cooped up all day in the house."

"She does, and you're right, she would be so disappointed. I hate leaving you and Dad, though."

"I know, baby, but we're fine."

She stands beside me and pulls me into a hug. "I love you, my girl."

"Love you, too, Mom."

Our quiet moment is suddenly interrupted by Avery, who comes racing into the room, shouting, "I'm reeeeee-aaaaaaaddddddyyyyy!"

Mom gives me one last squeeze before she pulls away, a massive grin on her face. She beams at me before she turns to Avery, "I don't know about you, Cora, but I think Avery is ready. What do you think?"

Turning my attention to my exuberant five-year-old, I agree, "I'm also going to assume she is ready to go."

Avery smiles brightly at me, "I've got my shoes on, and I've got my new sticker book, so I can give one to Jakey and Jasper."

"That is very thoughtful," Mom says, before turning to the counter to retrieve the plates of food she made for her and Dad. "I'm going to let you girls get going, and I'll take our dinner back to Granddad before it gets cold. I love you both, and please say hello to the family."

"We will!" Avery exclaims. "Tell Granddad I love him!"

I can't remember the last time I've seen her this excited. No, check that. Just a few days ago, when Jasper came over as he had promised, she nearly broke the glass in all the windows with her squeals of happiness.

"I will. See you girls later, and have fun."

"Let's go, Mommy! We're going to be late."

I pick up the fruit platter. "Okay...okay! I'm right behind you."

As we walk across the street, I think about the week. We haven't seen Jasper in a few days, but we've texted. Everything seems to be falling back into a comfortable kind of routine. It's beginning to feel like Jasper and I are in our old sort of rhythm, or at least heading in that direction. I guess it's starting to feel easy again.

Of course, he and Avery haven't missed a beat. I love that for her. There isn't a better person in the world, and he loves her so much. I should've opened my eyes to all of this so much sooner. But I can't change the past; I can only make different choices in the future.

Jasper's Jeep pulls into his parents' driveway as we step off the sidewalk from my parents' yard.

"Jasper!" Avery shouts.

"Avery, do not run in the street. You need to wait for me."

Jasper hops out and heads toward us.

"How are my favorite ladies this evening?" He asks, just as he reaches us. Avery immediately jumps into his arms, and he easily catches her in his embrace.

"Amazing!"

This girl has yelled every word she has spoken in the last ten minutes.

"Oh, yeah? And why are you so amazing?"

"Because it's Sunday dinner. I love Sunday dinners."

"I love Sunday dinners, too."

Jasper looks at me as we step onto his parents' front porch. "What about you? How are you today?"

"I'm pretty great. And if you both don't mind sharing them, Sunday dinners are my favorite, too."

"We will always share with you, right, Avery?"

"Right!"

Jasper sets Avery down and knocks as he opens the door, "Mom? Dad?"

His dad peeks around the corner from the kitchen. "Jas, I'll never understand why you always need to knock. This is your house. Your brothers don't knock before entering; even your sister doesn't." Jasper, Avery, and I close the door behind us. "Ah, Cora…Avery, welcome! We're so glad you're here."

"Dad, I knock because I don't live here anymore, and I think it's considerate to at least alert you. It's not like I wait for you to answer."

"Hello, Mr. Nallen. Thanks for having us," I say, stepping around him through the door. "We brought a fruit platter."

"Is Jakey here yet?" Avery asks.

"Avery, please say hello to Mr. Nallen first. Greeting people when you first see them is polite," I gently chide her.

"Sorry, Mommy." She turns back to Jasper's dad. "Hi, Papa Nallen."

Jasper quirks his eyebrow at me and mouths, *"Papa Nallen?"*

I shrug my shoulders and quietly whisper, "I'll explain later." Jasper gives me a small smile and nods before we turn our attention back to his dad and Avery.

"Avery, my girl, I believe Jakey is out back with his dad and Uncle Ty playing on the swings, and I'm certain he will be very excited to see you," Mr. Nallen says.

"Can I go out back, Mommy?" Avery asks excitedly.

"Sure, baby." Before I can say more, she darts out the back door. I set the fruit platter on the table.

"Where's Mom?" Jasper asks his dad.

"She just went upstairs to clean up. Your mother has been on the go all day long."

"Not surprised. So, is everyone else here already?" Jasper pops a blueberry in his mouth.

"Everyone's here but Kelsea."

"When I talked to her earlier, she did say that she may be a little later, but she'd be here before we eat," I chime in.

"That's good to know," Mr. Nallen says as he seasons the meat in.

"How's the new grill? I'm assuming you'll be putting it to good use tonight?" I ask.

"You bet! I don't know why I waited so long. Don't tell my wife. I said that since she's been telling me for years that I need a new one."

A grin spreads across his face, but quickly disappears when we hear a voice from the doorway connecting the kitchen to the hallway. "I heard that!"

Jasper and I look at one another, and we can't help the laughter that escapes.

Mr. Nallen gives both of us a look of mock betrayal, then gives us a smirk, and glances back in his wife's direction.

"You didn't hear a thing," he winks at her, and as soon as she gets close enough, he pulls her against him and kisses her square on the lips before she even knows what is happening.

"That's our cue," Jasper says, instantly taking my hand and turning us for the back door. I'm still laughing as Jasper pulls me behind him.

As soon as we're outside, Jasper turns to me and lightly touches my mouth. "It's not funny! That was …weird." I can't help myself; his comment only makes me laugh harder. Jasper pulls me even closer. "Stop," he laughs, his eyes shining down at me. One last giggle escapes before my laughter dies in my throat as I become aware of our proximity and how breathtakingly handsome he is.

Jasper must recognize that the light-hearted moment has passed. I stare into his beautiful eyes, and my gaze drifts to his lips.

"Cora," my name leaves his mouth in a raspy whisper. Then he's inching closer.

"Hey, you two, whatcha doin'?" Tyler's voice breaks through, the world around us returning to focus.

"I…ah…I don't see anything. Does it still feel like something is in your eye?" Jasper reacts, trying to play off what Tyler just walked up on.

Blinking rapidly, I reply, "Umm, no, I think it's gone now."

We both look at Ty. He looks happily suspicious at

what he just walked up on.

"Oh, what did you say, Ty?" Jasper asks.

"Uh, huh, okay, if we're going to play it like that," Tyler says, then continues, "I was just saying hello. I thought you might have forgotten that most of us are here, too."

"Mommy!" Avery shouts as she runs up beside us. Children really do have perfect timing, I think.

"Yeah, baby?"

"I'm thirsty."

"Here, I'll take you to get something," Jasper says, taking her by the hand and leading her away.

I watch them walk to the other side of the patio deck, where the cooler of ice-cold drinks is. Every time I see them together, something tugs at my heart. And after what just happened...God, what did just happen? Jasper—I was feeling something I pushed away years ago. Was he feeling it, too?

"Those two are something special, aren't they?"

I was so engrossed in my thoughts that I forgot that Tyler was still standing there. When I turn and look at him, he's not watching them; he's staring at me. I returned his gaze for a moment, trying to read his expression. There is something more behind his statement. Feeling a bit uncomfortable, I turn back to look at the subject of his comment.

"Yeah, they are," I say almost wistfully.

"We're thrilled you're back, Cora. We've all missed you," Tyler pauses and then adds, "He missed you. Your leaving nearly killed him, so please be sure of whatever you're thinking. And I know—I know you have a lot with your dad, but I'm just asking as someone who loves him and frankly loves you, please be certain."

My eyes flash up to his, and our gazes lock for one split second. Then, Ty walks away to join his brother and Avery. That was the most serious statement I've ever witnessed from him, and I'm not sure how I feel about it.

Before I can get too deep into analyzing what Ty said, Rosie and Drew walk up the steps from the yard, followed by Parker and Abbey. Each Nallen brother is carrying a child, and Jakey is following closely behind his parents. As soon as they see me, they all wave and greet me excitedly.

I have no choice but to put aside all the thoughts and emotions swirling in my head from the last five minutes and join the group. This isn't the time, but if there's one thing I know, I will have to figure out what all of this means soon.

JASPER

What the hell was I thinking? The reality is, I wasn't thinking. My brain ceased to function when the sudden urge to kiss Cora flared up, the presence of my family fading from awareness for a brief, tempting instant.

After all this time, how can she still get to me this way? After all the time that had passed. The absence of her in my life. I thought I'd moved past these feelings. These urges.

As we sit at the table eating dinner, my mind drifts to these thoughts. The usual Nallen family chaos gives me some reprieve from the emotions that hit me fast and unexpectedly. Cora sits across from me, and I can't help glancing in her direction periodically. Once or twice, her attention was on me. I wonder if she is thinking the same things I am. Did I upset her? Is she angry with me for nearly kissing her in front of my family and Avery, consequences be damned? Because if I'm honest, that is what I almost did. I almost pulled her tight against me and kissed her until she begged for more. I'm thankful for Tyler's interruption, even if I've caught his knowing gaze looking my direction more than once this evening.

I'm not looking forward to that conversation because, knowing Tyler, he will not let this go.

"Jas, how's that project going at work?" Dad asks.

I snap my head up, "Oh, uh…it's going well. We should complete it within the next week, which will be a welcome break."

"That's great. I know you've been working hard on this one. Maybe you'll be able to relax for a bit now."

"Speaking of relax, I'd say it's about time for a little brotherly fun," Parker chimes in.

"Yeah, it has been a while since we've all gone out," Drew adds.

"Oh, really?" Abbey says, eyeing Parker. "Well, then I think that calls for a girls' night, right, ladies?" Parker shakes his head and takes another massive bite of his food.

"I'm in," Rosie says, giving Drew a cheeky smile. He

grins back, leans into her, and kisses her lips lightly.

"How about this Saturday, Kelsea...Cora?" Abbey looks at us, waiting for confirmation.

Kelsea shrugs, "Why not!"

"Absolutely, I'll just need to make sure Mom is okay watching Avery."

Everyone's eyes are bouncing between all of the girls. Tyler looks like he might explode if he can't make some sarcastic comment, and Drew seems to be enjoying himself. Parker and Abbey keep side-eyeing one another with annoyance. They must have argued over time spent away from Sydney because it almost feels like we're in the middle of their battle. Drew knows it, too. I can tell by the look on his face.

"Perfect! Then we're on for this Saturday!" Rosie says, clapping her hands together.

"And so are we!" Tyler announces.

"Sounds like a plan," Drew and Parker say in unison.

All eyes swing my direction. "What?" I ask, feeling their stare.

"Don't be a dumbass, Jas. Also, you won't get out of it, so don't even try!" Tyler announces. "You're in for guys' night on Saturday."

"Who said I didn't want to go?"

"Your face," Drew retorts, and all of my brothers start laughing.

"You guys are ridiculous. I'm there."

My mom finally turns her attention away from Avery and my nephew, Jakey. "I think it sounds like a lovely idea for you all to have a night out. Things have been heavy and busy for all of you in different ways, so have fun. We'll watch the kids."

"All the kids?" Dad questions, his eyes growing wide.

"Yes, all of them. We did have four children all within a few years of each other, so I think we're up to the challenge. And if Cora is okay with it, we'll even keep Avery. I think she will help keep Jakey occupied."

Avery's eyes light up, and I realize she has been following the conversation. That little girl is one bright five-year-old, never missing a beat. "Can I, Mommy?"

All eyes turn to Cora. When I gaze in her direction, she is looking at me, oblivious to the fact that everyone at the table is waiting for her response.

"Mommy?"

She snaps out of it then, "Sorry, baby. I didn't mean to ignore you. I think it might be helpful since Grandma's usually caring for Granddad. Thank you, Mrs. Nallen."

"Yay!" Avery shouts then high fives my dad.

I look back at Cora, and she's grinning at Avery. I see happiness in her smile, and I feel that pull in my chest again.

The conversation carries on, bouncing between everyone with ease. I'm quiet as usual, observing, and most of my attention is on Cora. I can't stop thinking about the near kiss. Old buried feelings are rising to the surface. The way this night feels like simpler times, before Cora and Avery left, and I was so hurt. I didn't think I could ever heal from that. I don't think I was even sure I'd be able to move on after we had our talk, where we laid everything out on the table and promised to move forward.

But tonight, I see new possibilities for the future and old feelings resurfacing. The crazy part is that I can't quite decide if I'm comfortable with any of it. There are still so many unknowns. I know we said we'd be friends, but could we be more?

As if my mom can read my mind, she asks, "So Cora, curious minds want to know if you're back permanently. Can we expect you and our Avery girl to make your home here?"

Cora's face turns thoughtful as she seems to contemplate Mom's question. I didn't realize it at first, but I was holding my breath, waiting for her answer. Will she leave again? I hadn't really thought much about that because my mind only seemed to focus on the fact that she was here to help her mom. I've only thought of her spending time with her dad. I hadn't really thought of the future. But the cold, hard truth is that Mr. Connolly will not recover. It's only a matter of time, and if God is merciful, he will not allow him to suffer much longer. All those feelings I experienced all those year ago when she said she was leaving flood me and have me paralyzed.

"Honestly, I'm not really sure right now. I haven't thought much past tomorrow. But I don't have any plans of leaving any time soon."

My breath releases. It's loud enough that Kelsea turns her head in my direction and gives me a look of sympathy. I hate that look. It's the same look each family member gave me whenever they saw me for at least six months after Cora left.

"Well, that makes sense. I just hope you know we are

here for you," Rosie adds to the conversation. In her typical way, she is trying to ease the tension and sorrow that fill the air around us. It has always been one of my favorite things about my sister-in-law, her ability to care so deeply and show it in subtle ways.

Everyone murmurs their agreement. In typical Tyler fashion, when he's uncomfortable with real emotions, he says, "Parks, what did you do to piss Abbey off this time?" Dude is always stirring the pot.

Abbey looks at him incredulously, "I'm not mad. Why would you think I'm mad?" She glances from Tyler to Parker.

Drew and Rosie try to hide their smiles. Kelsea rolls her eyes. Cora looks at me and raises her eyebrows, a smirk on her face. My parents occupy themselves with the kids.

Parker gives an "I'm going to kick your ass" look at Tyler before turning to Abbey, "Babe, ignore Ty. You know how he is."

"Yes, I do know how he is," she glares at Ty.

Tyler gives her his biggest shit-eating grin. He's always loved to push Abbey's buttons because she is one person who can match his sarcasm. We're all used to it by now, and ironically, I find the friendly bickering sort of comforting. Focusing on their antics got me through a lot of hard days right after Cora left.

The evening continues in its usual manner: full of laughter, chatter, the occasional screaming kid, and conversation. As I look around, I realize there were days I never thought I would see Cora sitting here with my family on a Sunday night gathering again. A feeling of hope begins to creep in, and there is nothing that scares me more when Cora is involved.

CORA

I finally got Avery to settle and fall asleep. She is always so wound up after she spends time with the Nallen family. I don't blame her; they have an energy that just makes you feel happy and alive.

And they've always made me feel the same way. The way they love each other, tease, support, and drive each other insane, it's all an amazing part of their group dynamic. It doesn't matter if you're not blood. When one of them loves you, you become a part of that dynamic too. You become family.

Alone in my room, I sit in the overstuffed chair next to my window, looking out into the night sky. The lights still shine in Jasper's parents' house across the street.

It was a good night. My mind drifts to the conversations that flowed so easily. It feels like they've been one unit for a lifetime, but really, it's only been a few years since Rosie and Abbey married into the family. But they're seamless; you'd never know they haven't been a part of the group forever.

Rosie, sweet and thoughtful. In a lot of ways, she is just like Mrs. Nallen. She complements Drew perfectly, and he, her. You can see how strong their love is with every look they give one another. I envy that.

Then there is Abbey and Parker. Both headstrong and confident, and their love for each other is exactly like their personalities. Unbreakable. It's like they're the only proof you need that soul mates exist.

Kelsea, with her strong sense of self-worth. And Tyler's sarcastic, brother bear attitude rounds out the whole. Every person brings their own individual superpower to the force that is the Nallen family. And I can't help but want that, too. I was part of that once. Why is it that I'm only seeing that now?

But I'm scared. That near kiss …I felt it all the way to my core, and that was without even feeling Jasper's lips against mine. I fear we can't get back to where we once were, but I know without a doubt, especially after tonight, that I want to try. I've just got to figure out if Jasper is willing to take that chance again.

The first tear slips down my cheek, and a shiver runs up my spine. Wiping it away, I crawl beneath the blankets of my childhood bed.

Now, as I lie here in the dark, a sudden sorrow overcomes me. And I begin to weep for the years I lost with Jasper. With the Nallens. For the years I took away from Avery. I mourn for what my mom, Avery, and I will lose when my dad leaves this earth. My God, what the Nallens will lose because they not only brought me into their fold, but they also brought my parents in, too.

But I'm back, and this time fear won't stop me from reaching out for the possibility of being where my happiness exists…in a world with Jasper.

Because if there is one thing I realized tonight, it's that my trepidation of losing myself in Jasper is small compared to living without him again.

Sixteen

JASPER

I walk into The Roasting Company two days later for a mid-day pick-me-up. It has been a long couple of days at work, meeting after meeting—proposal after proposal. I'm exhausted.

I haven't seen Cora and Avery since they left my parents' house after dinner. I wanted to walk them home, but she insisted they'd be fine and left before I could argue. It left me wondering why—was she trying to avoid me and discussing our almost kiss?

Maybe it was for the best because I'm sure not what I would have said. I don't know what I was thinking, so how could I explain or apologize? Was she mad? I've wondered, but she talked to me during dinner, and we've exchanged texts since then.

"Jasper, mate! It's so nice to see you. Your brother and

Rosie were in this morning, and Cora just came in with her sweet little angel a few minutes ago. They're at the table over there in the corner," Andrew says as I walk up to the counter to order, and my gaze turns in the direction he's looking. A small smile creeps across my face.

Avery is standing before Cora. She seems to be telling her a story, waving her little hands in the air. Her facial expression is animated with every word she speaks. Cora sits at the table, grinning at her daughter in the most loving way and listening intently.

Turning back to Andrew, I order, "I'll take a large drip coffee with just a touch of half and half."

"Got it. Anything else?"

"That will be all."

I pay and wait as Andrew makes my order. He's quick and reaches over the counter to hand it to me. "Cheers, mate!" he says enthusiastically.

"Cheers," I reciprocate, raising my cup in the air.

When I turn around, I can see Cora has made Avery sit down at the table with her. I wind my way through the tables. As I approach them, Avery spots me first because Cora's back is to me.

She shouts my name with excitement, "Jasper!" and hops out of the chair, sneaking past her mother and throwing her arms around my legs. Cora's face lights up, and my heart beats faster at the sight.

"Fancy seeing you here," I say, rubbing my free hand over Avery's back as she squeezes me tighter.

Cora stands up to greet me, too, pushing a loose curl behind her ear. "Hey."

"Hey," I say back.

"I stopped in to grab a cup of rejuvenation, and Andrew pointed out that you two were sitting over here."

"Do you have time to join us?"

Before I can respond, Avery lets me go and pleads with me to stay. "You have to stay! Mommy told me she would get me a treat if I finished my sandwich. If you stay, I can share my treat with you."

"Well, I don't know how to pass up the chance to share a treat with my favorite five-year-old."

Looking back up to Cora, I wink at her, and she mouths "thank you" in return.

"How about you and I go back to the bakery display so you can pick out what we'll have, and Mommy can sit here and enjoy the rest of her lunch?"

"You don't have ..." Cora begins to say before I interrupt her.

"Cora, I've got this. It's fine," I tell her.

She nods. "Avery, please hold Jas's hand.

"I will, Mommy."

Her tiny hand slips into mine, and we walk away. I swear I can feel Cora's eyes on us the entire way.

As Avery's eyes scan the display case filled with cookies, pastries, and donuts, I glance back in Cora's direction. She abruptly stands, and her eyes go wide. Even from here, I can see the look of dread on her face. Her gaze is focused on the space just beyond where Avery and I stand.

Following her gaze, I turn, and standing there is the one guy in the world that I hate with every fiber of my being. He'd left town years ago, but apparently, he's back.

Tommy Warner. The town asshole and the guy who got Cora pregnant at a party one night and then wanted nothing to do with her or the baby. He tried forcing her to get an abortion, and when she refused, Tommy threatened her. I wanted to kill him, and if it weren't for my brothers, I would have done it. Seeing him again, here, so close to Cora and Avery, I feel the rage hot in my chest all over again.

I look back at Cora, and she is still frozen in place, like she's afraid that if she moves, he might see her.

Avery. My head swivels in her direction. "I know what I want," she says, as she whips around toward me, grin wide on her face.

I quickly step toward her and bend down to her level.

"Which one?" I ask, trying to sound calm. Praying he hasn't noticed us, because if there is one thing I know about Tommy, he will, in fact, make a scene.

"The chocolate cake-sant!"

God, I love this girl. I feel my need to protect her vibrate through me.

"You mean, the chocolate croissant?" I state, rubbing my hand gently over her head.

"That is what I said, chocolate cake-sant."

I smile because she is something special, but I can feel the possibility of war raging behind me.

"Sounds perfect, I'll get it. Why don't you run over and tell Mommy what you picked, and I will bring it over after I pay for it."

"Okay!" Avery shouts without argument and runs in the direction of Cora.

Watching as Avery makes her way through the tables, I lift my gaze to Cora, and we lock eyes. I give her a nod, then slowly begin to rise to standing level.

"Hey, Nallen. I see things haven't changed much around here. You're still following Cora around like you're her watchdog," Tommy says from behind me.

Taking a deep breath so I can keep my cool, I calmly turn to face him.

"Warner," I say, hatred coating his name.

He involuntarily takes a slight step back. He's tall, but I'm taller by at least two inches. I've always liked this advantage. Tommy's never been smart enough to know when he should read social cues. Even though I just took a step toward him and am now looking down at him, a cocky smirk rests on his face. But it's his eyes that give away what a coward he is.

"Get whatever you came in here for and leave," I demand, quietly.

His lip tips up even more in one corner. "This is a public place, Jasper. You can't make me leave. And I doubt much has changed over the years. Mommy and Daddy raised you to be proper and polite, so there is no way you'll cause a scene to make me. Especially in front of that little girl of Cora's. Speaking of, maybe I should introduce myself."

Before either of us even realizes what I'm doing, I grab a fistfull of his shirt and pull him against me. Through gritted teeth, I grind out, "You stay away from them, or I will make you regret ever being born."

For once, he has the decency to look scared for a second. "Isn't it my right to talk to my little girl?"

Blind rage pulses through my veins, and my ears are ringing. I pull my other fist back, ready to connect, when someone grabs my arm with all their strength.

"Jas, not here. She is watching." Tyler's voice is in my ear. It's now that I grasp what I'm doing and the scene I'm causing. His words clear my blurred vision. "Let him go; he isn't worth it," he continues.

My grip gradually releases its hold on Tommy's shirt, and I take a step back, my breathing becoming steady. My head swivels in Cora and Avery's direction. Cora is a little closer, and Avery is holding her leg, a look of uncertainty on her face. The entire coffee house is silent and looking in our direction.

The cocky smirk returns, "Big brother, nice to see you're rescuing your little bro from an ass whipping once again. Smart."

From the corner of my eye, I see Tyler enter Tommy's personal space. Tyler is even bigger than I am, so the impact is greater. It's the reason we all call him a bear. His voice is cold and intimidating, two things you never want to push Tyler to. "First off, Warner, Jasper doesn't need me to rescue him. You do. And second, you come anywhere near anyone in my family, which includes Cora Connolly and her little girl, and you won't need to worry about how Jasper will react because you will have me to answer to every other Nallen brother, you worthless piece of shit."

I place my hand on Ty's shoulder without taking my eyes off Cora, then I speak in a hush, harsh tone. "Warner, I think you should do the right thing for once in your life and leave this building. Find another coffee house in town to frequent."

A loud huff escapes Tommy, "You think I'm staying in this shithole of a town for long? I'm only here to visit my dad, then I'm out."

"Good," Ty states, the coldness still lingering in his words.

Tommy backs up, hands in the air, after he reads our faces one last time. The cocky grin is long gone. He glances over my shoulder; I step forward with the intention of fulfilling our threats.

"She's still one hot little piece."

I lunge for him as he slips through the door. I think about going after him for one split second until Tyler says, "No, Jas," with an older brother authority that he never uses.

As soon as the patrons of the coffee shop know he's gone and nothing is going to happen, the buzzing of conversation starts up again.

My attention instantly returns to the two most important people in my life, who both look scared, but there is also relief written across Cora's face. I start to make my way to them, forgetting Tyler and everything else that happened in the last five minutes. Before I even take three steps, Andrew is standing in front of me, holding a small brown bag extended out to me. "You almost forgot the chocolate croissant, mate. And I think you're going to need it."

My eyes meet his, I take the croissant I never had a chance to order, and quietly thank him before he walks away. I continue to make my way over to Cora and Avery, and I can feel Ty shadowing me a few steps back. As soon as I reach them, I whisper "I'm sorry" to Cora, and I can now see the tears in her eyes. Then I drop to my knees in front of Avery, waiting for a cue from her before I move closer.

"Jasper, that man was mean," she says before reaching out for me. I pull her against me, and she leans into my chest. "He scared me."

"He is mean, baby girl, but there is no reason to be scared. I would never let him hurt you."

Shaking her little head, she says, "I wasn't afraid he would hurt me. I was afraid he'd hurt you," then she wraps her arms around my neck and squeezes tight.

"He can't hurt either of us. I wouldn't let him, and neither would Ty."

Avery pulls back, nodding. "Can we have our chocolate cake-sant now?"

"I think we could all use a chocolate milk, too," Tyler says before I can even answer.

"Yes!" Avery shouts.

Setting Avery down, I stand back up. "Really, man?" I question, looking at my brother.

"Yes, really," Ty says, then reaches out for Avery's hand. "And my gal, Avery, is going to help me order them for all of us."

She beams up at Ty. "I think that is a fan-castick idea," Avery tells him.

"Fantastic," he corrects.

"That's what I said, silly. Fan-castick!"

Tyler's face shapes into the perfect apologetic look and says, "Oh, excuse me. My mistake."

"That's okay," Avery replies frankly.

Tyler covers his smile, and the two of them walk off together. Sometimes, Tyler can be surprisingly intuitive. Cora hasn't made a sound. I need to talk to her, and Avery can't be here when I do.

Gently, I reach for her hand and say her name, "Cora."

All at once, her free hand covers her mouth, and the first tear slips past her lids, sliding down her cheek. She holds the sob in, and I pull her out the side patio door to get her out of eye view of the entire coffee shop.

Luckily, the crowd had started to dissipate, and no one was out here. We're alone and, thank God, because just like I thought, she breaks. I bring her into me, and she sinks into me. I let her cry while I gently rub my hand in a circle over her back.

"Oh God, Jasper," she finally says. "I…I've been gone so long that I forgot about all the worry of one day running into him." She pushes back and wipes the tears away, her voice steadier now. "I wasn't prepared. What if he talked to her? What if he told her who he is?"

"But he didn't, Cora. And I wouldn't have let him get another step closer to either one of you."

"What if you weren't here?"

"But I was, and the what-ifs don't matter," I tell her, reaching back out to her so I can touch her again. Seeing her this upset and frightened makes me feel protective.

"What if he hurt you?"

"He couldn't. He wouldn't."

"God, how could I? How could he be Avery's dad? She's so good. So perfect."

For some reason, the red-hot anger fills my chest again…no, not anger, but jealousy. So, I reach for the right thing to say. Anything I can say to take away what Cora just tried to give him by calling him Avery's dad.

Stepping close to Cora, I take her face in between my hands and hold her. Our eyes lock on one another, hers swimming with tears, and mine nearly matching hers.

As gently as I can, I convey everything I think she needs to hear. "Cora, listen to what I'm about to say. It's time to stop beating yourself up over one mistake you made when we were young. But if you really consider it, it wasn't a mistake at all because it gave you Avery…gave all of us Avery." I caress her cheek lightly with one of my hands, and she leans into it. "She is good and perfect. But that has nothing to do with him. It's all you. She is you in every way, and if it were possible, I'd say you were the only one who had a hand in creating her. And never call him her dad again. He isn't her dad. A dad is always there, protects you, loves you, and puts your happiness first. Tommy Warner has never done any of those things. Avery doesn't need him. Do you hear me? He can't touch you or her, and he never will. Because I won't let him." I lightly kiss her cheeks. First on the left and then on the right. And she lets me.

The next thing I know, Cora is wrapping her arms around my middle and holding me tight. "Thank you, Jasper. Thank you for always being on my side. For always being here for me and for forgiving me when I cut you out.

I promise I thought it was best." She looks up at me before continuing, "But I was wrong, and I won't make that mistake again."

"We both made wrong choices. We're Jasper and Cora. We can get through anything."

The door suddenly swings open, and Avery comes barreling out.

"Mommy...Jas, I was tired of waiting for you to come back in."

Tyler walks out the door behind her, "Sorry, I held her off as long as I could."

Cora walks over to Tyler and takes him off guard when she throws her arms around his neck. "Thanks, Ty." I hear her whisper.

"Anytime, Cor. I'll always have your back. We're family," he tells her as he hugs her back.

Avery pulls on my pant leg, getting my attention. "Jas."

"Yeah, sweet girl."

"Sorry, but Ty ate your half of the chocolate cake-sant."

Tyler grins, "You mean, croissant."

"That's what I said, cake-sant," she insists, placing one hand on her hip.

I look at Cora. "See? She's just like you."

Cora smiles at me gratefully.

Seventeen

CORA

Avery skips along the sidewalk in front of us. I've been watching her closely, trying to decipher if she is still worried about the interaction between Jasper and Tommy. But she's been her typical, precocious self since then. Playing with Tyler before he left to head back to work. Telling Jasper about her one-sided conversation with my dad this morning. And even now, she has a smile on her face while she hums a tune I can't quite pinpoint.

"You really don't have to walk us to our car, Jas. I'm sure you probably need to get back to work," I insist.

He takes my hand and squeezes it. "Cora, I want to, and it's fine. I'm not under any time constraint."

Squeezing his hand back, I shrug my shoulders. "Fine, if you insist."

"I do." Jasper releases my hand, letting it fall in between us as we walk side by side. My hand still tingles from his touch, and I long to take his hand in mine again.

I don't know if this overwhelming feeling to be closer to him is because I'm finally accepting the possibility of us, or if it is lingering adrenaline from all the emotions of the last half hour. My feelings seem to be simmering at the surface, and they are swirling together. So many thoughts—worry and happiness and longing. I'm just feeling so much, and Jasper is at the center of it all.

Once we reach my car, Jasper opens the door for Avery, and she climbs into her car seat. He secures her in and bends forward, kissing her on the forehead. She pats him on the back as he leans in.

"Bye, Jasper. I hope to see you soon. Maybe tonight?" Avery says as Jasper straightens up and stares down into the back seat at her.

"I'm not sure I'll be able to come by tonight, but I will be over tomorrow to visit your Granddad, like always."

No matter how busy he's been at work, Jasper has visited my dad every Wednesday. From what Mom has told me, this started long before Dad got sick, and I moved back.

She frowns but accepts his response. "Fine, but it would've been better to see you again today."

"Avery…" I start to remind her that Jasper is busy, but he interrupts me.

"Avery, I couldn't agree more, but unfortunately, I have a very important project to finish tonight. But I promise I will be thinking about you the whole time and wishing I was with you."

"Okay, me too," Avery responds, then says, "And I bet Mommy will be doing the same."

My cheeks grow red, and while I want to deny her presumption, I can't. Not to mention, I really didn't know how to protest without making it more obvious that she's right. I realize now that I will be wishing for exactly that.

"Well, that would be nice," Jasper says. "Bye, sweet girl."

He closes the door and looks over the top of the car at where I'm standing next to the open driver's side door. He just stares in silence.

Nervously, I push the ever-errant strand of hair behind my ear. "Well, uh…bye. See you tomorrow."

Stepping back, he says, "Yeah, see you. Be safe and have a good night."

"Bye, Jas," I say, then I slide into the car behind the wheel and close my door.

Starting the car, I give one last look in the direction Jasper walked, watching him for a moment, once again trying to figure out just what all these feelings really mean.

Sighing, I finally pull out of the parking spot. Just before I turn out of the lot, I glance in the rearview mirror and see that Jasper has stopped and is now watching us drive away. In a way, it reminds me of the day we left town all those years ago. All I can think now is that I hope he knows I'm not interested in leaving again, and I hope that is what he wants too.

● ● ●

It's Saturday night, and it's time for our girls' night. I almost didn't think I was going to go tonight, but I'm glad I decided to make it happen. This week has been a little much, but it will be nice to get out and spend some time with the Nallen girls.

Jasper came over on Wednesday, as he had promised, to visit Dad, and then he had dinner with me, Mom, and Avery. It felt wonderful to have him there, and it gave all of us a moment of reprieve from the worry of how much Dad had deteriorated over the last couple of weeks.

The moments he's awake are fewer and fewer. His nurse says that they're giving him enough medicine, so he doesn't suffer too much, but it's also the reason he isn't alert more often.

That's one of the reasons I wasn't sure I was going to make it out tonight with all the girls. I didn't know if I should leave Mom, especially to take care of Avery, when she has my dad to worry about.

But Mrs. Nallen came over to visit Mom yesterday and suggested again that Avery stay the night with them since she and Mr. Nallen were watching their grandkids. She convinced me that it would be easier on her if Avery helped keep Jakey occupied. I'm not that confident in Avery's five-year-old abilities to keep anyone calm and occupied, I told her jokingly. We all laughed, then she and Mom insisted that I go out and enjoy myself. Mom said she would be backup and profusely thanked her friend for taking Avery for the night.

So now here I am, hopping out of the Uber in front of Kelsea's condo, in hopes of enjoying a night out with all the Nallen girls. I thank the driver and then make my way up the walkway, slowly. I'm not sure what I was thinking when I decided to wear these three-inch heels and this skirt that barely hits past mid-thigh.

When I reach her front door, I wrap my knuckles against it.

Within seconds, the door swings open, and Kelsea is already walking away as she greets me. "Hey, I just have to put the final touches on my face, and I'm pretty sure Rosie and Abbey will be here any minute. Grab a drink from the fridge if you want." She didn't even glance in my direction.

"Hey, sounds good," I say as I follow her in, shutting the door behind me. "Did you even know it was me?" I ask loudly as she disappears into the bathroom down the hallway.

Peeking her head out through the doorway, she responds, "I assumed. I wasn't expecting anyone…Whoa! Girl, look at you!"

Conscientiously, I rub my hands down my front. "Umm, does it look bad? Is it too much? I wasn't…"

Kelsea steps fully into the hallway and interrupts me, "Cora, far from it. You're hot, and now I think I need to change."

"Oh. You look incredible, don't change. And are you sure this isn't too …I don't know, I haven't really been out in a while. "

"I'm positive. You're gorgeous."

"Thanks."

She steps back into the bathroom but keeps talking to

me. I look in her fridge and pull the drink she offered out for myself.

"So, when you say you haven't been out in a while, what do you mean by a while?"

"Like over a year," I say, sheepishly.

"You haven't been on a date in over a year!"

"Oh, it wasn't a date. I went out with a couple of girls from work. I tried to go on one date about a year after I moved to Arizona. It lasted about twenty minutes."

"Basically, you're saying your last date was four years ago, and it only lasted as long as a shower? "

"Yep, that's what I'm saying."

"You were gone for four years and never met anyone? Never dated?"

"There was never anyone who made me laugh, or whom I felt I could trust. Plus, I had to consider Avery. She came first." I thought back to life in Arizona and the different men from the office who asked me out, or even the neighbor three doors down who was kind, handsome, and utterly relentless in his pursuit of me. I still couldn't bring myself to allow anyone in. "It's not that I didn't meet people or have the opportunity."

Kelsea steps out into the hall again, staring at me. "Then, what stopped you?"

I stare at her because I can see from how she looks at me that Kelsea expects more than a generic answer, but that is exactly what I give her. "I don't know."

"Don't you?" She asks.

Suddenly, there is a loud knock on the door, startling us both and saving me from the turn our conversation had just taken.

"Shit, that scared me," I say.

Kelsea laughs, "Saved by the knock, I guess. Can you answer that? I'm pretty sure it's the girls."

"Sure thing," I say, feeling relieved to avoid the direction of that conversation as I go to the door, pulling it open.

Abbey's hands are raised in the air as soon as the door opens. She shouts, "Wooo hooo, ladies! Let's do this!"

Rosie's standing beside her, a giant grin on her face as she rubs her pregnant belly. "It's been a while since she's had a night out," she says, angling her head toward her best friend.

I laugh and wave them in just about the time Kelsea enters the living room.

"Dang, girl! Those legs in that skirt!" Rosie says as she follows me in.

"That's what I was thinking too," Kelsea agrees, adding, "I mean, you two look fabulous too."

"Personally, I think we're all hot," Abbey shouts.

"Good lord, Abbey, what did you drink before you got here?" Kelsea asks. "Did my brother make one of his concoctions?"

"Nope, I made my own by adding an extra shot when he handed me the one he made me," Abbey says, winking.

"Oh, man, this is going to be a fun night," Kelsea says sarcastically.

Rosie and I laugh. I like Abbey. She's funny and confident, and she takes no bullshit. She's the perfect match for Parker.

"Isn't that the plan?" I ask.

"Damn right it is! So, let's get this party started. Rosie is the designated driver!" Abbey bellows.

Rosie shakes her head while patting her belly again, "Thrilled to take one for the team."

I smile at her, and she smiles back.

"Well, ladies, shall we get this party started?" Kelsea asks.

We all whoop, and one by one, we march out the door for what we hope will be a fun-filled girls' night out.

Eighteen

JASPER

Tyler tips back the beer the waitress just set in front of him while we wait for Parker and Drew. I sit in front of him, staring up at the television over the bar while the scores of all the games from earlier in the day scroll across the bottom of the screen.

"So, are we ever going to talk about the other day?" Tyler asks.

Without looking at him, I shrug. "What's there to talk about?"

He taps the table in front of him to bring my attention to our conversation. When I look at him, he nods, as if saying, "Okay now I can continue."

"Oh, I don't know. Maybe how you almost lost your shit in public and in front of Avery." He takes another long pull from the bottle in his hand before continuing.

"Or maybe how intense your conversation with Cora was after?"

"There's nothing to talk about. Tommy Warner is an asshole, and he got too close. He gave up his rights to go anywhere near Cora and Avery a long time ago. I won't let him hurt them."

"Yeah, maybe so, but you looked like you were going to kill him, and what good would that do anyone? I mean, then you wouldn't have your chance to be a real family with your girls."

"Dude, what the hell are you talking about?" I ask him. That old familiar ache fills the pit of my stomach. The ache I hadn't felt in years until the last couple of weeks, and it's only gotten more intense. "They're not my girls."

"Come on, Jas. You know it, and I know it. You're falling in love with Cora all over again." Tyler pats me on the knee. "Not that you ever got over her in the first place."

"Loving Cora has never been the problem. Or Avery, for that matter."

"Then what? If you're admitting it, what's the deal? What had you two so emotional after that run-in with Tommy? And don't try to blame him. It was something more."

"Look, Ty. I don't know where Cora's head is at right now. Honestly, I'm not quite sure where mine is either."

"Jas, it wasn't that long ago at Mom and Dad's house. You two were inches from kissing each other without a second thought about the fact that every one of us was standing within five feet of you. Now you're saying this display of emotions between you and Cora was solely based on what just happened."

"You're wrong. I was about to kiss her. But I doubt she was about to kiss me. Cora has never lost her inhibitions with me before. Why would things be any different now?" I ask him. "And as for the other day, she was emotional over the run-in with Tommy. She was worried about Avery, and can you blame her?"

"I think it was more than that."

"It wasn't."

"Whatever you need to tell yourself."

Tyler isn't backing down, and I haven't processed everything I've been feeling. I thought I'd pushed these emotions out of my mind. Maybe that's the problem; my mind isn't where they reside, they're in my heart. Our eyes lock in a battle of wills, and right now, in this bar, and on this night, I'm refusing to have this conversation with my big brother.

"Hey there, little brothers," Drew's voice comes from one end of the table. "What's going on here?"

"Yeah, did we miss something?" Parker says from the opposite end of the table.

"No," I say. "Yes," Ty says. Both of us answer at the same time without looking away from one another.

"Right," Drew says as he and Parker pull out a stool and take a seat.

"Our little brother here is being stubborn. I had to save him from certain jail time a couple of days ago and …"

"Excuse me?" Parker interrupts.

"Tommy Warner is back in town, and he thought it might be a good idea to talk to Avery and Cora, but thankfully, Jasper was there to intercept. And this was in the middle of The Roasting Company, so as you can imagine what a shock for me when I walked in and Jas here has one fist full of Werner's T-shirt and the other raised to knock him into next week."

"Should've let him do it," Drew says. "I hate that piece of shit."

"Really, Drew?" Parker asks.

"What? Come on, Jas wouldn't have gone to jail…for long," Drew responds.

"God, would you all shut up? I don't want to talk about this tonight. We dealt with Tommy, Cora and Avery are fine, and that's that. Ty was a big help, and I appreciated it."

"So touchy," Parker declares.

At that moment, the waitress walks back up to the table.

"Hey, guys. What can I get for you two, and are you two ready for another?" She directs her question at Parker and Drew, then points to me and Ty.

"We'll each have a Blanton's on a single rock, and two more Sierra Nevada in a bottle," Drew orders.

"Got it. Be right back," the waitress says.

"I think the girls are coming here tonight, too," Drew tells us.

"Yeah, I'm pretty sure Abbey said the same," Parker remarks.

"I haven't seen them yet," I say.

"Yeah, he would notice," Ty says.

"What? Shut up, Ty."

"You keep dodging the Cora conversation, and I'm just

saying that if the girls had come in, you would've noticed."

"Yeah, what is happening there? Did you finally apologize to her?" Drew asks.

"I did, and she apologized too. We talked things through and we're good now."

"And so, what does Ty think you're avoiding then?" Parker questions.

Renee, the waitress, has impeccable timing because she arrives back at the table with all of our drinks to save me from having to answer the question.

"Here ya go. Do you want to start a tab?"

"Yes, please…take this card," Drew insists.

"Thanks, I'll be back to check on you in a few, but wave if you need anything."

"Now, back to the conversation at hand," Drew says.

If I quit trying to ignore the questions, they'll let this go. For as long as I can remember, my family has been obsessed with knowing every detail so they can understand my relationship with Cora.

"Fine, I'm struggling with what I've felt for Cora most of our lives, how I dealt with her leaving four years ago, and her coming back. I don't know what to think or feel. And I sure as hell don't get the idea that anything has changed for her, so all that tells me is that I'm going to get hurt again."

Tyler looks at me and shakes his head, "I think you're wrong. I think you've always been wrong about Cora's feelings and her reasons for leaving."

"You're crazy," I tell him, shaking my head.

"Nope, it was something that she said when you

walked away from her at dinner last Sunday after you almost kissed," he retorts.

"Wait, you and Cora almost kissed?" Parker says, sounding shocked.

"They did, and then I watched Cora the rest of the night. She was paying close attention to Jasper's every move for the rest of the night. You should talk to her and tell her how you feel," Tyler insists.

All three of my brothers are looking at me intently, and I know they won't let this go unless I agree.

"Fine. If I promise to speak with Cora, can we let this go for the night?"

"Yes," they all agree.

"Then fine, I promise. I will talk to Cora and figure my shit out."

Parker raises his glass, then Drew and Tyler follow suit. They all wait for me to join them. Releasing a loud sigh, I lift my beer and nod at my older brother to proceed.

"To brotherly love, forcing one another to face our fears, and a fun night!"

Drew, Ty, and I clink our drinks with a whoop of agreement.

I realize I've been so distracted by the conversation with my brothers that I didn't know how packed the bar was. My eyes roam over the room, wondering if we missed the girls arriving for their night out.

"I don't think they're here yet," Drew hollers over the music and the crowd, leaning toward me so I can hear him better.

I acknowledge him with a thumb-up. There is no use

in denying that I was looking for them, and he probably was, too.

Parker waves to the waitress for another round, and we all sit back silently for a while, watching as more and more people walk into the bar.

"Tell us what's new with you, Tyler," Parker asks. "Any new prospects?" Tyler's face always goes blank when we mention his love life or lack thereof. Parker pushes a little more, "You can't always expect us to be the topic of conversation."

"There isn't anything to tell. I work, and I see some people, but nothing serious. And I don't plan on there being anything to report any time soon. I'm not like all of you."

"What the hell is that supposed to mean?" I ask.

"Each of you has always wanted to find someone you feel completes you. Not me," Ty quips.

"Dude, I just asked a simple question. You don't have to get so defensive," Parker says.

Once again, Renee arrives just in time and drops our drinks at the table. "I'm supposed to tell you all that this round is paid for."

"Uh, okay...by who?" Drew asks.

Renee turns around and points across the room to a group of four familiar faces, smiling back at us. "Those four ladies over at the bar." Renee salutes them and shouts over her shoulder as she walks away, "I'll be back around soon."

We all wave at the girls and raise our drinks in their direction. I try to get a clear view of Cora, but there are too many people between us, and where the girls are standing, I only have a partial view of her.

"Who wants to bet that those four get us in trouble tonight?" Ty asks.

Parker, Drew, and I lift our hands in response. This may be a long night.

Nineteen

CORA

Conversations and loud music swirl around us, and I'm trying to hear Abbey's story about the time she and Rosie spent two hours getting ready for a night out with Drew and Parker when she suddenly went into labor.

Rosie laughs and says she hopes that doesn't happen tonight and ruin our first girls' night out in ages.

Kelsea orders all of us a cocktail and a shot each, except for Rosie, and then Abbey insists we order the guys some, too. She just spotted them across the room at a table. They look so engrossed in a discussion that none of them has spotted us yet.

My eyes immediately seek out Jasper, hoping for a glimpse of him.

We aren't close enough to them, and too many people

are crossing my line of sight, but I can imagine the look on his face—he has a kind but intense look. He's aware of what is happening around them, but his attention is on his brothers.

"Cora, did we mention how hot you look tonight?" Rosie asks, as she snags a seat at the bar, after a couple left with drinks in their hands.

Accepting my drink from Kelsea, I answer, "Only about seven other times." I flash her a grin, so she knows I'm joking.

"Because it's true," Abbey exclaims.

Kelsea reaches across me to hand Abbey a shot, then picks up another one from the bar and hands it to me, before taking hers in her hand. Rosie lifts her water, and we lift our shots.

"To friendship and sisterhood," Rosie says.

"To fun and laughter," Abbey adds.

"To happiness and health," Kelsea declares.

"To finding love and holding onto it," I say without thinking. Their heads turn to me, and curious looks are on their faces. Our drinks are hanging in the air between us. I don't know what else to do, so I shout, "Cheers to the night!" This draws them back to the toast at hand, and we all tap our glasses together and throw them back.

A few minutes later, I'm definitely feeling the effects of the shot and the drinks I've had both here and at Kelsea's. Abbey has pulled us all out on the dance floor multiple times, and her excitement and enthusiasm are rubbing off on us.

As much fun as I'm having, I've spent much of the last

hour searching for Jasper.

"They're still over at the same table they were at when we walked in an hour ago," Kelsea says, leaning as close as she can to my ear.

I pull back and try to look confused. God, I hope I look confused.

"Oh, come on! Don't give me that look."

Abbey twirls around us, hands in the air. "What are you two talking about?"

"Cora's incessant need to have Jasper in her sight," Kelsea tells her, a grin on her face.

Abbey stops dead, mid-twirl, and whips around toward me. "Say what?"

"Kelsea! It's not what you…" I drift off.

Now we're all standing still in the middle of the dance floor, staring at one another. From behind Abbey, Rosie peeks around, looking only slightly miserable.

"What happened?" Rosie asks.

Abbey tilts her head to her best friend and sister-in-law and says, "We're waiting for Cora to explain why Kelsea just said she can't stop staring in our sweet and handsome little brother-in-law's direction."

I thought it only happened in cartoons, but Rosie's mouth literally formed an "o" shape.

"Let's not make this a big deal," I beg.

They all keep watching me, waiting for more. But I don't have more to give them, or at least, I don't think I do. I know what I feel, but I don't know what to do about it. I also don't know what Jasper feels, so I'm stuck at a crossroads.

"It kind of feels like a big deal, though," Rosie says. Kelsea and Abbey are nodding in agreement.

"Oh my God, can we just get another drink?"

Rosie, Kelsea, and Abbey all look at one another, then back to me. "Sure," they all say together.

We wind our way back to the bar, and luckily, there's a seat for Rosie.

"Thank the pregnancy gods that there is a stool available; my feet are feeling about four sizes bigger than normal."

Abbey orders us all shots and then turns back to where Kelsea and I are standing. She glances over my shoulder. "They're all still there, totally focused on each other like they're hanging out in a living room. Parker promised to let us have our night and not crash it."

"That's sweet," I say. "They all get that from their dad, don't you think, Kels? I mean, your dad is probably the kindest and most attentive husband to your mom. So respectful."

"Yes, it would be nauseating if it weren't so great."

The bartender finally brings us the shots and hands them out. Rosie shakes her water glass with a smile. We all count to three, tap our glasses, then slam them back. This one went down much smoother than the first one, and that tingly feeling I thought I felt earlier is definitely running through my whole body now.

Abbey picks up the conversation where we left off. "Parker is everything I could hope for in a husband, but if I didn't feel the urge to kick him in the shin at least once a day, I'd think it was all a lie. Like, what is up with his inability to pick up his socks? He leaves them everywhere."

"Oh my God, Drew, too! And he can't seem to shut a light off when he leaves the room." Rosie chimes in. "What is up with that?"

Kelsea shrugs, "Don't look at me. Y'all had a choice, I didn't."

I laugh, and a small snort slips out, making me laugh harder.

"Hello, ladies, how about you let us in on the joke?" A guy towering over me crowds into the space next to us, and several other guys come in behind him.

I instantly stopped laughing and took a step to the side, closer to Kelsea.

Abbey steps forward, but before she can say anything, a familiar face moves between us and the other guys.

"Kelsea Nallen…Cora Connolly? Aren't you two all grown up?"

"Noah Miller, is that you?" I beam. It had been ages since I've seen him. He spent a lot of time with Parker and Drew when we were growing up, but he moved away for college when they graduated.

"It is," he says, giving me a once-over. "Looking good, Ms. Connolly." His eyes drift over to Kelsea, and his gaze runs up her body until their eyes meet. Kelsea hasn't said a word; she stares at Noah with a look I don't think I've ever seen on her face. A little mix of longing and pure hatred. "Kelsea, how are you? Where are your brothers?"

I guess Noah's friends decide that maybe this isn't working out how they'd hoped, so they step around us and up to the bar.

I gently elbow her in her side, prompting her to finally speak, "I'm fantastic, and my brothers are just over there." She points her finger over his shoulder, then turns and puts her back to him.

Abbey peers at Kelsea, then turns to Noah and sticks her hand out. "Hi, I'm Abbey Nallen, Parker's wife." She points at Rosie and continues, "And that is Rosie; she is married to Drew."

Noah says, "Oh wow, nice to meet you both. I grew up with your husbands."

"Noah, Drew, and Parker were best friends. Noah left for school…," I look at him with a questioning look before continuing, "once he and Parker graduated and he disappeared."

Noah looks at me and shakes his head, smiling, "I wouldn't say I disappeared. I just wasn't in Santa Cruz."

"How long have you been back in town?" I ask, side-eyeing Kelsea, because I can't figure out why she is acting so weird, for the life of me.

"I just got back tonight. After about six months, I left school and joined the Navy. I was on active duty, and we just returned to the States." Noah explained.

Well, that does answer a lot of questions. Noah and Parker's senior year of high school began when Noah's parents passed away in an automobile accident, and his grandparents took him in. It was a challenging year for him. Noah's grandparents moved to Ohio to be closer to their other daughter after he graduated, and from what I'd heard, everyone lost touch.

"Wow, thank you for your service," Rosie says. "I bet

the guys would love to see you."

"All the boys are over there," I add.

Suddenly, a heavy arm is slung over my shoulder. "Noah, who is this sweet little thing?"

I try removing his arm, but it won't budge. Kelsea turns around and gives him a look that makes me want to run away, but the guy doesn't budge. "Look, creep. Get your hands off of her."

"Stevens, what the hell? Let her go," Noah says, taking a small step toward us as his friend pulls me in closer to his side. "What the hell, man? Don't start shit here. Let her go."

A deep voice from behind Noah growls, "Yeah, Stevens. Get your fucking hands off of her." Looking over Noah's shoulder, I see all four Nallen brothers standing like a brick wall. I'm not sure who said that because all of their faces look intimidating and angry.

Stepping forward, Noah grabs the jerk holding me by the shirt. "Fucking let her go and walk away."

"I think you should listen to your friend, or I'm pretty sure you'll have all four of my brothers to deal with, and I promise you don't want that, Navy or not," Kelsea hisses from next to me.

Stevens slowly releases me, and Noah lets him go once he does. "Fuck, Miller. I thought…"

Putting his hand on the guys shoulder, Noah points toward their other friends, who had retreated earlier. "Just leave, Stevens."

He gives Noah one last fuck-off look, then walks away. As soon as he does, Kelsea pulls me to her, and Jasper is beside us. I hadn't noticed before, but Abbey is standing closer to Rosie now, and they're holding hands, watching like they were waiting for a brawl to break out.

Jasper bends down a little to look me in the eyes, "Cora, are you okay?"

"I'm fine; it's no big deal," I shrug. Then I say, "It's not the first time some guy tried to put his hands on me without permission. If you had given me another second, I would've had just the right position to knee him where it counts."

Jasper grins, and my heart skips a beat.

"God, Cora, I'm sorry about that. I want to say he isn't usually an asshole, but I can't," Noah apologizes.

"Noah Miller? Is that you?" Parker's voice carries over the loud music.

Jasper's head snaps in Noah's direction, and his eyes widen. A slow smile crosses Noah's face, then he slowly turns to come face to face with his old friend.

Twenty

JASPER

I should've known and kept my hand down when Tyler offered the bet. Parker, Drew, and I had to pay Tyler twenty bucks each after we almost rearranged the face of the jerk who had his hands all over Cora.

I could have at least taken the obvious odds when Kelsea, Abbey, and alcohol are involved. Although I'm not certain that would have worked out either, Kelsea or Abbey had nothing to do with that guy and his inability to make good choices.

After the incident and the shock of seeing Noah wore off, we all played catch-up. Our two nights out groups merged into one.

Drew bailed about an hour ago because Rosie was exhausted. Noah promised to stay in touch and then left to search for his Navy buddies. I still can't believe Noah joined the military.

"It was good seeing Noah, right?" Cora asks us.

"Hell, yeah," Parks agrees.

Abbey starts to say something, but she lets out a huge yawn instead. Parker stands up and takes her by the hand. "Come on, Babe. Let's get you home." He twirls her into his arms and plants a kiss on her mouth. She giggles and wraps her arms around his neck.

"Are you picking me up in a bar?" She asks, a broad grin on her face.

Parker smirks at her. "Yes, just like the night we met. I'm taking you home with me and having my way with you on basically ey... " Abbey lightly swats his arm to cut him off, and he laughs a loud, boisterous laugh. One that he doesn't allow to slip out often.

"Okay, you two, take it home," Tyler says, looking both disgusted and delighted by Parker and Abbey's display of affection.

Everyone laughs except Kelsea, who hasn't said much for a while and is currently tossing back another shot at the bar alone. What is that about?

"I think I'm ready to go, too," Cora says. "Hey, Kels, I guess it's just the two of us sharing an Uber."

"I'm not ready to leave yet," Kelsea says, slightly slurring.

"Okay, well, I guess I can take one alone," Cora responds, and Kelsea gives her a weird head shake.

"Hey, I can take you home," I say.

"Yeah, and I've got Kelsea," Ty says.

I mouth, "Good," to him. When I turn back to Cora,

she's staring at me, but she doesn't respond.

"Cora? Did you hear me?"

Ty raises his eyebrows in my direction and then looks at Cora. I shrug. Then he walks over to the bar and sits next to Kelsea, who is once again waving down the bartender.

Cora suddenly returns from wherever her mind had gone just now because she finally says, "Oh, that would be great."

We say our goodbyes. Tyler promises he won't leave Kelsea's side and will get her home safely.

As Cora and I walk to my apartment to get my car keys, I watch her from the corner of my eye. She's looking around like this is the first time she's ever walked this street. A sort of awe and wonder paint her features, and the moonlight highlights her beauty. Because Cora is beautiful, she always has been. She is all warmth and charm with her velvety, chocolate brown curls and coffee-colored eyes. And when she allows herself to relax and be in the moment, all her worries slip away and transform her into something breathtaking.

Breaking the silence, she says, "Jas, I really missed this place. The crisp ocean air at night and the smell of clean salty air."

"I can't imagine living in a different place," I reply, then realize I'm walking alone. Cora stopped a few steps behind me.

When I turn around, she stares at me again, like she wants to say something but is unsure whether she should.

"Cora?"

"You almost kissed me. Why?" She blurts out the

words that I wasn't prepared for.

Putting my hands in my pockets, I look at my feet, searching for the right way to answer her.

"It's not like it would be the first time I kissed you." I don't know why I said it, but that's what came out. I look back up at her.

She takes one step toward me, shaking her head slightly. "That was years ago. You stopped being my friend after that. You only just forgave me for ..." Trailing off, she shakes her head a little harder as if trying to clear her thoughts. I remain quiet, waiting. "I think you had feelings for me then, so that's different. But then so much changed while I was gone. Why did you almost kiss me NOW?" She emphasizes the last word.

"Because I still have those feelings for you. Because at that moment, you looked so beautiful that I couldn't think of anything else. I didn't care that we were standing in my parents' backyard, surrounded by my family. I only saw you. Thought about you and the way your lips would feel against mine. As hard as I've tried, I've never stopped wanting to kiss you. I've never stopped having feelings for you. Is that what you want to hear?"

Before I know what's happening, Cora steps forward, lifting up on her toes, and pulls my face down to hers. "Kiss me now," she whispers, her breath hitting my lips.

I don't have time to think about what is happening or take in the fact that this is something I've always wanted her to ask me. There is only time to take the one thing I've always dreamed about.

I pull her closer, search her eyes for one last second,

and gently press my lips to hers. She sighs, and it sounds like relief. That pushes me over the edge. I need more. I need to be closer. I need everything that is Cora. This desire becomes more urgent. With this kiss, we become one.

Her hands move around my waist and under my shirt, and her touch pulses through me.

Pulling away, I'm stunned with an intense yearning as her hands slide around me. She takes my hand, leading me in the direction we were walking.

"Your house, now," she demands.

I don't say anything in response. I wouldn't even know what to say if I could speak. My focus is solely on Cora and the doorway she just opened.

When we reach my condo, we barely make it through the door before pulling at one another again, kissing, touching, and exploring.

"Cora," I rasp between kisses. She doesn't answer. "Cora," I say once more, gently taking her shoulders and pushing her back so I can look her in the eyes. I see a fire in her I've never witnessed, and it makes her even more beautiful; her lips are swollen from our searing connection. She's incredible, and I want her more than I've ever wanted anything else. My voice trembling, I say, "If we do this, there is no going back. I won't survive losing you again."

Her hand softly touches my face, "Jasper, I understand the repercussions of us taking this step. It changes nothing."

We are still for one quiet heartbeat, then we move back to each other with a sudden, desperate need.

It feels perfect. Magical. It's everything I've ever wanted.

Twenty-One

CORA

I'm kissing Jasper. I've never been kissed like this, and it's never felt this perfect. And there is no way I'm ever going to stop.

All at once, he lifts me into his arms, our mouths still fused by desire and need. Pushing his bedroom door open, Jasper walks in and slowly sets me to my feet at the end of his bed. Breaking apart, we look at one another and allow ourselves to take in what is happening.

Jasper reaches one hand up, caressing my cheek. "Cora, you're so beautiful."

A blush creeps over my cheekbones, and I whisper, shyly, "Thank you."

"I just want you to be certain that this is what you want because, like I told you earlier, if we do this, then this is it. It will be me, you, and Avery. There will be no turning back. There is too much at stake."

Resting my hand over his, I squeeze softly and lean my face into his hand. "Jas, this is what I want. I denied this for too long. I want…no, I need you."

Swiftly, his mouth is on mine, and he murmurs against my lips, "I need you, too."

Our mouths and hands roam over one another. The touch is more reverent and lingering as if with every motion we're noticing each other for the first time. It feels like we are committing ourselves to this newfound memory.

Piece by piece, we begin to remove our clothes; we're no longer acting as if we are starving for these affections but simply savoring them. When we finally stand bare before one another, we both release a breath. A small smile touches his lips, and I wonder why it took me so long to really see him. Reaching out, I lightly touch Jasper's chest and glide my fingertips over the bronzed contours.

With soft lips, he traces a line from my collarbone to the hollow of my throat, sending a rush of pleasure through my body. A faint moan escapes me, and I let my head fall back, to give him more access. I never want these feelings to stop.

Jasper kisses a trail all the way until his mouth lingers above mine. He doesn't say a word, but his eyes convey everything he is feeling in that moment. I hope he can see the same reflected in mine.

He wraps my arms around his neck, lifting me until my legs surround his waist, then he kisses me. Gently, enticing me to open more so he can deepen the kiss. Turning, he begins lowering us to the bed until he is hovering over me.

Lifting himself, he looks down at me, "God, you're so beautiful."

I smile, and it widens across my face. I've never experienced this kind of happiness before. The kind where I feel alive and sexy and where I'm told I'm beautiful. "So are you," I tell him, and Jasper returns my smile with his own.

Reaching over to his bedside table, he slides open the drawer before returning to the small space he's left between our bodies. He begins to fumble, so I touch his hand and say, "Wait, let me do it." He nods, and I take control, a slight moan leaving him.

I move my hands, stroking him and enticing him to kiss me again with an urgency stronger than before. Suddenly, his lips move from my mouth and cover my right breast, suckling and nipping gently with his teeth. As if he doesn't want to leave my left breast out, he moves to that one and does the same. I'm moaning and moaning his name, begging for more, and when I do, he makes one sudden thrust forward until he completely sheaths himself inside of me.

"Jasper," I call out as he calls out, "Cora."

Our bodies freeze in motion for one blissful second, his passion-filled gaze locked with mine. Then all at once, we move together slowly at first, then faster. I meet him thrust for thrust, all the while our lips explore whatever part of the other it can reach.

The sensation of splintering into a million pieces builds and builds until I don't think my body will hold for one more second. I've never felt anything so wonderful and sensual in my life. Our bodies move as one until the very moment we shatter, and I'm certain our souls become one.

JASPER

From the moment I entered Cora, I knew I had been right all along; she was meant for me, and there could never be anyone else. After we reached that earth-shattering climax, I rolled over and pulled Cora into me, tucking her into my side. Her arm rests across my chest as she kisses my chest tenderly, then says, "That was amazing."

"Beyond amazing," I reply.

She giggles and tries burying herself deeper into my side.

Kissing the top of her head, I ask, "Do you need to let your mom know that you won't be home tonight?"

Cora yawns then answers, "No, I told her I was possibly staying with Kelsea, so she shouldn't expect me, and Avery is staying at your parents."

"Good," I tell her. "Get some sleep."

She nods, "Goodnight, Jas."

"Goodnight, Cora."

Her breathing slows, and I know she's asleep.

My mind is swirling with the emotions of the night. I think back and try to determine if I saw this coming. It's what I wanted for so long, but after she left and during the years of separation, I never imagined we would end up here. In some ways, I'm afraid of falling asleep because what if she regrets this when she wakes up? What if I forced all these feelings that I tried burying so long ago, for fear that if I didn't, they'd bury me? What if Cora wakes up thinking this was all a mistake? What if she is vulnerable because of all she is going through with her dad? If she told me we could never happen after tonight, I'd never recover this time. I'd fall to pieces.

What am I doing? I'm ruining the greatest night of my life with worries from the past. I have to trust what Cora's eyes and body told me. She trusts me. She cares for me. And maybe she even feels the one thing I've always wanted her to feel.

Maybe, just maybe, she loves me. Hope starts to creep in and push away the doubt that was trying to take over. Maybe she loves me.

Because as much as I tried to forget her and close my heart to her, she still resides there, and I still love her.

CORA

My eyes open, light trickling in across our naked bodies, mine curved against his.

Blinking, I try to clear the sleepy haze from my vision. The slight rise and fall of his chest under my cheek tells me that Jasper is still asleep.

Quietly and gently, I sit up and look down over his form lying beside me.

He has to be the most beautiful man I've ever laid my eyes on. His tawny skin and long, lean body are what dreams are made of. Jasper has been right in front of me all these years, and I never allowed myself to really look at him for fear of ruining the bond we had. He was harder to resist after Avery was born, and that only increased my fear. I tried so damn hard to do what was best for him, and all I did was hurt him. And Avery and I in the process. I've never been so wrong about something in my life.

Looking at him here, so peaceful like this, makes me want him all over again.

The urge to crawl over him outweighs any other need, so that is exactly what I do. I straddle his waist and begin peppering his chest with kisses until his eyes flutter open. "Good morning," I say against his skin, my voice heavy with need.

Lifting my head, I look at him, and a slow grin covers his face. "Good morning to you," he says.

With one swift move, I'm on my back, and Jasper is covering me. His kiss rekindles the fire we lit last night.

Twenty-Two

JASPER

I t's Sunday, and that means dinner with my family. After the third round of lovemaking, Cora and I finally pulled ourselves out of bed. Of course, we tried showering, and that only led to more sex.

Finally, we dressed, and I took Cora home. Instead of driving back, I decided to stay and spend time with my parents.

We climbed out of my Jeep, and I snuck one last kiss before watching her walk across the street to her house. Just before she entered, she turned back, a bright smile shining on her face, and waved.

"Holy smokes," I say aloud, leaning back against my Jeep. Last night happened so fast, and this is the first chance I've had to catch my breath and let it sink in. I refuse to analyze it. I prayed for this, and now I need to allow it to happen.

"Who put that shit-eating grin on your face?"

Drew's voice sneaks up from beside me, startling me.

"Shit, Drew. You scared me."

"And you ignored my question," he retorts. Rosie is smiling next to him and swats him on his arm.

"Leave Jas alone," she says, before addressing me. "What are you doing here so early?" She rises on her tip-toes and softly kisses my cheek.

"I ...ugh, I just thought I would come by and visit with Mom and Dad a little early."

"That's so sweet," she says, crossing the yard to the front door.

As Drew passes me, he whispers, "You're full of crap, and you know it."

I shake my head at my brother and follow him and Rosie to the door. Before I walk, I glance at the house across the street one last time, like I've done practically my whole life. Except this time, things are different, and I don't think I've ever been as happy as I am right now.

"Uncle Jas!" Jakey calls as soon as I'm over the thresh-old. He's running toward me, and trailing behind him is Avery with a grin spread wide across her face. Jakey in-stantly wraps himself around one of my legs while Avery launches herself in the air and into my arms. "Oof," I let out a woosh of air.

"Jasper, I've missed you," Avery tells me.

Pulling on my jeans, Jakey shouts, "Me, too!"

"Jacob Nallen, get off your uncle and let him fully en-ter the house before you attack him," Rosie gently scolds her son. She walks over to where I'm standing and pries Jakey from my leg.

"It's fine, Rose," I whisper to her to avoid negating what she told him.

"Jas, you're such a sweet uncle."

"I'm sorry," Avery mutters, looking a little sheepish.

This instantly gets my attention. "For what, sweet girl?"

"For not letting you fully enter the house before I attacked you," she says.

I smile at her, and Rosie lets out a little giggle before she straightens her face and says, "Oh, sweetie, I wasn't talking about you."

"Well, we're just so happy to see Jasper. He's our favorite person," Avery tells Rosie.

"I know, and between us, he's my favorite person too. But you have to promise not to tell Uncle Drew, Uncle Ty, Uncle Parker, or Aunt Kelsea & Aunt Abbey." She winks at Avery.

Avery crossed her heart with a giant grin, "I promise, I won't."

"Well, now that you both have boosted my ego, I think we should see how we can help make dinner."

Rosie grins down at Jakey, who she's still trying to pry off my legs. "What do you say, Jakey? Should we go with Uncle Jas & Avery to find out how we can help Grandma & Grandpa?

The four of us go in search of my brother and parents. When we find them, my mom is prepping some chicken while my dad and Drew are leaning against the island, chatting.

"Jas, you're early," my mom says when she sees me enter the kitchen.

"I thought I would come early to see if I can help and visit a little."

"Jakey thought he came early to be his jungle gym and entertainment," Rosie jokes as she enters the room behind me.

"Dad and Mom were just regaling me with how last night went with three kids under six. Apparently, our kids are easier than we were," Drew laughs.

I laugh out loud. "Well, none of you have a Ty yet," I say, pulling a laugh from Drew. Avery and Jakey laugh, too, although I'm pretty sure they have no idea why.

"Don't pick on your brother when he isn't here to defend himself," Mom

says, then adds, "You all had your difficult moments."

This time, Dad is laughing, and Avery and Jakey again join in.

I start tickling them. "What are you two laughing at?" I ask, and they both fall to the floor, rolling around in a fit of laughter.

Before I know it, Jakey is wrapped around one of my legs again; this time, Avery is on the other one. I'm laughing now just as much as they are, and I get a little lost in the overwhelming happiness I'm feeling. There's been a shift in my world, and everything finally feels in place. I don't know exactly where this thing with Cora is headed, but I shared with her what I hoped for. And I think the message was received with complete understanding and agreement.

CORA

When I open the door to the Nallen house, I hear laughter coming from the kitchen. It's a mix of giggles I recognize. A smaller laugh that I can only assume is Jakey, and then two others that I've heard thousands and thousands of times over my life. Jasper and Avery's laughter would stand out to me anywhere. But this time, the way it seems to be perfectly in tune hits me straight in my heart.

I follow the sound down the hall, and when I enter the kitchen, the scene before me hypnotizes me.

Jakey is holding onto Jasper around his leg, while Jasper lifts Avery into the air; both have the biggest, brightest smiles. It hits me, she's happier than I've ever seen her, and so is he. And they are the two people I love most in this world. I want things to always be this simple. I want the three of us to be together and be carefree.

"Cora, hello, honey. We didn't hear you come in," Mrs. Nallen says.

Jasper's head snaps up, and our eyes meet. I give him a slight smile before turning my attention to his mom. "Oh, I hope you don't mind I let myself in; I heard these three laughing and I just had to find out what was going on in here."

"Mommy!" Avery shouts. "I missed you, but seeing Jasper made me forget a little."

I walk over to where they're standing, "Oh well, I'm glad Jasper cheered you up."

"Oh, yes, he always cheers me up," she says.

"Me, too," I tell her.

Jakey lets go of Jasper's leg, hops up, and takes off running, yelling, "Meeeeeee, toooo!"

Drew steps forward, "Well, let's face it. Jasper apparently makes everything better."

"I think so," Rosie says. "Cora, thanks for a fun night last night. Did y'all stay out much later?" Rosie's Texas accent occasionally slips in; as if she could get any cuter or sweeter, her voice puts it over the top.

"It was fun. We … didn't stay much later," I say, avoiding eye contact with Jasper. Then I address Mr. and Mrs. Nallen. "And thank you again for letting Avery stay here last night. It was a huge help and relieved so much stress."

"Cora, sweetie, we love Avery, and she will always be one of our babies," Mr. Nallen tells me.

The feeling I get when he says this is so familiar because it is how I've always felt with the Nallen family: loved, accepted, and part of something special.

"Thank you for that, it means so much. It always has," I respond.

"Will your mom still be joining us tonight?" Mrs. Nallen asks.

Nodding, I reply, "Yes, she was just sitting with Dad, but should be here in a bit."

"Oh, honey, is he awake right now?" she asks.

"He was, but it doesn't last too long nowadays. It's getting harder for him to stay awake."

Rosie gently rested her hand against my arm, "Oh, Cora, I'm so sorry."

"Me, too. I just don't want him to suffer."

Drew walks back in, Jakey tucked under his arm. "I think taking this guy out in the backyard to release some of this energy might be a good idea. Avery, do you want to play with us?"

"Oh, yes, please!" She wiggles a little, and Jasper has no choice but to set her down. She hops up and down around Drew and Jakey. "Let's play Cowboys and Robbers."

"Sounds like a great idea," Drew tells her.

They head out the door, and I turn to ask about helping, "Is there anything I can help with? I'm pretty sure Mom is bringing banana bread."

"And when Abbey picked up Sydney this morning, she said they would bring a salad. I think we're covered. Why don't you all go outside and relax? Your dad and I have things under control."

"If you're sure, Mom," Jasper says.

"We are," his dad says.

"I think I will put my feet up; they are swollen today. I think it was all the standing and dancing last night," Rosie sighs.

"Poor thing," I say to her. "Come out and sit with us and rest."

The three of us disappear outside and leave Jasper's parents dealing with Sunday dinner. Now all we need to do is go relax and hope no one asks too many questions about last night. I've managed to dodge them so far, but when all Jasper's siblings are under one roof and they have any suspicion, they will not stop until they figure us out.

The only thing about that is that I haven't even figured

out what Jasper and I are doing, so I definitely won't be able to handle a Nallen family interrogation.

Twenty-Three

JASPER

I can feel Cora's nerves; it's as if they're radiating off her and finding their way into me. Whenever we make eye contact, I wonder why we didn't talk more this morning about what last night meant. Because it meant something, and it changed everything.

Drew is playing with Jakey and Avery in the yard, while Rosie sits with me and Cora, her feet propped up on a stool in front of her. Rosie absentmindedly rubs a hand over her belly, a soft grin on her face as she watches my brother gallop around the yard. He's assumed my regular role of playing horse for Jakey's cowboy.

"Maybe I'll go check on my mom to see if she needs anything before everyone arrives," Cora says, standing.

"I'll walk with you," I tell her, pushing myself out of the seat. This will be my opportunity to chat with her alone.

Cora looks over at me but doesn't say a word. Instead, she turns to Rosie and asks, "Do you mind if I leave Avery?"

"Don't be silly. Of course not," she responds.

"Thanks, we'll be right back," Cora says.

We turn and make our way into the house, pausing only a second to let my parents know we're going to check on Mrs. Connolly.

Walking side by side, Cora and I don't speak until we step off the curb from my parents' front yard. "I guess we should've talked about the two of us a little more than we did," I say.

Looking over at me, Cora gives me a slight smile. She laces her fingers through mine. "Maybe, but I think we were enjoying the touching."

"Yeah, I think we had a lot of time to make up for in that department," I tell her.

"Does this feel weird?" she asks, lightly squeezing my hand.

I glance down at her profile as we walk to her parents' front door together. "Holding hands or us?" I give her a smirk because I know what she means. I'm just trying to keep the conversation lighthearted.

"You know what I mean."

"I do." Stopping before we step up on the porch, I turn Cora to face me. Motioning my hand between us, I say, "This? Nothing about this feels weird. I mean, how could I ever think that is weird when it's exactly what I've dreamed about for most of our lives?"

A small, worried smile plays across her face.

"Doesn't it worry you that what we've spent our whole lives building, all the trust and all of this love, will be ruined if we don't work out? And now I've got Avery to consider. She loves you so much. And…"

I interrupt her, "I love her, too. Why wouldn't we work out? Think about it, you know me, and I know you—better than we know anyone else. Even with the last few years of silence between us, what we have is unbreakable. We only lost our way because of miscommunication and fear. I'm done being scared, Cora. Life is too short to let this possibility slip by. Stop overthinking it, and open your eyes to see how incredible you, Avery, and I could be together."

Cora stands and says nothing. She closes her eyes and takes in a few deep breaths, letting them out slowly, and I wait. I don't know what I'm waiting for other than for her to say she can see what we could be, too. Because there is nothing I believe more. Every choice and every step we've taken since she and Avery returned has renewed my hopes for our future. I may have buried it deep, but it never left my heart.

Opening her eyes, a wide grin spreads across her face. "I think I've always seen it, but I'm not sure I was ready to believe it until now."

A smile so big spreads on my face that matches hers, "Are we doing this, then?"

Nodding her head, she says, "We're doing this."

"We're doing this," I repeat, leaning in until our lips briefly touch.

Cora sighs softly, and we rest our foreheads against each other's. We stand like this for only a moment, letting the idea sink in.

When we pull back, she asks, "Can we hold off telling everyone? I want to talk to Avery first. I know she's only five, but she gets these kinds of things."

"Cora," I say, placing my finger under her chin and gently tilting her face up so her eyes meet mine before I continue. "We can handle this however it makes you feel comfortable." Then I give her a quick peck on the lips.

"Plus, it's probably best we do not announce our relationship at Sunday dinner. Can you imagine the crap my siblings would give us?"

She laughs, "Tyler would be unbearable."

"I'm not sure Parker and Drew would be much better. Then there's Kelsea, you never know how she will react."

"True on all accounts, but Kelsea would maybe surprise us. My mom and dad will be …," she trails off. The look on her face tells me that she is thinking of her dad. I pull her into a hug.

"They'll be happy, just like my parents will be. I'm reasonably sure they've all been waiting for us to get our heads and hearts on the same page," I tell her.

Releasing our embrace, Cora gazes up at me, unshed tears glistening in her eyes, and says, "There is no doubt, especially my dad."

"Let's get in there and see if your mom needs help before we go back. We do not want to be standing out here when the rest of the Nallen squad starts arriving and catches me kissing you or something."

"But you aren't kissing me."

"I will be if I keep standing here looking at you, knowing that I can kiss you and touch you in all the ways I've wanted to for so long."

"Oh, really?" she beams.

Smacking her playfully on her butt, I reach for the door handle and say, "You have no idea how badly I want to skip dinner, but alas, we can't."

I leave Cora standing outside the door to her parents' house, shaking her head with a grin still on her face. "I'm thinking I like your idea better than the reality."

Laughing, I pull her through the doorway. That anxious feeling I felt coming from her before has completely disappeared. If I'm being honest, mine is gone, too. Mission accomplished.

I can't remember the last time I've felt this happy, and I don't want it to end.

Twenty-Four

CORA

I t's a typical Santa Cruz evening. A slight ocean breeze, creating a chill in the air. Our first official date is going perfectly. Why wouldn't it, though? Jasper and I have never been at a loss for things to discuss, even though we basically know everything about one another. Aside from the last four years, we've pretty much spent most of our days together.

Sure, four years is a long time to be apart, but it did give us lots of things to talk about on our date. As sensitive as the topic of our time apart is, we did fill in some blanks.

We decided that our childhood beach would be a nice place to go after dinner. Every minute has been going as well as you would hope a first date would go. But my first date with my best friend is going perfectly.

As we walk along the beach, I ask, "Do you think anyone has suspected we're together?"

It has been three days since we saw everyone at the family dinner, and everything seems quiet. The Nallens rarely are quiet…about anything. I'd need a moment with my dad to process everything. Dad has always been the most level-headed person in my life, and he helps me handle most of my significant changes or decisions. And taking this step with Jasper makes me feel anything but composed. Admitting that I have feelings beyond friendship for Jasper is like going skydiving. It's a rush, a freefall, full of exhilaration, and the experience is something you never want to end. But I need someone to help me feel a little more grounded, and Dad is always so good at that.

"I doubt it. We didn't act any differently than we have our entire lives," he shrugs.

"True, you didn't touch me once," I say this with a hint of disappointment, and it gets his attention.

"Hey! We agreed to keep it quiet until you could tell Avery. If one tiny thing between us seemed different, one of them would have sniffed it out and sounded the horns."

My laugh comes out fast and loud. He is so right; if they knew, we'd know. Grinning over at me, Jasper pulls me to him. The sound of the waves crashing against the shore surrounds us. He wraps his arms around my waist, then brings me even closer and leans his head down until his mouth is on mine. That pulse of electricity that shoots through me every time he kisses me creates a moan that passes my lips. I don't know how I walked away after the first time we kissed, but I did. I blame it on the fact that I've never felt this kind of feeling. The sensation I got when his lips were on mine scared me then, but now I never want to let him go.

"Cora," he murmurs my name as he deepens the kiss.

My arms wrap around him tighter, trying with all their power to bring him closer. Then reality sets in when the frigid cold of the surf hits our feet, like an ice bucket to dampen our overheated moment.

Letting out a yelp and completely ruining the moment, I try to jump into his arms to escape getting wet. First, it's too late, and second, I take him completely off guard. As he catches me, Jasper begins to stumble backward and lands on his back in the wet sand, letting out an audible groan.

We both lie there for at least thirty seconds before we bust out laughing.

"Oh, my gawd, are you okay?" I ask him between giggles.

Chuckling, he says, "I'm always okay when you're on top of me."

I look down at him, and that's all it takes for my laughter to stop and my lips to be back on his. I just can't get enough of him. And he doesn't miss a beat; Jasper is completely in sync with me, kissing me, touching me, until the whole world fades away.

He was right when he said we had a lot of time to make up for.

That is, until the freezing water of the Pacific Ocean laps against us once more, and we're reminded just where we are.

"We'd better get back to our cars and get dried off.

Once the sun goes down, we'll be icicles." Jasper helps me up off the sand and does his best to knock the beach off both of our clothes.

"Who are we kidding? I'm already freezing," I laugh.

"This is definitely no Arizona. You were gone a while, but you couldn't have forgotten these Santa Cruz temperatures," he says, as we walk hand in hand back to where we parked our cars.

"No, I never could seem to forget a lot of things about this place, no matter how hard I tried." I don't look at him when I say this, but I can feel his gaze on me. That tingling feeling sweeps over my body, and it isn't from the ocean breeze.

There's a silence between us until we reach our cars.

Jasper unlocks his Jeep and gets into the back. He digs around for a few seconds before producing a towel. He hands it to me so I can use it first.

"Just so you know, no matter how upset I was with you and, regardless of how hard I tried, I could never get over what I felt for you."

Glancing up at him, I find his eyes looking so serious and full of a kind of sadness that I never want him to feel again. "Jas, I really am so very sorry. I did what I thought was best."

Jasper takes a step toward me until we're toe to toe, and while I'm considered tall, my eyes still only reach his mouth. Now that he's closer, I have to tilt my head back a little further. "Cora, you don't need to keep apologizing. I didn't tell you that to make you feel bad. I said it so you knew that you could trust what I feel for you, and so you can stop beating yourself up over leaving. Maybe it gave us both time to grow." He brushes a loose curl from my face. "I know I didn't see it this way before, but I think it was a chance to look at our time apart as validation of what we are to one another."

Raising up on my tiptoes, I press my lips tenderly to his and pull away. "Thank you."

"Thank you for finally taking the chance on me."

"I've always chosen you, even if neither of us realized it," I tell him. "Thank you for a wonderful night. This has been the best first date ever."

"Thank you. Now, let's get you in your car so you can get home to put Avery to bed." He opens my door, and I hand him the towel, but he shakes his head in refusal. "No, use it to put down on your seat. I have another in the Jeep."

"Jasper Nallen, always prepared and always considerate."

He shrugs, "I'm a surfer. Of course, I carry towels around in my Jeep."

"Yeah…yeah," I say, then I wrap my arms around his waist for a quick hug. He kisses the top of my head. "Goodnight, Jas. I'll talk to you later."

"Goodnight, Cora."

After I slide into my car, he closes my door. I buckle my seat belt and give him one last wave as I pull away. I see him in the rear-view mirror, still watching me until I turn the corner.

His words play over and over in my mind. Maybe he's right, maybe we were given a chance to realize what we mean to another.

• • •

I got home just in time to start Avery's bedtime routine. I'm thankful I've rarely missed one, and it's always been a time for her and me to chat about things on our minds. She's five, so usually it's things like, "Why does the girl next door have pink hair and why can't she have pink hair?" But sometimes, the topics take on a serious note, like, "Why did Granddad get sick, and do I believe in heaven?"

Often, I wonder if bathtime and our bedtime routine allow her mind to focus on all the things she's kept tucked away during the day. Either way, I love this part of our day. I started telling her about things that I'm carrying around in my head, too. I figured if she shares, then I should share, too.

I'm running my fingers through her damp hair to loosen the curls enough to keep the knots from forming before I braid it for the night, when she asks, "Mommy, why does a dog bark and a cat meow?"

Looking at her heart-shaped face in the mirror that's almost identical to mine, I can see she is very serious. I can't help the small smile starting to form on my lips, so I do my best to hide it. "Well, that's a good question. I think it's because when a dog barks, it sounds like the word, and when a cat meows, it sounds like that word." That is literally the worst explanation I could've given, but I don't think I could have come up with anything else.

The other great thing about these conversations with Avery is the fact that she is only five years old, and for the most part, she accepts anything and everything I say as the word of God.

"Oh, that's funny," she says, simply as her lips tilt slightly up at the corners.

"It is, isn't it?" I agree.

"Mommy, do you think we can see Jasper soon?"

I want to talk to her about Jasper, but I am still trying to think of the best way. She loves him so much, and I just want to be sure this is everything we hope it will be. I'm worrying again, and I just need to trust my heart and his.

I finish her braid and turn her to face me. "I think we can, sweetie. Come on, let's get you in bed. I want to talk to you about something."

"Okay, Mommy. Can we see Jasper tomorrow?"

She's a relentless little thing, I think with a grin as she climbs into her bed, under the covers. I crawl in beside her, and Avery tucks herself between my arm and chest.

"I think we can ask him," I tell her.

"Yay, I miss seeing him when he isn't here."

"Me, too, baby."

"Do you think he misses us when he doesn't see us?"

"Actually, I do. And do you know how I know?" I ask her.

Avery shakes her head no with a yawn.

"Well, he told me that he does. Remember how I told you that Jasper and I have been best friends since we were kids?"

"Yes, he was your first friend when you, Grand, and

Granddad moved here."

I smile, thinking of that first day he came to our door with his mom. I could tell she made him come with her, but he smiled and was polite anyway.

"That's right. He is kind…"

"And funny," she interrupts.

I laugh, "Yes, he's funny. He likes spending time with us. And he loves you."

"I know, he does," she says.

"How do you know?" I ask out of curiosity what she will say.

She sits up and looks at me. "Because he told me, and because in that picture you had in our old house."

"The picture?" I ask; now I really am curious.

"The one where we're at the beach and I'm a baby. He's smiling at me like you do."

"Like I do?"

She's practically on top of me now, and she places both of her tiny hands on either side of my face. Holding my face, she puts this wide grin on her face and says, "Like this," she says, then continues, "and that's what you look like when you tell me that you love me."

I don't know what I did to deserve this smart, funny, and loving little girl, but life would be unbearable without her.

"Well, I do love you, and I think you're right. Jasper loved you even in that picture."

"He looks at you like that, too, so I think he loves you, too. Do you love him?"

I kiss her on the nose. "Lie back down so I can tuck

you in," I tell her, and she does as I say. "I think I do, so are you okay if I tell him that?"

"Uuuuumm," she says with exaggeration. "Will I get to see him more?"

Leaning down, I hug her. "If it will make you happy."

"It will make you happy," she says.

"What?" I'm thrown off and not for the first time tonight.

"You're always happier when we're with Jasper. And so am I."

I hug her again. "Goodnight, baby. I love you."

"I love you, too, Mommy. Goodnight."

Twenty-Five

CORA

When my eyes open, it's still dark outside. I'm tired, but I've tossed and turned all night. I just couldn't get comfortable, not to mention my mind was consumed by a million thoughts. My dad. Jasper. Avery. Mom. All of my choices. And the list goes on and on. I reach for my phone on the nightstand, and the phone illuminates with the time, four-thirty a.m. That is an awful hour to wake up.

Setting the phone back down, my head falls back to the pillow. I stretch my arms above my head and extend my legs to work out all the kinks in my body. As tired as I am, there is no way I'm falling back to sleep, so I do the only thing I can think of. I throw my comforter off of me, pull on my sweatshirt over my head, and slide my feet into my slippers, then I head downstairs.

I do my best to be as quiet as I can as I make my way to the one place I know I will find a little clarity and comfort, even if he isn't awake to give me his two cents.

Silently, I push open the door to my dad's room and tiptoe across the room, taking a seat in the chair next to his bed. His breath is coming in shorter pants than they were even a few days ago. My heart breaks each day. When he is awake, he reassures us he isn't in pain, but I'm not certain he is being entirely truthful. I think he is trying to spare us the extra heartache.

Pulling my knees up to my chest, I watch him. I watch his chest move up and down in a slow rhythm.

My thoughts begin to drift to all the things swirling around, like there's a tornado in my mind. What would he think about me and Jas? He always tried to push me to follow my heart. Why has he always known me better than myself? Maybe because he is my dad. The person who watched me grow up, make mistakes, have successes, and stood by me as I changed into the person I am today. He watched Jasper and me lift one another up and walk side by side if either of us needed support. Did Dad always know?

"You know, I can see the wheels turning in your head, and it's exhausting me," he croaks suddenly, startling me.

Putting my hand over my heart, I squeal, "Oh my God, Dad. You scared me!"

He starts to chuckle, but, of course, it turns into a cough. I sit up quickly to give him some water. Once he finally stops, I put the water down.

"I'm sorry about that. You know how jumpy I am."

He does his best to smile.

"I'm also sorry I woke you up," I tell him.

Finding his voice again, he whispers, "I'm glad I woke up. What has you worried?"

"Everything?" I say, with a sad smile.

"Cora."

He only says my name, and even though it's a whisper, I can still hear the tone he's used with me my entire life when he knows I'm playing games and trying to stuff my feelings.

"Dad, what will I do without you?" A lone tear slips down my cheek.

"Honey, you'll live the life you have."

"It's not that simple," I tell him.

"Oh, but it is." He signals for more water, so I oblige. Then he continues, "My life and your life are connected by love, but not by necessity. Your mom and I gave you life, and you're meant to live it for as long as you have it—just like I have."

"I love you."

"I love you, too."

"I hear you, but I don't feel ready to let you go."

"You'll never be ready. But you have Avery and your mother. You have Jasper."

I reach for his hand. "What is it about Jasper that you've always seen us as a unit, Dad?" I ask him this question because his answer is important to me. I ask him because I know what I see in Jasper, but I've always struggled with trusting my instincts and choices, even if I have no reason to doubt myself when it comes to the boy, now man, that has always been my best friend.

"That's easy, Cora. You know the answer, but I will tell you anyway," he says, a slow smile giving his face a little life that wasn't there before. "Jasper is good. He's kind and honest. He is so many things, but best of all, he sees you, and because of that, he loves you so unconditionally. It is all a parent wishes for their child."

"I think I love him, Dad," I confess, more tears falling. "And we're finally opening up to the possibility of our relationship being more than just two kids with a lifetime of friendship. Do you think that it's too much to ask for from God—that I can have him as my friend and partner for a lifetime?"

When I look at him now, Dad's grin is still in place, and there are tears in his eyes, waiting to fall. "It's what you deserve and what I've known you were both meant to have your whole lives. I'm just glad you've both finally realized it and you're taking that chance. It's all I've wanted for you, Cora."

Dropping to my knees, I gently lay my arms over him in the best hug I can give him when he is lying down. "I love you, Daddy."

"I love you, Cora."

JASPER

Cora and I only briefly spoke this morning, and all she said was that she had sat with her dad this morning and that he was awake. She started to tell me about their conversation, but then her mom told her breakfast was ready, so Cora said she would talk with me tonight since I had meetings all day. I'm really anxious to hear how this conversation went with her dad. I know how much she loves and trusts him. He's her world and the one person who can help her work through things she's processing.

I came directly to her parents' house when I got off work, only stopping at my apartment to change. Cora, Avery, and Mrs. Connolly were out when I first arrived, so the nurse let me in like she's done many times before.

"Hi, Jasper," she greets me as she opens the door. "He was asleep when I checked on him a few minutes ago. I'm not sure about now, though."

"Hey, Harper, that's okay. I will just go sit with him for a while."

As she shuts the door behind me, she says, "I know he really likes it when you visit. How have you been?"

Harper has been doing in-home care for Mr. Connolly since he got sick and was sent home from the hospital. We haven't spoken much, but she has always been kind and empathic to everyone's feelings. And she's young, not much older than Cora and me. She seems to really care about creating a comfortable space for Cora's mom and dad.

"Well, he's important to me, and I think I'm being selfish because I need these visits probably more than he does," I confess.

"See it how you want, but I think it's special to him. He talks to me about all of you often, so I promise that when I say your presence is making a difference to him, it is."

"Thank you for that," I tell her, indicating I'm going to head into his room. "I'll do my best to let him rest."

She nods and disappears into the kitchen.

I push the door open, making my way to his bedside, and take a seat. His eyes are closed, and his breathing is soft. He looks even more frail than when I saw him on Sunday. I didn't think it was possible, but I think his cheeks are more sunken in, and the sorrow sitting in the middle of my stomach makes me feel a little queasy.

His eyelashes begin to flutter a little, then freeze. I'm trying so hard not to disturb him too much.

"I can sense you even in my sleep. I'm not sure why you and Cora think I can't feel you both ogling me with my eyes closed."

With a small guilty laugh, I apologize. "Sorry about that."

"That's what Cora said this morning."

I smile a full, genuine smile because it warms me inside to know his sense of humor is still intact.

"You finally convinced our girl to give you a chance, huh?"

"Yes, sir. I think I have," I reply before adding, "I hope you're still okay with that."

"Don't be a damn fool, Jasper. You've never been one

before, so don't start now. I'm more than okay with it. I've never minced my words with you, so you already know that, don't you?"

"Yes, sir. Thank you. I'll take care of them. All of them."

He coughs, and his eyes close. I start to reach for his water, but he weakly waves me away with his hand. After a few breaths, he says, "I have no doubt, son. It's why I'm at peace. I know they will have you and your family. There isn't anything more I can hope for."

"Can I ask you one question? It's not for right now, but it is for one day. For when Cora is ready?" I ask.

"You have my blessing, Jasper."

CORA

As we pull up, Jasper is walking across the street from his parents' house. He had texted me that he had visited with my dad for a little while, but then Dad was tired and had fallen asleep. He had walked over to say hello to his mom and dad before we got back with dinner.

I hop out of the car about the same time Avery climbs out of the backseat. Ever since she learned to unbuckle herself from her car seat, I'm lucky she waits until we come to a complete stop.

"Jasper!" She bellows as she runs towards him.

He easily sweeps her into his arms and keeps walking

toward me.

She clings to him like she hasn't seen him in years, rather than a few days.

"Avery, my girl! I'm so happy to see you," he tells her, and she grins from ear to ear.

He eyes me from over her head and winks. When did Jasper start winking at me? I'd generally think it was cheesy and weird, but that was kind of sexy.

"Hey, Jasper," my mom says, pulling a few bags out of the car.

"Hi, Mrs. Connolly. Need some help with those bags?" Jasper asks as he sets Avery down.

"I think I have these, but there are a few more, and the pizza we picked up for dinner," Mom tells him.

"Got it," he says, then turns to me when he reaches my side. "Hi, there. Are the rest of the bags in the back?"

"Hi. They are." His hand grazes the back of mine as he walks by. A shiver runs up my spine.

"Mommy, can I carry the pizza?" Avery asks.

"Why don't you help Jas with one of the bags, and I'll carry the pizza," I tell her.

I can read the look on her face that she's considering arguing with me for a split second before she skips over to Jasper's side. He's got the back of my mom's SUV open, pulling the bags out and looping the handles over his arms. He must have heard our conversation because he hands a bag to her, and she resumes skipping into the house.

He lifts his head in my direction and grins. Man, I love that face. I carry the pizza, and Jasper follows behind me with the rest of the bags.

Just before we reach the porch, I say as quietly as I can, but where he can still hear me, "I told Dad."

"I know, he told me."

"Oh."

"We'll talk more later," he tells me as I reach the door.

I nod, then say, "You can leave those at the bottom of the stairs."

"No problem."

When we get in the kitchen, Mom and Avery are already setting the table.

"Avery, did you wash your hands?" I ask.

"Yes, Grand had me do it."

We all take a seat around the table, and I open the box, placing a slice on Avery's plate.

Taking a slice for myself, I pass the box to my mom, then Jasper. We all take a bite before we say anything. Of course, Avery starts the conversation.

"I love pizza," she says with her mouth full.

"Me, too," Mom, Jasper, and I all say at once.

"I don't know who decided we should have pizza tonight, but I love you," Jasper mumbles between bites.

"See, Mommy? I told you that Jas loves you."

I nearly spat my food out of my mouth. Mom coughs, but I can tell it's totally fake, like she's trying to distract herself from the awkwardness that Avery just sat all of us right in.

I'm afraid to look at Jasper, but I decide to glance in his direction, and he has a huge Cheshire cat grin on his face.

"You're a smart girl, Avery," Jasper says and looks right at me.

"I know," she says. "You have that smile on your face."

"Avery," I say, remembering what she told me last night and wanting to redirect the conversation.

"What smile?" Mom says. My head swivels to her, and I can see her curiosity piqued.

Oh, God. I don't know how to stop this flow of conversation without making it worse. I want to laugh and cry at the same time. Am I dying from embarrassment because my face feels warm, and my chest feels slightly tingly?

"You know, the smile Jas gives Mommy and me because he loves us. He had it when he was looking at Mommy just now."

Mom's mouth forms an "O," and I'd crawl under the table if I thought I could get away with it.

Jasper's eyes widen, and then his smile slowly grows wider. "You bet I love you," he says, all teeth.

"See? I knew it," she says, still oblivious to my discomfort with this whole conversation.

Mom regards me, and I briefly make eye contact with her, silently begging her not to question any part of this conversation. She takes the last bite of her pizza and quickly changes the subject. "Who is excited by the fact that pizza means no dirty dishes!"

We all raise our hands, and the conversation naturally turns to other things. We discuss our day and what each of us did, including our shopping trip with Mom. Since pronouncing his love for Avery, Jasper has turned a little quiet and introspective, leaving me wondering if I should be worried.

Once again, Avery waves her hands through the air

in an animated explanation of how she caught a banana slug in the backyard. He's captivated by her. It's silly that I would feel jealous that he didn't profess his love to me right now, but why would he in front of my mom?

One, we're only supposed to be friends in front of our family still; two, he hasn't even told me that he loves me when we're alone. Maybe the better question is—am I ready for him to say those three words?

Twenty-Six

JASPER

I watch as she throws her head back in laughter. I've just told her a story from when we were little and how Tyler pulled Drew's pants down in front of his crush at the time. Drew was so pissed, and Tyler never had a chance once Drew got his revenge. It was a thousand times worse, and so was Drew's punishment. Drew didn't care, though; he had successfully locked Tyler out of the house naked for six hours straight one day with no way to hide.

I think this was the year before Cora moved in across the street, so I think Tyler was eleven and Drew was fourteen. Being eight at the time, I always listened when Drew threatened my life, even if it meant not helping Tyler. I learned my lesson not to mess with Drew.

There are very few memories before Cora. We were only nine when she moved in, and being the youngest left me a little invisible until her. But the second we met, she saw me, and I saw her.

Just like now, the way her eyes shine when she laughs.

"God, Tyler has obviously never known when to say no to his impulses," she says, smiling.

The cool, ocean breeze whips around us as we sit side by side on a beach on West Cliff near the lighthouse. There is nothing like a picnic dinner out here at sunset.

"No, and I doubt that will ever change," I tell her, returning her grin. "I still can't believe you've never heard that story."

"I know; I almost forgot there were Nallen family shenanigans before I moved in."

"I'm pretty sure there were Nallen shenanigans in the womb."

Taking a small bite of her burrito, she shakes her head slightly, then once she swallows, says, "Your poor mom."

I take a large bite of my burrito, and with a mouth full, I agree, "No doubt."

After that, we sit in a comfortable silence for a little while, seagulls soaring in the distance, the sun going down, and a few dedicated surfers waiting for the perfect wave. This place really is breathtaking. Glancing briefly at Cora, I can't help thinking about the other night at dinner with her mom and Avery. All the talk about love. There is no doubt that I've never stopped loving Cora. I've always loved her, but does she love me? Or am I just comfortable to her? Safe? I want to trust what seems to be happening between us. And I want to tell her and show her just how much I love her every day. I'm just not sure I'm brave enough to risk having my heart trampled again.

"I missed you so much," I say.

It's all my heart would allow in that moment. A thought that sounds so random right then, but really, I've wanted to say it since she got home. Yet it's only a minute part of what I'm feeling. It wasn't at all what I intended to say, but those three words just weren't ready to come out.

Cora's head slowly swivels in my direction. She doesn't say a word at first. She only watches me, then she reaches her hand out tentatively, as if she touched me, I'd disappear. Her hand hovers only a second before she touches my face. I draw in a breath as she cups my cheek and stands and crawls onto my lap. I welcome her, and she brings her lips to mine, just a soft touch, then she pulls back.

"You have no idea how much I missed you. Longed for you," she finally says.

Her mouth fuses with mine once more, but this time, she deepens it quickly, and a low moan slips from between our lips. I pull her closer, and we kiss like we're trying to convey something more than we're both willing to say.

Pulling back, I say, "Let's get out of here."

She nods her head and slides out of my lap. We gather up our things, toss our trash in the bin nearby, and head to my Jeep. As we walk, we interlock our fingers, and I lean over, placing a quick kiss on her lips, and Cora's facial expression brightens.

"Uncle Jas!"

Cora and I both freeze, and I feel her squeeze my hand before letting it go. Plastering a smile on our faces, we turn around and find Drew and Rosie with Jakey strapped in his stroller about ten feet away. I try not to make eye contact with either adult and instead, focus solely on my nephew.

"Hey, buddy!" I call out.

He waves vigorously, shaking his whole stroller, looking so happy to see me. Drew pushes the stroller closer, and Rosie sidles up beside him.

She's the first to speak. "Hey, Jasper and Cora. It's so…uh…surprising to see you both."

"Surprising is a subtle way of putting this encounter, babe. The word that describes what I'm feeling is shocked," Drew adds.

I begin to say something, but Cora beats me to it. "We were going to tell everyone; we just wanted a little time together without having to explain this change. We just wanted some time to savor it first."

Rosie swats Drew on the arm. "Y'all don't owe us a single explanation. It's none of our business. In fact, it's no one's business but yours. Right, Drew?" She keeps our eyes on us when she has to nudge him into speaking.

Drew is watching us both. His eyes linger a little more on Cora, like he is trying to read her. It's kind of weird because it seems to be coated in a little distrust.

"Right, Drew?" Rosie says, again.

"Actually," he starts and then stops when he looks me in the eyes. He sees the threat that lies there if he opens this door right now.

When he doesn't finish his sentence, I lace my fingers through Cora's again and say, "I get it's a shock. But we've talked a lot since Cora came home. This is a good thing. We're good."

"I'm glad," Drew says. "I just didn't expect this yet. We've all wanted this for a long time, but...well, it doesn't matter."

"Can you let us tell everyone else? We were going to let you all know at Sunday dinner," I tell them.

"Absolutely, it isn't our business to tell," Rosie says, immediately.

I look at Drew, and he is once again staring at me. I give him a nod of my head, letting him know I understand him, and we'll talk.

"Uncle Jas, Avery?" Jakey says.

Squatting down in front of him, I give him my attention. "She's at home, buddy."

That seemed to be enough of an answer for him, or it was the distraction of the golden retriever that just walked past us, because he suddenly moved his attention elsewhere.

"How are you feeling, Rosie?" Cora asks.

Rosie looks down at her protruding belly and rubs her hand across it. "Huge," she sighs.

"Babe, you're nearly nine months pregnant. Give yourself a break," Drew says.

"Listen to your husband," Cora tells Rosie.

Rosie shrugs, "Fine. I'm great, but tired of being pregnant." She gives us all one of her usual warm smiles.

Jakey lets out a loud squeal, once again reminding us he is here.

"Well, we'll let you two get going, plus I think Jakey is beginning to lose his patience and needs to move."

Rosie and Cora hug. Drew and I fist-bump. Then Drew

approaches Cora and pulls her into a hug. She squeezes him back, then I notice her body slightly stiffen. When they pull apart, Cora smiles, but I can tell her mood has shifted somewhat. I can't help wondering why, but Rosie interrupts my spiraling thoughts when she hugs me around my waist. I bend down slightly into our embrace. "I'm happy for you," she whispers, then steps back and waves as the three of them walk away. She is so sweet and good; my brother is one lucky guy.

After they disappear down the sidewalk along West Cliff, I reach for Cora's hand, and she looks up at me. "What did he say?" I ask.

"Who?"

"I know he said something that upset you, Cora, because your face changed."

Shaking her head, she tries leading me in the direction of my Jeep. "Nothing."

"Cora, just tell me."

"Fine, he said not to hurt you again."

"I'm sorry," I tell her, tightening my hold on her hand as we walk together.

"Jas, don't be. Drew is just looking out for you, and I did, in fact, hurt you."

I don't say anything, because what is there to say?

"See? You can't deny it, so if it makes Drew feel better to say it, then I'm okay."

"He loves you, too, though," I tell her. I don't know why I feel like she needs that reassurance.

"I know he does, Jas, but he's your older brother first. It only stung a little because I did that, I hurt you. It was just a reminder of what I did."

We reach my car, and I open the door for Cora. She climbs in, and before I close the door, I lean in and give her a quick peck on the lips. Shutting the door, I make my way around and slide into the driver's side.

"You're coming back to my place?" I phrase it like a question rather than a statement.

"If it's still okay."

"It's more than okay," I grin.

Since my condo is close, it doesn't take long for us to get to my place. We park and make our way to the door; the tension that hung between us after our interaction with Drew and Rosie has dissipated.

I hang the keys on the hook just inside the door as Cora puts her bag down on the small table in the entry.

Walking into the living room, Cora spins around to face me as the last of the light from the setting sun trickles through the curtains.

"What should we do?" she asks, a sly smile on her face.

I stand close enough to press my lips to the exposed skin of her collarbone, so I don't hold back. Trailing kisses up the column of her neck, I breathe, "I think something that involves a lot of kissing and touching." I don't stop until I'm hovering over her mouth.

Her breath hitches, and she sways forward, meeting her lips to mine.

With our mouths fused together, we deepen the kiss, and my body begins to vibrate with need. We must both feel it because we simultaneously reach for each other's shirts, breaking the kiss long enough to lift them over our heads.

Wanting her like this feels desperate and out of control; I've never felt this way before. Only with Cora. Only for Cora. When neither of us is wearing a single piece of clothing, and we're standing in my living room, staring at one another, I know that I have never and will never be this intimate with another woman again. For me, Cora is it. These few seconds we take each other in solidifies what we are now, and if I have my way, what we will be forever—one.

Stepping together and resuming where we left off, I kiss every inch of her body, and she allows me that liberty, then she returns the favor. The pleasure of this night soaks into every move we make. My touch is meant to let her know she is worth it, all the heartache and every happiness we've ever had together. It's to let her know she is perfect.

Picking her up, I carry her into my room and lay her in the middle of the bed, our eyes locked in a gaze clouded with need.

I make sure we're protected before I cover Cora's body with mine.

Her eyes are closed, and she's making a low whimpering sound when I take her breast into my mouth. They're perfect, and she is so damn beautiful. Between the combination of the sounds she's making and my own imagination, I don't think I can take much longer of not being inside her.

"Cora, open your eyes," I gently demand.

Her lids flutter open, and desire is swirling there. I want to see the look in her eyes the moment I enter her. I kiss her mouth hard once more before pulling back, aligning myself with her, and in one swift move, I push all the way into her center.

"Jasper," she screams my name. She says my name as if she is worshiping me.

"Oh, God...Jasper," she continues as I keep rocking into her, my own breath coming in short, rapid pants. I feel her clinching around me every time I bury inside her completely. Her face contorts into a look of pure ecstasy.

Together, we move in sync as if our bodies were made for one another. It's in this now that I know it doesn't matter if she loves me or if she will ever love me. I love Cora Connolly with every part of my being, and I'm telling her.

I'm telling her with my body right now, and I will find a way to tell her with words later.

"Cora," I say her name with reverence as I fill her one final time, both of us falling into this explosive oblivion together.

I fall to her side, pulling her against me. Before either of us speaks, we're both overtaken by pure exhaustion.

Twenty-Seven

CORA

The distant sound of a phone ringing pulls me from my deep sleep. I blink twice and rub my eyes; the ringing stops, then starts up again a few seconds later.

Sitting up, I look around the room. Jasper lies next to me, still asleep.

Where is the ringing coming from? Then I suddenly realize it's the ringtone that plays when my mom is calling. I throw the covers back and run out into the living room, completely unfazed that I don't have any clothes on, panic setting in. I flip on the lights because it's pitch black. And why is my mom calling in the middle of the night? I told her I was staying out tonight. I didn't volunteer who I'd be with, and she didn't ask, but I think she knew.

Where is my damn phone?

It starts ringing again, and I finally realize it's coming from my purse that I left on the entry table. I dig it out and grapple with my phone before sliding my finger across the screen to answer.

"Mom?"

"Cora, thank goodness. I...your dad, we're at the hospital. He's... "

"Mom, I'm coming," I interrupt her. "Oh, God, Avery. Where's Avery?"

I run around the living room, gathering my clothes. Where the hell is my shirt?

"Avery is fine. She is with the Jasper's parents," she says.

From behind me, I hear Jasper's quavering voice, "Cora? What's going on?"

There it is; I finally find my top buried under Jasper's jeans. I don't even answer him as I begin to pull my jeans over my legs, at the same time, I'm trying to hold the phone between my ear and shoulder.

"Cora?" This time, Jasper seems more awake when he says my name like a question. I hear the concern behind it, but I can't focus enough to soothe him.

"Mom, where are you exactly? Are you in a room? Where?"

"I'm in emergency. They have your dad in the back and haven't let me back yet."

I can hear the worry in her voice, and that only exacerbates my own.

"Mom, I'm coming. I will be there as fast as I can get there."

I hang up the phone and pull my top over my head. Suddenly, two hands are on my shoulders.

"Cora, stop. What is happening?"

I finally look at him, and now that I do, I lose it. The fear and the tears overwhelm me.

My body shakes, and I fall into him.

"Baby, please tell me."

"My dad...hospital," I hiccup between sobs. I give myself a mental scolding. I can't fall apart. I don't have time to fall apart; my mom needs me. My dad needs me.

Pulling myself together, I push back out of Jasper's embrace.

"I need to go," I say, calmly now.

"I'll take you, let me throw my clothes on."

Taking a step back, he doesn't take his eyes off me until I nod in acknowledgment that he can help me. By the time I locate my shoes and put them on, Jasper is coming out of his room dressed and ready to go.

"You have everything you need?" he asks.

"Yes, they're at Dominican Emergency."

My head is swirling with the same anxiety and fear I heard in my mom's voice. I don't know if I'm prepared for all of this.

Jasper and I rush out of his house. He opens the door of his Jeep for me, I hop in, and within seconds, he is in the driver's seat.

"Avery?" He asks as if he suddenly remembers.

"She's with your parents."

"Thank God. Put your seat belt on," he says, pausing to bring my hand up to his lips, pressing a kiss tenderly on my fingertips before he continues," Cora, I'm here for you, remember that."

I look at him and nod, then turn to stare out the window as we pull away.

• • •

My eyes are heavy as I look up at the ceiling of the hospital room where my father now lies in an unconscious state. Although his breathing is better, they have him on oxygen to help.

Apparently, Dad had extreme difficulty breathing, which can be common with neuroblastoma. Luckily, Mom had been sitting with him at the time and was able to get him help quickly.

She's sitting in the chair next to his bed now, her head resting on his bedside. I, on the other hand, am wide awake, riddled with guilt. I've been so selfish, worrying more about my relationship with Jasper than about helping focus on my dad's care.

Jasper. He wanted to stay here with me and Mom. I insisted he leave and left no room for him to make any other choice than to go. He told me he was going to his parents to make sure Avery was okay. I thanked him and then turned and walked away.

My mom promised him we would give him an update when we knew anything. I said nothing. The guilt kept creeping in—I was too wrapped up in him and missed the moment my mom and dad needed me the most. Mom didn't say anything after Jasper left, but I could feel her watching me. I know there are questions, but before she could ask, they came in and told us that Dad had been put in a room.

> I text Jas: Hey, they have Dad in a room now. He's stable for now, and they're allowing me and Mom back. We will check back in.

> His reply is instant: Thank you for the update. Do you need me to bring you anything?

That was three hours ago. I never answered, so two hours ago, I received another text.

> **Jasper:** I hope you're okay. I know this isn't easy. Let me know if you need anything.

Then, half an hour ago, he texts again.

> **Jasper:** Thinking of your dad, mom, and you.

I left it unanswered.

"Are you going to tell me what is going on?"

Mom's voice startles me. "Mom, shit. You scared me." I lean my head back again, resuming my position.

"Sorry, are you going to tell me why you pushed Jasper out like that?"

"You needed me. Dad needed me. Jasper is a distraction right now."

"First, seeing you pull up at midnight with Jasper was a bit of a surprise, but not altogether unexpected. But you're in shut-down mode, and if I can see it, then he can see it, too. Don't start doing that thing you do," she says.

I don't look at my om as she speaks; I keep my eyes focused on the same ceiling tiles I've been looking at for the last couple of hours. That thing I do. What does that mean?

"Cora Anne Connolly, do not ignore me."

She only uses my middle name when she thinks I'm being spoiled and unreasonable.

"Mom, I'm not ready," I finally say, sadly.

I hear her move before saying anything, then I feel her standing in front of me.

"Cora, look at me," she gently demands.

If I look at her, I might lose the last bit of control I have right now, but I do it because she isn't going to go away. I sit up and bring my gaze to hers.

"This is happening whether we want it to or not. We can't control that, so trying is futile. You're only going to hurt yourself more. Pushing Jasper away when you need him most will definitely hurt you more. You've tried that before, and look where it got you. Your dad wouldn't want that for you."

Mom reaches her hand out to me, so I take it. She gently pulls me to my feet and into her embrace. And I let go of everything I've been trying to hold at bay. I cry. I cry for what we're about to lose. I cry for all the heartache and despair that is flooding my system now that she opened the gate.

"I'm scared," I tell her through my tears.

"Me, too," she whispers, and I can hear the pain in her voice.

A throat clears from the doorway. I pull out of Mom's tender hold to find Dad's doctor standing just inside the room.

"My apologies. I'm wondering if I can speak with you, Mrs. Connolly," he says.

Wiping her tears away, she says, "Sure."

"I'll go get some coffee and call Jasper to check on Avery."

Mom nods, and I leave the room.

Once I'm back in the waiting area, I pull my phone out of my pocket.

"Hey," his voice comes through the phone. "I was just thinking about you."

"Hey, how's Avery?" I ask, immediately.

He's silent for one split second, then he says, "She's fine. Rosie brought Jakey over, so she is preoccupied."

"That's good," I say.

"Any updates? My mom has been asking me."

"He still hasn't woken up. The doctor is in with Mom right now, that's why I decided to check in on Avery."

"I'm sorry you're hurting," Jasper says.

"Me, too," I say.

I don't know why I'm putting this wall up. I can feel myself doing it, and I need to stop. My mom is right. I need to be brave. I need to let Jasper in because I need him. I want him. But we have to wait so I can be present for Mom and Dad. There is so much I want to say, and I can tell he can feel the block between us, too, but I don't know how to ease his mind right now. Everything I want and need to say to him has to be in person and has to be later. I just need to put the brakes on us for now.

"I know your heart is breaking, Cora. But please don't

shut me out. I'm here for you."

Tears prickle at the edge of my eyelids.

"I know, Jas. I…we'll talk soon. I will keep you posted. Give Avery a kiss for me," I say.

"Okay, I'm not going anywhere. And of course, I will. She's fine, so don't worry about her."

"Thank you. Goodbye, Jas."

"Bye, Cora."

Twenty-Eight

JASPER

It's been three days, and Mr. Connolly still hasn't woken up. Avery has been with me for the most part, and we've been staying at her house to give her some sort of normalcy. We've been eating dinner with my parents, and during the day, Rosie has brought Jakey over.

As for Cora, I've seen very little of her, and when we do talk, our conversations are short.

She's exhausted and in pain. It's hard to witness and even harder to be pushed to the sideline. In a lot of ways, I shouldn't be surprised. She tends to do this; she bottles things up, trying to hold herself up during the heaviest times in her life. She's strong, but I wish she'd give a little. Admit that she needs help. Accept help.

I'd be lying if I didn't admit her distance has me worried. Partly because this time, her walls seem even more directed at me. And here I am, being selfish when my focus should be on Mr. Connolly and how much pain their family is going through. I shouldn't be worried about what this will mean for Cora and me.

"Jasper, do you think Mommy will be home to sleep soon? Is Granddad in heaven?"

Avery's questions pull me from my thoughts.

"No, sweet girl. Granddad is not in heaven yet, and I'm not sure when Mommy will be home to sleep. She did tell me that she would come home to have lunch with you today, though."

"Oh, good. I miss them. Mommy, Grand, and Granddad."

"I miss them, too," I tell her. Then I pull her into my lap and hug her.

"I'm glad you're here," she says.

"Me, too."

Suddenly, there is a loud knock on the front door, and Avery immediately hops off my lap and beelines it for the front door.

"Avery, don't answer that door unless you know who it is?" I yell after her.

Standing, I head in the direction Avery just ran.

"It's just Drew and Kelsea! I know them, so I'm opening the door," Avery yells.

My brother and sister greet Avery, and their familiar voices are a relief. I walk into the room as they come in, and Avery closes the door behind them.

"Hey, little bro. How's it going?" Drew asks.

Kelsea stands beside him, her eyes intently focused on

my face, like she's searching for some kind of secret.

"As good as it can be. What brings you two over?" I ask.

"I'm going back to finish drawing my picture for Granddad," Avery announces and skips out of the room. We all watch her disappear back in the direction of the kitchen.

Putting my hands in my front pockets, I wait for the answer to my question. When they say nothing and just study me, I ask, "Well, are you going to answer?"

"No reason other than we were worried about you," Kelsea says. She still has that look on her face.

"Worried about me? I'm fine," I say.

"Rosie said you seemed upset and..." Drew starts to say, then I interrupt. "Of course, I'm upset. Aren't you? Mr. Connolly is dying." My voice was raised at first, and then I remembered Avery, so I lowered it. "I don't want to talk where Avery can hear; let's go sit out back."

They both nod, and we make our way through the kitchen to the back door.

"Avery, my girl, Drew, Kelsea, and I are going to sit out back. Don't go out the front door, and if you need anything, we'll be right there," I say, pointing outside to the patio.

"Okay," she says without looking up.

The three of us step outside and all sit down around the table.

"I know what you're doing, Drew, but you're worried for nothing. I'm fine."

"What am I doing, Jas?"

"All of you are getting all protective, like you always do when it comes to me. You all think Cora will hurt me again. And don't think I don't know what you said to her the other day when we ran into you and Rosie. I'm sure you didn't hesitate to tell Parker, Ty, and Kelsea," I motion toward her as she sits silently, watching me, before continuing, "about me and Cora."

Kelsea perks up, "You and Cora? Drew hasn't said a word to me about anything. What about you and Cora?"

"You're wrong. Rosie made me promise I'd keep my mouth shut until you two were ready to let everyone in the family in on the fact that you two are together."

"What? You and Cora are together? Since when?"

I rub my temples and put my head in my hands briefly. Shit, now the twenty questions will begin.

"Since the night we all went out."

"That was a month ago! And you didn't tell any of us? Mom? Dad?"

I shake my head. "Only Mr. Connolly."

"Why is this a secret? Why wouldn't you tell us?" she asks.

Now Drew is silent. He's the one watching me.

"Because we wanted to have a moment to let it all sink in. We wanted a moment with just the two of us, without any of your comments or opinions. I didn't want to hear your worries and Tyler's jokes or Drew and Parker's big brother concerns. Cora wanted…"

Drew leans forward, "Cora wanted what?"

I shrug, because when I think about it, what did Cora want?

"Exactly. You know I love her like my own sister, Jas. But she nearly destroyed you once. We watched you crumble when she took Avery and left like you without even considering you. We hurt when you hurt."

Shaking my head, I try defending both myself and Cora. "She didn't mean to hurt me, and actually, she hurt herself in the process. She knows she made the wrong decision now. And she never made me promises; she was only the friend she'd always been. It's not her fault that I had new expectations."

"You love her," Kelsea says softly.

My throat clogs with emotion, but I manage to say, "Yes."

"But does she love you? Because if you don't know and she hasn't told you, why are you taking this risk again? Will you survive this loss again? I don't think you will, and I'm not sure your friendship will recover if this detonates in your face again."

Kelsea doesn't usually talk like this, and it makes me wonder what is prompting these kinds of thoughts, because it sounds like this is coming from experience more than worry.

"I don't have the answer, and how can I find out when Cora has all of this going on right now?"

"Rosie also said it seems like Cora is avoiding you," Drew says, his tone softer than it was a few minutes ago. God, he's pitying me, and there is nothing worse than when one of my brothers pities me.

"She has a lot on her mind."

Kelsea reaches her hand across the table and lays it over

mine. "Don't sink again with her. Fight for her when you feel you're ready, but don't wait too long, and let her build up this wall that we all know she's building. Remember, we've been friends with Cora just as long as you have."

• • •

Cora had come home around lunchtime just as she promised she would. I went to my parents to give them some alone time with Avery. She didn't try to stop me, and while I insisted on leaving, she didn't stop me, and a part of me felt the fear I thought I'd put away pry open again.

Kelsea and Drew's concerns this morning probably didn't help either.

Avery and Cora just showed up at my parents' house, and she updated them on her dad. My mom was, of course, just as concerned for her and Mrs. Connolly. Cora promised they were fine.

After about half an hour, Cora stood, "Well, I think I'd better get back to Mom and Dad. Thanks again to all of you for your help with Avery."

Mom and Dad each give her a long hug. "Of course, honey. We love you all. We're family."

Cora gives my mom a warm smile, and even though it doesn't reach her eyes, I'm glad to see some sign of her behind the sadness lining her features.

"I will walk you to your car," I say.

"You don't need to do that," she says.

"I know I don't, but I want to."

She nods. The look on her face is a little nervous for one brief second. Cora and I haven't been alone since that early morning when I dropped her off at the hospital. It's only been a few days, but there has been some shift, I can tell.

Avery and Cora say goodbye, and Mom distracts Avery with cookies while Cora and I slip out of the house.

Walking side by side in silence, we head across the street to her car.

When we reach her car, I open her door for her, and just before she slides in, I lightly grab her wrist, stopping her. "Cora, wait," I say.

She doesn't look at me.

"Cora," I say again.

"I can't do this, Jas."

"What did I do wrong? Why aren't you talking to me?"

Her head slowly turns toward me, her eyes filled with unshed tears.

"You didn't do anything wrong. I did. I lost sight of why I came home, and I wasn't with my mom and dad when they needed me most. I was being selfish."

My hand reaches up and caresses the side of her face. She flinches a little, then leans into it.

"No, you weren't being selfish. My God, Cora, stop punishing yourself. Stop punishing me. You and me, this is what your dad wanted."

"What?" she says, her eyes wide with surprise.

"He's been scolding me for years that I've never told you how I felt about you. He believed we were meant for each other," I say, sucking in a breath, willing myself to be brave enough to continue. "God, Cora. I'm so in love with you. I've always loved you, and I want to be here for you, comfort you, and be what you need."

She takes one step out of my reach, and my hand falls.

Shaking her head, she says, "I can't do this now. I …I need to get back."

"Cora, please…"

"I said, I can't do this, Jasper," she turns and slides into the driver's side of her car.

Putting my hand on the door before she can close it, I say her name, "Cora."

She doesn't look at me. She stares straight out the front windshield as tears fall down her cheeks. My heart is breaking. With her hand on the door, she pleads with me one more time, "Please." It's all she says.

I'm defeated, so I simply say, "Okay, I have Avery, don't worry about her." She nods, then I close the door and take a step back.

Cora doesn't look in my direction again. She backs her car out of the driveway while I stand in the same yard we met at just nine years old and watch her drive away... again.

How do I hold on?

Twenty-Nine

CORA

The heart monitor echoes through the dark hospital room. It's the only noise in an otherwise silent space. Mom went home to shower while I stayed here with Dad. The silence is deafening. I so desperately want to hear Dad's voice one more time, but he hasn't woken up yet. The doctors said it's unlikely he will at this point, but Mom and I are still hanging onto some hope.

I sit here next to him, watching him, and my mind swirls with all my fears, all my longing, and everything that has happened in my life. In the life my dad gave me. All the adventures that he and Mom took me on. The love he poured into me. How he was always there for me, on my side, no matter what. How I never felt lonely, and I always felt loved.

I think about the day we moved to Santa Cruz and how

a boy my age came over with his mom to make her happy by greeting the new neighbors. I think about the inevitability of that same young boy and girl becoming best friends. I don't think he really wanted to be my friend back then; I practically forced myself into his life. Jasper was just too kind to ignore me or push me away. Instead, he opened his heart, and I changed his mind.

"Jasper told me he loves me," I whisper into the dark, silent room. I pretend my dad can hear me, but the sound of the machine tells me a different story. "But I'm afraid. He put himself out there, told me he loved me, and I just drove away."

Leaning forward, I take Dad's frail hand into mine. It's cold and lifeless. I hate that because my dad has always been the warmest person in my life. He was like the sun, always shining light on my mom and me, warming us with his love and humor. Our biggest fans.

"Jasper told me he loves me," I say again. "He said you scolded him. I would've liked to have seen that. What he doesn't know is that you scolded me, too, for the same reason. But I didn't listen. I didn't tell him I love him, Dad. I didn't say anything." A tear slips down my cheek. "Why do I keep hurting him? Why do I keep hurting myself?"

From behind me, Mom's voice fills the quiet space. "That is what we have always wanted to know." My head turns in her direction. She takes a step toward me. "Cora, stop punishing yourself. You have been mine and your dad's greatest blessing. We've always wanted you to just allow yourself to be happy."

"Oh, Mom. I don't deserve Jasper."

"Cora, stop," she says, then rubs her hand tenderly over my hair. "Sweetie, I'd like to tell you that your dad and I agreed with your decision to leave us. To leave Jasper. But I can't. We've known that boy has loved you for a long time. And the man he's become is no surprise. We always suspected that you've loved him just as long, but for some reason, you put up a barrier. You put him up on a pedestal from the moment you met him, but what you didn't realize is that you've been standing right next to him up there that whole time. You just thought you were standing below, looking up at him."

"I've hurt him too many times, Mom. I hurt him again today."

Mom doesn't say anything at first; she only regards me with a contemplative look on her face.

"You don't give him enough credit. You need to trust him and his love for you because, Cora, you're too smart not to. You need to make room for the reality that Jasper is it. He is your happy ever after. The one who sticks by your side and is loyal, because he has never shown himself to be anyone different. You need to trust yourself and what you see in him. It's the same thing your father and I see in him."

Sighing, I let what she has just said sink in. She allows me this time and doesn't try to fill the silence between us. Instead, she steps over to Dad and looks him over, lingering on his face. I watch her and see the reverence she has for him. The love I witnessed my entire life, but now it's something more. Something I never paid attention to or maybe just didn't recognize until now. I see not only love, but a devotion and intimacy so pure that no one would ever be able to penetrate it. Their own world where only the two of them exist.

And then, it hits me. This is what I've been so afraid of. Having this and losing it one day. This is what Jasper and I have; we have this same bubble of devotion and loyalty. And instead of allowing it to happen and protecting it, I've been sabotaging it before someone else could. I thought I was protecting us, but I was completely wrong. Nothing will ever break what Jasper and I have because it is everlasting. As this realization hits me, I suck in a sharp breath.

"You love him," Mom says without looking away from my dad.

"More than my own life," I whisper.

She reaches her hand back to me. I take it, and together Mom and I sit in silence as she mourns the love of her life.

After a long time, Mom speaks again. "Cora, don't wait too long to let him know. Life is short and unpredictable. Don't waste any more time."

• • •

A few hours later, the doctors came in to check on Dad and told us it probably wouldn't be much longer. I decided to call Jas and let him know.

Pacing outside the hospital, a cool evening breeze blowing around me, I make the call.

As soon as he picks up his phone, I speak. "Jas. I ..." I can feel the emotions start to suffocate me.

"Cora, what is it?"

His voice is so full of concern. It's as if our last conversation never happened. It's as if he never said those words, and I never walked away after.

"Uh, I…Jas, Dad is not going to be with us much longer. I think you should come."

Silence hangs on the other end of the line. I hear a long, sorrowful sigh.

"Jas?"

It takes a few seconds, but he finally responds, "I'm here. I will be there soon." I could hear it in his voice that he was crying. Just one more reminder that I haven't really considered his feelings about Dad dying. They were close, and I know he loved him. They loved each other.

"Should we let Avery come?" I ask.

More silence. Then he clears his throat.

"That's your decision, Cora. I will do whatever you want. You're her mother."

"I'm asking your opinion. You're her…," I trail off, then say, "I would like your opinion."

"Okay, then I think Avery deserves a chance to say goodbye."

"You're right. Do you think you can talk to her before you get here? Explain?"

"Of course. We will be there soon."

"Thank you, Jasper. For everything."

"You never have to thank me; I choose to be here for you and Avery. For your dad and mom. Always. Like my mom said, we're family. See you soon, Cora."

"See you soon."

Thirty

JASPER

A very never fails to amaze me. She's beyond her years, and I can confidently say that Cora and I made the right decision to let her say goodbye to Mr. Connolly. She touched his face, held his hand, and kissed him on his cheek. She told him to have fun in heaven, as if it would be the time of his life.

She could teach the rest of us a lesson on death and goodbyes.

Because now, I'm sitting here alone next to a man whom I love like a father. A man who picked me up repeatedly when I fell off my bicycle, if my dad wasn't around. He listened to me when I felt like I needed space from my family. He was one of the single greatest men I've ever known.

"I'm having a hard time finding the words I want to say

to you," I begin. "Even harder when I'm not certain you can hear me."

Only a slow heartbeat beep from the machine responds, and I take that as a sign.

"I'm going to miss you; we all will. There will be a hole in our family, but we will never forget you. I will spend the rest of my days honoring you." I have to pause to keep the tears threatening to fall at bay. "I finally took your advice and told Cora I love her. It didn't go exactly like I hoped, but I promised you I wouldn't give up. I did that once, and it was my greatest mistake."

His face shows no sign that he hears me, I only know he is here because of the slow rise and fall of his chest.

"I won't push her, though. Maybe she will never love me, but I know I can never love anyone else. I tried." I wipe the tears that escaped. "I promise I will always take care of all of your girls. Rest well; we'll all see you again one day."

Standing, I lean over him and hug his fragile body. He always hugged me goodbye, so it felt appropriate.

The door opens, and Mrs. Connolly comes in.

"I hope I'm not interrupting you," she says.

"Of course not. Avery and Cora went to the cafeteria for a snack." I say, then continue, "I think Cora wanted to give me a moment."

She walks across the room and takes Mr. Connolly's hand carefully.

"I can give you…" I begin to say, but she waves me off with her free hand.

"No, stay. I've said my goodbyes well before we made

it here," she says. "Of course, it doesn't make this easier, but I don't want him to suffer anymore. I want Cora, Avery, and me to have more than the memories of his illness. I want the memories of the husband, father, and grandfather he was to outshine these last days forever in our minds."

"He will always shine in mine," I tell her.

"Well, you certainly shone in his," she says. "He loved you like his own."

"I loved him."

Seconds hang between us before Mrs. Connolly says, "Don't give up on her, Jasper."

Stunned by her comment at first, I hesitate before saying, "I don't think I could even, if I wanted to…I tried."

This time, she turns and looks directly into my eyes.

"I know you did, and I'm sorry you were hurting like you were; you had every right to move forward when she left the way she did. But if I'm honest, I prayed that you wouldn't ever move on, and she would come to her senses. Even if Jim hadn't become ill, I think Cora would've eventually come home. She always asked about you. As hard as she tried, she never moved on."

"Thank you for telling me that," I say.

She only nods with a half-smile and turns her attention back to Mr. Connolly.

● ● ●

Mr. Connolly was gone by the next morning. Cora texted at five a.m. with the news.

Cora: Dad is gone.

Me: God, Cora. I'm so sorry. Sending you and your mom my love.

Cora: Thank you, Jasper, for everything. I will talk to Avery later; we'll be home soon. Everything has already been arranged.

Me: I'll be here.

Cora: Jas, I almost don't want to leave, or this will be real.

Me: Cor, I know it's hard, but your dad isn't there anymore. He's in a better place.

I saw the conversation bubbles play across the screen as if she were typing a long response until, they stopped, and then only a couple of words appeared.

Cora: Thank you.

It's been a week since that text message. Today was the funeral, and we're all gathered at the Connollys' home afterward. Cora has been so focused on today, her mom, and her grief that we've barely had one minute to ourselves. I just keep replaying Mrs. Connolly's words from the hospital and the few interactions Cora and I have had in my mind; that's what's keeping me sane.

This thing between us is important, but everything that is happening is the most important thing right now.

"Hey, little brother, how are you holding up?" Parker says as he walks up and stands next to me.

I've been hiding in the corner, observing everyone as they move in and out of the house.

"I'm here. It's hard to believe he's gone," I say. My eyes lock on Cora; she's standing on the opposite side of the room, talking to Rosie and Abbey.

"I think this is the first person we've lost that we've been super close to, and I'm feeling a bit overwhelmed by it myself," he says. "How's Cora?"

"Hurting, but honestly, we haven't had a chance to talk much."

"Oh, I'm sure she is. Do you think she'll leave again?"

My head snaps in his direction. "Why would you say that? Did you hear something?" I ask, fear and anger hugging my words. I don't even care how loud I am.

He holds his hands up, "Hey…hey, Jas, no. I just thought, maybe."

"I'm sorry," I say, but I don't elaborate.

"What's going on? You okay?" Parker asks as he walks up.

I look back in Cora's direction, and this time, she's watching me. She has a look of concern on her face, and then someone walks into my line of view to talk to her, and the moment is broken.

"I'm surprised Drew and Kelsea haven't said anything," I tell him.

"They haven't," he says, then pauses, looking at me with a raised eyebrow. When I don't say anything, he continues, "Maybe you want to fill me in yourself."

"Not now," I say. "It's not the time."

"If you say so, but Jasper, make sure you are just as honest with yourself as you are with everyone else," he says.

My heart is outside my chest right now, standing across the room. That is as honest as I can handle right now.

Thirty-One

CORA

Staring out into the darkness that covers our front yard, I can see the lights at the Nallen house are still on. Jasper is still there, most likely sitting with his family, enjoying some sort of dessert Mrs. Nallen made.

Dad's funeral was nice. It was just as he wanted, filled with friends and family that he valued. Simple. He wanted it to be a time of happy memories so we could hang onto those throughout the day instead of sorrow.

The Nallens were the biggest part of making that happen, and I'm so grateful.

Jasper gave me my space, but I felt him watching me throughout the entire afternoon. Anytime I looked up, my eyes would always find his, looking directly at me. It seemed as if he were waiting to save me. I could feel him reading me, too, and I know he could tell that I was hanging on by a thread. He knows me too well.

Sipping my tea, I can't help but wish he had stayed so I could sit with him in this silence now.

"What's on that mind of yours?"

My mother's voice comes from the doorway of the house as she walks out onto the porch. She walks over and takes a seat in the rocker next to mine.

"Just the day. Dad," I say.

"Jasper?" Mom asks.

I look at her from the corner of my eye, a soft smile playing at my lips.

"And Jasper."

"When are you going to put yourself and him out of this misery?"

"Misery?" I ask. Sometimes it's easier to pretend I'm oblivious to the feelings I'm having and that I've been pushing Jasper away again.

"Cora Anne, stop playing dumb. Why are you prolonging this hurt? Why are you punishing yourself and Jasper?"

"Mom, I don't want to talk about this today."

"Sweet girl, Life is going to keep happening—today and even with your father gone."

The emotions of the last week begin to bubble inside me again. I'm trying to process all of this because I don't want to make a mistake.

"He loves you," she says when I don't respond.

"I know he does," I say.

"You love him, too, Cora."

"Am I what he needs, though? That is the question I'm trying to answer. I hurt him once. His friendship is the air

I breathe, but the love I feel for him is my every heartbeat. How do I risk all of that?"

She leans toward me, but I keep my eyes on the house across the street.

"Look at me," she gently demands.

When I do, the look in her eyes is full of sorrow and concern. She has something to say and deserves my attention. I want to hear what it is.

"You don't get to decide what Jasper needs. He decides that, and you should always remember that. But you do get to decide what you need, and I think we both know that it's Jasper. Quit wasting time."

With that, she pushes herself out of the rocker, kisses the top of my head, and leaves me sitting alone to process what she's just told me. Mom has always been straight and to the point. It's one of the many things I loved about my childhood and my parents. I always knew what they thought and where they stood in any situation.

Taking another sip of my tea, I close my eyes and rest my head back on the chair.

What do I need? I think to myself. Mom said I get to decide what I need, and that is the only thing in my control. But how does that impact Jasper's needs? Her words roll around in my mind. Jasper has a choice, and all I can do is ask him to choose me and forgive me for taking so long to recognize that he is all I need. He is what Avery needs, too.

Sitting up, I take one last look across the street. I want to run there and beg him to be with me and never leave. But sleeping on it is a better idea.

Tomorrow, I will go to him.

I picked up my phone and found his name in my text messages.

Me: Goodnight, Jas. Thank you again for everything.

I wait for a response. For anything from him. After a few minutes, I realize it may not come, so I stand and make my way into the house. I just hope tomorrow isn't too late.

• • •

JASPER

"I'm probably going to head out soon," I tell my parents. "Kels, do you need a ride?"

For the third time tonight, Kelsea is in her own little world. If I think about it, she's been off for the last month or so, a little distant and introspective. Completely different from her norm.

"Earth to Kelsea," I say again.

"What? Yeah…sorry, I guess I was spacing out," she says.

"You've been doing that a lot lately," I say, then continue, "I just asked if you wanted a ride rather than Ubering home. I'm about to leave."

"Sure, that would be great," she responds.

"Kelsea, honey, are you all right?" Mom asks.

"I'm fine. It was just an emotional day, and I'm tired,"

Kelsea says.

I don't believe her. There's something more going on with her, but knowing my sister, she will want to process whatever is bothering her, and then she will come to one of us. If we push her, then she will push back, and it won't be good for any of us.

"Okay, well, I'm glad you're riding home with your brother instead of alone in one of those strangers' cars," Mom says.

Kelsea rolls her eyes, and I laugh.

"Honey, that's how people get around these days. It's not like your daughter is just hitchhiking and hopping in just anyone's car," Dad says.

"Hmmm, well, it's almost exactly what she is doing. I'll never really understand it."

Standing, I look at Kelsea and grin. "You ready to go?"

"Yep," my sister says, then she kisses our mom on the cheek and hugs our dad.

I do the same and say, "We'll let ourselves out. Talk to you soon."

Kelsea and I leave through the front door and head for my Jeep.

My eyes move to Cora's house of their own volition. It's completely dark. I can't help wondering if she's asleep because she just couldn't fight the exhaustion any longer, or if she's lying awake full of sadness.

I wonder if she is thinking of me or if she really is done with us. Our communication has been limited, and while I know she's had a lot going on, I can't help fearing this shift is permanent.

Kelsea and I get into my car, and I pull my phone from my pocket to plug it in. That's when I notice a text message from Cora, the notification bright on the screen. It came in about twenty minutes ago.

"Are you afraid to read it?" Kelsea asks.

Looking up from my phone, I shake my head. "No, why would I be afraid?"

"I don't know, Jas. Maybe because you're hoping she's going to give you any sign that she loves you back, and how much it will hurt if this is just another text. You told her you love her, right?"

"Yes, but I wasn't expecting her to say it back."

"Really? Fine, perhaps not right in the moment when you said it because she was in the middle of a lot of heavy shit. But you can't tell me that you haven't hoped she would give you some sign that she sees you and that she loves you in the same way you love her."

I stare at Kelsea for a few seconds, and then, without responding, I open Cora's text message and read it. My heart does sink a little, and I feel angry that Kelsea was right. I'm back where I was four years ago. Completely and fully head over heels in love with my best friend, and she still doesn't fully see me or the possibility of us. I set the phone down and start the car. I can feel Kelsea watching me, pity in her eyes, and I sort of hate her for it.

"Are you going to respond?" she finally asks as we pull out of the driveway.

"No," I say, firmly.

Her eyes penetrate me for a few more seconds, and when I show no sign of explaining myself further, Kelsea turns and stares out the passenger side window. She looks sad and distant again, as if she is experiencing her own heartache.

Thirty-Two

JASPER

I can't seem to relax or quiet the mental noise in my head, my thoughts playing on constant repeat with no end in sight. I kick the covers off and turn on my side, trying my best to get comfortable. Tonight, it's impossible.

Parker's comments and Kelsea's behavior. Cora's text message. The last days of Mr. Connolly's illness and every day leading up to the funeral. The funeral itself. In fact, it's every moment and every word that Cora and I have spent together or spoken since she got back into town. All of it. My brain just won't shut off.

I pull my pillow out from under my head and push it over my face, as if that will help block it all out.

"Ugggggghhhhhh!" I scream into the pillow.

Wait, was that the doorbell? I pull the pillow off my head and sit up in bed. There it is again. This time, there is no mistaking that someone has just rang my doorbell. Rolling myself out of bed, I glance at the clock on my bookshelf as I walk by. The display shows two o'clock in the morning brightly on the screen. Who could be at my door at two in the morning? If those little punk teenagers are out doing the whole doorbell-ditching thing again, I'm going to handle it with a little less understanding this time.

I shuffle my way down the hall. The bell rings two more times by the time I reach it, and when I swing the door open, I'm prepared to chase the little shits.

Instead of a group of teenage boys running for their lives, I find Cora standing there, looking miserable and restless. When she realizes I've actually opened the door, a look of shock briefly crosses her face, as if she's forgotten that she was the one who drove to my house and is knocking on my door in the middle of the night.

When I really look at her, I can see that she's been crying. I wait in my own shock to see if she's going to speak, but she doesn't. She just stands on my doorstep, staring at me like she's forgotten why she's here.

"You didn't text me back," she finally blurts out.

"No," I respond. I don't know what else to say.

"You didn't text me back," she repeats.

As if I just realized we're still standing in my open doorway, I say, "Come inside."

She walks in, and it's then that I notice she is in some thin pair of pajama shorts, a tank top, and a cardigan sweater. She must be freezing.

"Did you get out of bed to come over here?" I ask, running my gaze up and down her body and still feeling confused as to what is happening.

She looks down at herself, her cheeks turning a light shade of pink.

"Yes, I…I couldn't sleep," she says.

"Because I didn't text you back?" I ask.

"Yes…no…yes," she says, looking defeated. "I mean, yes and no. There are other reasons, but…why didn't you respond?"

"I don't know," I tell her. "I needed a minute."

"It has been more than a minute," she says.

"Cora, what is going on?"

She is making sense, yet she is completely irrational—not at all like herself. Cora is methodical and rational in everything she does and every decision she makes. Showing up here at two in the morning, rambling, is the opposite of the Cora I know.

"Do you hate me?"

Her question hits me like a slap across the face. Why would she say that? Think that?

"What? I could never hate you."

"I've hurt you and deserve it, so of course you could hate me. You stopped talking to me almost completely for a full year and only through occasional text messages for the next three years. Even through all those years, you always replied to me. Tonight, you didn't even respond to a simple text message. I hurt you again," she says, sorrowfully.

"Yes, you hurt me…again, but I would never. I just needed to step back for a beat," I say.

"Jasper, I'm sorry."

"I know you are," I immediately tell her. Because I do know she is sorry. I've never thought Cora could ever hurt me intentionally.

"I need you. You're my best friend," she tells me.

"You're my best friend, too. But I…," I trail off.

What? What more can I say? What more do I want to say? Yes, you hurt me. Yes, you're my best friend, but I don't know if I can live this life so close to you, but never be able to love you as more than my friend.

"There's a 'but' in this scenario, and that is the problem. You're drawing a line between us," she says.

The hurt I'm feeling turns inside my stomach and comes out as anger, "My God, Cora! What do you want from me?"

She flinches and takes a step back, as if my words whip at her.

My breathing is coming a little faster, and I run my fingers through my hair and pull, then hang my head like I want to stuff every thought and feeling back inside.

She's staring at me, and I can see she wants to say something, but she's trying to work up the nerve.

"Damn it! Say something because I'm tired of being the one who keeps laying his heart out for you to reject. I'm tired of being the one who tries to convince you that we are meant to be together forever as more than friends. I felt it every time we made love and saw it every time I looked into your eyes."

Cora takes a step back toward me, her head tilted as she caresses my face with her gaze.

I can't do this right now. I can't bear to hear that she

doesn't want this kind of love from me.

"Please leave," I say.

CORA

I could barely breathe. When I looked at the clock, it had been four hours, and sleep was no closer to overtaking me than when I first lay down. I knew it was futile. Not even the exhaustion from the day could make me fall asleep.

So, I got up without thinking and immediately got in my car. All I could think was, am I too late? Primarily, after he didn't even text me back. I've hurt him enough to make him decide the fight wasn't worth it.

I cried the entire way to Jasper's house. I was prepared to beg and plead with him, but I froze when he opened the door.

"Please leave," he repeated for the second time after I didn't make a move when he asked the first time.

These words and the look on his face are a blow to the chest. I'm losing him, and I've got to do something now. My mom's words play in my mind.

"Not yet," I tell him. I have something to say first, and if you still want me to leave after that, then I will respect your wishes."

I can see his hesitation at first, but then he nods.

"I remember the first day I ever saw you. Your smile.

The clothes you wore and how your hair fell over your eyes. I used to love it when you pushed it out of your eyes. I watched you from the window of our living room. It was before you came over with your mom to welcome us to the neighborhood. I saw her say something to you and each of the boys, and you were the only one who walked over with her. I could see you were reluctant, but you did it for her." I tell him.

"Parker, Drew, and Ty refused. I could tell it disappointed her, and I hated disappointing her," he says.

"I know. Even then, you were always considering others' feelings. I knew from that moment how special you are and wanted to be your friend."

Jasper turns away from me. "Cora, is there a point? Can't we reminisce some other time?"

"No, we can't. I need to say this now, and I need you to listen, please."

With his back to me, he says, "If that is what you need."

"The years went by, and I began to see you differently every day, or maybe I just understood my feelings better. My heartbeat raced a little faster when I was around you, and I felt butterflies in my stomach whenever you touched my hand."

As I tell my story, I see Jasper's shoulders heaving with emotion. He doesn't say anything and keeps his back to me, so I continue, "But then one day, I heard Greg Martin tease you about being in love with me, and you said we were just friends. I felt devastated because I wanted both, and when I told my dad, he said that maybe you didn't want to mess up our friendship. And when I asked why we couldn't have both, he said it might not work out. And that stuck with me." I know it was not his intention to have me deny my feelings all these years, but I worried about it, Jasper. I was scared that I could lose you, and that seemed like something I wouldn't survive. I wanted you so much, I believed I could never lose you."

Jasper suddenly whips around, throwing his hands in the air and steps toward me, "Why are you telling me all of this?"

Instead of stepping away, I steadily approach him until we are almost toe to toe. He freezes, and his breath catches.

"I'm telling you this because I never stopped feeling that way about you. I still love watching you push your hair from your eyes. I love watching you do things for people you care about to make them happy. I love how my heart moves in a faster rhythm when I see you and how I still get butterflies when you take my hand in yours. Don't you see, Jasper? I've been so afraid of our relationship not working and getting messy, even after all these years, that I pushed you away. I mean, who falls in love with their best friend when they are just nine years old?"

His eyes begin to look hopeful and fearful all at once.

Instead of stopping, I keep going. "I do. I fell in love with you that day all those years ago, and I never stopped. I love you for every reason I told you and much more, Jasper. I love you, Jasper."

His hands find my face, and for one second, his eyes search mine as if he is trying to decipher if my words match any feelings showing through my eyes. Then his lips are on mine. And I'm falling all over again.

Thirty-Three

JASPER

I didn't think I could keep standing here listening to another memory, another word, and then she started planting tiny seeds of hope that I wouldn't allow myself to feel.

Then Cora looks directly into my eyes and says the one thing I've waited years to hear her speak. I could see the truth and depth of those feelings right there in her soul. Cora loves me. She's always loved me. I do the only thing I can right then because speaking would've been impossible.

I kiss her.

I kiss her with every ounce of love I have buried inside of me. I show her with every caress of my lips against hers. Then I realize I'm crying, but they're happy tears, and she's crying, too.

"You're crying," she whispers against my lips.

"So are you," I breathe.

She throws her arms around me and starts laughing. It's the most beautiful, happy sound, and I don't want it to end.

"I love you so much," she says through her laughter, her tears still falling.

"And I love you," I say back.

Suddenly, she's kissing me again, but this time with more intensity and need.

"Make love to me," she says.

I don't hesitate to pick her up, her legs wrapping around me as I carry her down the hall and into my room. All exhaustion long forgotten.

When I get her into my room, I lay her on the bed and slide her shorts and panties off, kissing my way down her legs until they are completely removed. She slips her arms free of her cardigan and pulls the tank top over her head. She's naked and beautiful before me. We've been here before, but this time it's different because there is nothing left unspoken between us.

I pull my sweatpants off and climb over her, pressing kisses on her thigh, up every inch of her skin, until my lips once again reach hers. In one quick movement, I open my drawer and slide the protection of my stiff shaft. She moans as she watches me and pulls my mouth back to hers, deepening the kiss. Cora's hands run over my shoulders, down my sides, and then she cups my ass with both hands.

"Open your eyes and look at me," I pant.

She does as I say, still holding onto me. I position myself, and we keep our gazes locked.

Her hands tight onto my ass cheeks, she pulls me forward as I push into her, burying myself inside her. "Jasper!" she hollers, voice raspy with desire.

We don't break our connection with our eyes or our bodies, and I begin moving inside her with a cadence that matches her own. Slow and easy, building a sensation between us that has us both moaning with every move.

Cora pushes at my shoulder, indicating she wants me to turn us over. I roll us together until she is sitting on top of me, her legs straddled on either side of my hips. She leans forward, her tongue and lips assaulting my chest and neck until Cora reaches my mouth. She sucks on my lip and then pushes her tongue into my mouth. Taking control of our lovemaking, her hips begin to rock forward at a slow, languid pace, our movement creating a sensation that is making it harder for me to keep control. She sits up and keeps moving, looking down on me, and all my mind can focus on is how beautiful she looks with her curls falling around her shoulders and with that blissful smile on her lips.

The need to move faster, deeper, and harder into her is only exacerbated by every rock forward.

She must feel it, too, because suddenly that is precisely where Cora takes us, into a frenzy of lovemaking. Her tongue once again in my mouth, and now she's matching every flick of her tongue to the movement of her hips until we both reach the edge. With one last lift of my hips, I send us both over the edge into the most intoxicating orgasm I've ever experienced.

She falls to my chest, and I wrap my arms around her, keeping her close.

"I love you," she sighs.

"And I love you."

Thirty-Four

CORA

Is it wrong to be this happy when I just lost my dad? Separating those feelings has been impossible over the last few weeks as it is, but now, as I lie next to Jasper, drawing the infinity sign over his heart with my fingertip, I wonder if this happiness is fair.

I mean, my mom is heartbroken. I'm heartbroken.

But at this very moment, I've never been happier. I'm in love with Jasper and no longer hiding it—seventeen years of denying it, of pretending that we were nothing more than two ordinary best friends.

Never again.

I will never deny myself Jasper's love again. I won't deny him mine, either. Because I do, I love him in an all-consuming and precious way. He is the light in every dark moment.

And that is what I will hold onto now. In this black time of my life, Jasper's love will be my guide to everything that brightens my world. It's exactly what my dad wanted for me…for us. It's what my mom was trying to tell me.

I need him, and he says he needs me. We choose each other. Our love deserves this chance.

"This time felt different than before," he says.

I lift my head and rest it on my bent elbow on his chest. I lazily touch his top lip. "It's because we aren't holding anything back. Our feelings have been laid bare, and now we can feel them all."

He laughs a little.

"What? Too deep?" I ask, a slight grin on my face.

"No, I'm just happy," he says.

We stay this way in silence, his eyes closed, while I watch different emotions play across his face. He must be thinking, and I love watching him.

Suddenly, his eyes flash open. "Do you think Avery will be okay with us being a family?"

"A family?" I ask, trying to keep my feelings at bay, if I misunderstood him.

"Is that too much, too fast?" he asks.

"Too fast?" I laugh, slightly shaking my head. "Uh, no. Not too fast, especially since I've been dreaming of being a family with you since we were little kids."

Jasper gives me a serious look. "Cora, you've always been my family."

"You know what I mean. And I think Avery already thinks we're family anyway. She always has," I say.

"What do you mean, she always has?"

"When we were away, I kept a framed picture of the three of us from our last day at the beach together. You know from when she was a baby? As she got older, she would look at it and say, 'Mommy, this is our family.' I press my lips to his side. "She's always known what we couldn't put together," I tell him.

His eyes shiny with tears, he rolls toward me and kisses me deeply…tenderly, and then, as if he needed me more now than ever, Jasper makes love to me again.

And then again.

And again.

Now, there is no worry, hesitation, or sadness regarding the idea of Jasper and me. How could there be? We were meant to be together. As best friends and as lovers.

I get to live because I have both my oxygen and my heartbeat. We are perfectly fit together now, instead of in pieces.

Epilogue

JASPER

1 Year Later

Kneeling before them on the beach, I wait for their answer. Avery is dancing around us, twirling and laughing. Cora is staring at me, full of love and joy.

"Yes, I told you before that being a family with you... married to you, would be a dream come true."

She throws her arms around me, and I catch her. When Cora says yes, Avery starts shouting, "She said yes! She said yes!"

Our family cheers from the cliff above us, where they've been hiding while I propose. We're in the same spot where we took that photo of the three of us all those years ago. Our first family photo, as Cora loves to call it.

Cora is laughing and kissing me, then she glances over her shoulder and raises her hand, showing off her ring.

"About damn time," Tyler shouts as they all make their way down to the beach.

Jakey comes running past Cora and me, in pursuit of Avery, yelling, "About damn time!"

I laugh, and Cora says, "Uh oh."

Seconds later, Ty yells, "Ouch!" after Rosie swats him with her bag. "Tyler Nallen, if you don't stop teaching my son those naughty words, I'm going to kill you!"

Drew laughs until he realizes that Rosie is glaring at him.

"Hey, I didn't say anything," Drew says.

"Quit while you're ahead," Abbey suggests.

They all surround us. My mom and dad. Mrs. Connolly and all my siblings. Our family.

"Avery, bring Jakey back this way for a minute," I tell her.

They both come running back over to us. Drew quickly scoops his son up into his arms. Avery stops and plops down in the sand at our feet. We all gather in a circle where we can look across and see each other.

My dad whistles to quiet everyone down and instantly has all of our attention.

"I want to tell you all a little story. A true story, and one of my favorites," he begins. "This story is about a young boy, the last of his family, the baby. The one everyone admired for his tenderness and capacity to love. It's a story of a young girl who easily captured the hearts of everyone she met with her quick smile and pureness of heart, but especially the heart of that tender-hearted young boy."

From the corner of my eye, I see that Cora is already wiping a tear from her eye.

"Everyone who knew them knew they had a love and devotion for one another that was lasting and true. Of course, like all good love stories, the boy and girl took a little longer to figure out what everyone else already knew."

Now Cora isn't the only one crying. As I glance around the circle of our family, I see Abbey, Rosie, and even Kelsea wiping their own tears. I hear our moms both sniffle. Even Tyler looks on the verge of emotions that aren't normal for him.

"As we all know, this is the story of our Jasper and Cora. Cora has been a part of our family since they moved into the house across the street, but these two will finally make it official. So please join me in wishing them our warmest congratulations. To Cora and Jasper. We love you!"

Our family cheers, and in front of them, I take Cora into my arms, pull her close, and kiss her like it's the first and last time.

Because she is my first. My last. My always.

The End

About the Author

Shirl Rickman is a writer, a dreamer, and an optimist. A small town Texas girl currently residing in the San Francisco Bay Area with her beautifully blended family and their three crazy dogs. When she's not dreaming up new love stories, Shirl can be found reading and drinking way too much coffee. She loves kindness, laughing and meeting her readers.

Website
www.shirlrickmanauthor.com

Facebook
www.facebook.com/shirlrickmanauthor

Facebook Reader Group
www.facebook.com/rickmanrebels

Instagram
www.instagram.com/shirlrickmanauthor/

TikTok
www.tiktok.com/@shirlrickmanauthor

www.ingramcontent.com/pod-product-compliance
Lightning Source LLC
Chambersburg PA
CBHW061940170626
46813CB00006B/2479